EPOCH

EPOCH

Book Two

by Jewel E. Ann

Copyright © 2018 by Jewel E. Ann
ISBN: 978-1-7320897-2-3
Print Edition

Cover Designer: ©Sarah Hansen, Okay Creations
Formatting: BB eBooks

CHAPTER ONE

I'T'S NOT NICE to talk about someone behind their back. That's what they're doing. Griffin, my mom, his parents ... they're in the other room, jotting down my straitjacket measurements between hushed words.

Swayze had a breakdown.

Swayze thinks Doug Mann killed Erica.

Swayze thinks Doug Mann killed some girl named Morgan Daisy Gallagher.

Shh ... don't speak too loud. We don't want to wake her.

The police didn't believe me. I know I sounded crazy, but I'm not. I can't remember all the details, or even most of them, but he killed Daisy. And he killed Erica. Not all truths can be explained.

The door eases open.

"You're awake." Mom smiles the kind of smile one gives an unstable person. It's the don't-break-the-good-China smile.

I sit up, leaning back against the creaky headboard. Something between utter shock and complete numbness settles along my body. "I'm awake." Glancing at the nightstand, I frown at the pill bottle. "I don't think Dr. B would approve of you sharing your sleeping pills with me. They're prescription."

"Griffin didn't want to have to call your psychiatrist yet, so we just gave you one to help you calm down. You weren't yourself. The things you said didn't make any sense. I think the news of Erica and seeing her body triggered something. How do you feel now?" She sits on the edge of the bed, taking a hold of my hand. Her fingers trace the diamond of my engagement ring.

Mom, I'm engaged.

Oh, Swayze! I'm so happy for you.

We can't have that conversation now. Pain burns my eyes as the vision of Erica's body continues to brand a permanent place in my memory. I can't erase the picture of Doug's bloodied face or Daisy falling. I don't even know what universe I'm in. I feel like I know more than I should and yet nothing at all. It's so messed-up. *I'm* so messed-up.

In love.

Engaged.

Angry.

Confused.

Terrified.

"What time is it?"

"Eight-thirty?"

"It's late. You should get home. I'm fine."

"Eight-thirty in the morning, Swayze."

My attention shifts to the windows. Light seeps in through the holes in the blinds. Bright morning light. Not the dim evening sunset.

"I'm late." I toss back the covers. "Where's my phone? I need to call Nate."

"Swayze—"

"My phone ..." Jerking open the door, my feet slap against the wooden hallway floor. "Where's my purse?"

"Swayz, what's wrong?" Griffin jumps up from the sofa.

I spot my purse on the table and retrieve my phone. There

are three missed calls from Nate and two texts.

Professor: *You're late. That's not like you. I'm worried.*

Professor: *Taking Morgan to work with me. Please call me as soon as you get this. I'm worried.*

"Swayz—"

I yank my arm away as Griffin's hand rests on my shoulder. "I'm late. How could you let me oversleep?" I call Nate, taking long strides to distance myself from Griffin, his parents, and my mom without acknowledging them before locking myself in the bathroom.

"Jesus, Swayze! Are you okay?" Nate answers.

"I'm so sorry. I'll be there in thirty minutes. Something happened yesterday and I … I … I'm sorry. I'm on my way." Perched on the cold toilet seat, I run my fingers through my hair and close my eyes. Even darkness won't eradicate the haunting images.

"I have to get back to my class. Morgan is in my office. My colleagues are taking turns watching her. Are you okay? You don't sound okay."

The door handle to the bathroom rattles. "Swayz, open the door."

"I'm on my way." I end the call and open the door. "You can't just drug me. I have a job. Responsibilities." Shouldering past Griffin, I tear through every dresser drawer, looking for my clothes. I'm still not used to where my stuff is in his house—our house.

"You're not going to work today. Have you forgotten about yesterday?"

I shove my feet into my jeans. "In spite of your efforts to drug me, no, I haven't forgotten about yesterday."

"It was one pill. I thought it was a better alternative than letting you self-destruct in front of everyone. I didn't shove it down your throat. I handed it to you with a glass of water. You willingly took it."

I hook my bra and tug on my T-shirt. "Did you tell me what it was?"

"Yes."

I stop my frantic movements long enough to study him. He's not lying. I can tell. It pisses me off that I can't remember him handing me a sleeping pill. It pisses me off that I can't remember what I did that warranted him feeling the need to sedate me like an out of control animal.

With the heels of my hands, I rub my eyes, shaking my head. "I'm sorry ... I have to go."

Griffin bends forward, putting us at eye level while sharing his minty breath with me. "*I* took the day off to be here for you. How can I do that if you're not here?"

"I have to go."

"Then I'm going with you."

I laugh. "You're coming with me to watch Morgan today?"

He nods. "You're not driving. And if Professor Hunt knew what happened to you yesterday, he wouldn't want you watching his daughter today."

"I would never sacrifice Morgan's safety." I ball my hands in defense.

"It's me and you today, Swayz. Deal with it."

On a sigh, I grab my socks and shoes.

"Where are you going?" Mom asks when we make our way to the living room.

"Work."

Sherri and Scott shoot Griffin concerned looks.

"I'm going with her."

They give Griffin deliberate nods, redirecting their worried looks toward me.

"I'm fine. Really. But thank you for your concern."

"Call me when you get home later." Mom hugs me. "We have a lot to discuss."

Who knows what Griffin told them. I'll deal with it later.

"DOES ERICA HAVE family around here?" Griffin asks on our way to Nate's office.

I stare out the window, seeing everything and nothing in particular at the same time. "Yes."

"I'll look for something on her visitation and funeral."

I nod. "Thanks."

He doesn't say anything else, and I don't spur on the conversation. At some point we'll discuss Daisy. How can we not? But not now. I need to let these images speak to me before I can try to make anyone else understand.

I lead the way to Nate's office, dodging students milling around the hallways. It was dead in the building the last time I was here.

"You're getting a lot of attention," I say as we take the stairs to the second floor. "These girls are wondering what your major is so they can change theirs to have all the same classes."

Griffin shakes his head, but he can't hide his grin. A pang of jealousy slithers into my conscience. Does he like these girls looking at him? Or am I looking for anything to distract my mind from Erica, even if it's conjuring up ridiculous reasons to blame Griffin for being—Griffin.

"This way, rock star." I nod my head toward the door to Nate's office.

"I only want to be *your* rock star." He slides two fingers into my back pocket, giving me a playful tug as I open the door.

"I don't want a rock star. I like my grocery store guy." And Erica alive again. If I'm making a list of things I want, she's at the top.

"Hi," Donna, the blowout lady, greets us. "She's zonked."

I glance at a sleeping Morgan in her car seat. "Thank you for helping Nate—er … Professor Hunt out. I feel really bad for running late today."

She stands from his desk chair, closing her laptop and hugging it to her chest. "No problem. Here are the keys to Nathaniel's car. He said you'd swap vehicles so you would have a base for Morgan's car seat. He's parked on the east side. Lot C. First row on the right." Her gaze falls over my shoulder.

"Oh … Donna, this is Griffin. Griffin, Donna."

"Nice to meet you."

"You too."

"Keys?" I say to Griffin.

He fishes out the keys to my car. I toss them on the desk and take Nate's keys.

"Well…" I shrug "…I'll take it from here."

Donna snaps out of her dreamy state. It's the same way she gawks at Nate. "Good. Okay. Nice to see you and uh…" she serves Griffin a flirty smile "…meet you."

After the door shuts, I turn toward Griffin. "A good ego day for you. Now you know where to come if it ever needs a boost."

He smirks. "College. Work. Gym. Grocery store. It doesn't

really matter."

I smile. It's hard. With each step, the reality of what I saw yesterday sinks in a little deeper, permanently staining my memories and my conscience. The adrenaline that spurred me to get dressed and rush here has started to wear off.

Doug Mann is a killer.

My friend was murdered.

Daisy was murdered.

Nate didn't tell me that. He's never told me how she died.

"Where are you, Swayz?" Griffin pulls me into his arms.

"Erica's dead," I mumble.

He kisses my forehead. "I know. I'm so sorry."

"He killed her."

"If he did, I'm sure the police will figure it out. You definitely put him on their radar yesterday."

"Maybe. Let's go." I pull away. "Before Morgan wakes up."

Griffin lifts the infant carrier. My gaze flicks to his.

"If you don't trust me to carry her, then we have issues to discuss."

"I trust you with my life." I smile, stopping short of telling him that means I trust him with Morgan, because whether it's right or not, she's part of my life.

Slinging her diaper bag over my shoulder, I open the door to the dull chattering of students and instructors flowing in both directions. Griffin, with baby in tow, garners as many hungry female eyes—if not more—than Griffin without Morgan.

"Swayze?"

I turn. Nate catches up to us just before we reach the stairs. He gives Griffin a stiff smile. I'm sure it's the normal reaction to seeing a stranger taking off with his baby.

"Hey, I'm so sorry about this morning."

He shakes his head as if to brush off my apology; his gaze shifts to Griffin every few seconds.

"Nate, er Nathaniel … I mean Professor Hunt …" Nothing awkward about this. I'm starting to sweat. "This is Griffin. Griff, this is …" *Don't fuck it up.* "Professor Nathaniel Hunt."

Too late. I fucked it up, and the expressions on both of their faces confirms it.

"Nathaniel." Nate holds out his hand.

Griffin shakes it. "Nice to meet you."

"So is everything okay?" Nate asks, looking only at me.

"Yeah."

"No. Yesterday Swayze's neighbor—her friend—was found dead in the apartment above hers."

I shoot Griffin a slight scowl.

"Jesus … I'm so sorry. Swayze, why didn't you tell me? You shouldn't be watching Morgan today."

Griffin has an I-told-you-so expression pasted on his face.

"I'm fine." I'm as far from fine as one could be. "Griffin took the day off to help me out, even though he didn't need to take the day off."

Griffin's expression doesn't change. He thinks he knows what's best for me. And if I weren't so stubborn, I'd admit that it's true.

"So …" I shrug. "We're fine. Morgan will have double the attention. Double the care."

"Unless, you distract each other."

I try not to read into Nate's comment, but there's an underlying tone to it that bleeds distrust. Does he not trust me because of what happened to Erica? Is it Griffin? Does he really think I'd let anything happen to Morgan?

"We're good, Professor. But thanks for your vote of confidence."

Nate inspects me for a few more seconds before giving Griffin one final glance. "I have to get to class. Thanks for coming to get her."

"It's fine." I shake my head like it's no big deal. "See you later."

"So THIS IS the house my mom gushed over," Griffin says, carrying Morgan's infant carrier into Nate's house.

"It's just a house." I wash my hands at the kitchen sink.

"You have no desire to live in something like this?" He deposits the carrier on the floor and inspects the great room.

No. And neither does the Nate I remember.

"I want to live with *you*." I take Morgan out of the carrier.

She fists at her eyes and mouth, arching her back as I bring her to my shoulder. It's weird seeing Griffin in Nate's house, such a clash of my worlds.

"Having just enough?" He gazes out the window to the unarguably impressive yard, green and meticulously manicured. "Because that's what living with me is—having just enough."

Easing into the recliner, I grin. "Yes."

"Two small bedrooms and a dinky kitchen?" Griffin moves on to inspect the mantle. My tatted bad-boy-looking man wears the hell out of those faded jeans and black tee that looks a size too small with his cut chest and thick arms.

"Yes." I chuckle, finding his glimpse of insecurity adorable.

"Used vehicles? Detached garage? A do-it-yourself lifestyle?"

"Do I really have to answer you?"

He glances over his shoulder, hands tucked into his pockets. "No." He shoots me a grin before turning back around. "What's up with the camera in the corner?"

"Nanny cam or security … I haven't figure it out yet."

"He's watching us?"

"Potentially."

"Audio too?"

I laugh, looking directly at the camera. "Yes. The professor is a little creepy." Nuzzling my nose into Morgan's neck, I find my baby voice. "Isn't your daddy a little creepy? Yes … I think he is."

She giggles.

Griffin turns with a grin on his face. "She's cute."

"Yes … she's adorable."

He folds his body onto the sofa, fingers interlaced between his widespread legs. "Are you ready to tell me who Morgan Daisy Gallagher is or was?"

I shoot a nervous glance at the camera. Nate should be in class, but … "It's complicated."

"Well, good thing we have all day."

I hate these stupid cameras.

"Swayz, out with it. You completely lost it with that guy yesterday over the girl in that picture you showed us. I'm sure the police will revisit you as they investigate this guy. I need to know what's going on."

He's already said too much.

"We'll talk later." I nod toward the camera, giving him a tight smile. "Okay?"

Impatience tugs at his mouth, but he lets it go. I don't like how the thoughts in my head wedge their way between us. It scares me. The grim reaper disguised as little memories, crooking his finger at me, beckoning me to surrender. What if the day comes where I can't separate who I know I am from the impostor's voice in my head?

After lunch, Griffin rocks Morgan while I call my mom. She's texted me several times, just to check on me and see if I've made an appointment with Dr. Greyson. I agree to make an appointment. It's the only way to calm her nerves.

Wish someone would calm mine. It's impossible to think of Doug Mann and breathe at the same time.

"Aww …" I smile at my guy when I see he's rocked her to sleep.

Griffin with a sleeping baby on his chest … *this* makes me want one of my own. But it doesn't lessen my desire to be with Morgan.

Right here. Right now. It hits me.

Nate named his daughter after his best friend. He thinks he named her after *me*.

How will I ever explain all of this to Griffin?

We give our attention to Morgan for the rest of the day, but I don't miss Griffin's restrained smiles, like concern strangling happiness.

Who am I?

What's happening to my life?

Am I living in a parallel universe?

CHAPTER TWO

WE SAY A final goodbye to Erica.

A mother's weeps shatter the silence as the earth embraces the lowered casket.

Yet … Doug Mann lives in his apartment. A free man. A murderer.

The police questioned me again yesterday because they can't tie him to Erica's death—a death they are certain was an accident. An accidental drowning. Are you kidding me? A cardiologist accidentally drowning in a bathtub? I couldn't give them anything more than vague memories dating back to a time before I was alive. And they won't arrest him based solely on my gut, which swears with every fiber of my being that he killed her.

Griffin pulls into an empty parking lot as I stare at the hem of my black dress resting just above my knees. I should have worn tall boots instead of tights and heels. My knees knocked throughout the burial as chills pimpled along my skin. It's not that cold out. It's the memories—they're chilling.

"Look at me."

I lift my head, but I don't look at him. Behind dark glasses, my eyes focus on the nothingness around us.

"I won't be ignored any longer. The police questioned you. The funeral is over. It's time we talk about this. I've been patient, but it's time to tell me, Swayz."

I close my eyes. I open my eyes. It doesn't matter. The vision holds space in my mind. It doesn't need light to be seen, and it won't stop replaying. The real world fades like an echo, leaving this deep suffocating silence.

His bloodied face.

One drip.

Two drips.

Tears fill her brown eyes, reflecting the image of her killer. With a blink, life drains from her face, dissolving the fear, surrendering one final breath.

Static. Whoosh.

Complete silence.

The darkest darkness.

Warmth.

Serenity.

"Nate's childhood friend was Morgan Daisy Gallagher. I see her. I see him—Doug Mann. The cut on his face—raw and oozing crimson. They're just flashes, but they're real." I ease my head to the side, meeting Griffin's gaze, my brows drawn together. "Nate thinks I'm her."

"Her?"

I nod. "Daisy. Morgan Daisy Gallagher. His best friend. His daughter bears her name. And ..." I shake my head, maybe because I can't believe it—accept it—or maybe because I don't want to. "He thinks I know things about his past because I'm her. She's me." Continuing to shake my head, I sigh. "I don't know, but I supposedly know things about him that only she knew. I can give accounts of moments that happened to him only in her presence. I know things about him that he told her. Only her."

Griffin's lips twist, deepening the lines along his brow.

"You can't mean reincarnation."

"Nate thinks so."

"And you?" he asks with a hint of sarcasm.

"No." Drawing in a deep breath, I avert my gaze. "I … I don't know. The thing is … I didn't remember her until I saw Erica's body in the bathtub. And even then, it was just flashes of Doug's face, her face … her dying. I remember Nate. Not Daisy. If reincarnation is real, how can a soul retain memories of other people but not the person it was before this new life? It doesn't make sense." I laugh. "This is ridiculous. I'm attempting to give rules to a phenomenon that may not even exist. And by doing so, I feel like I'm acknowledging that the rebirth of a soul is a definite possibility." Closing my eyes, I press my lips together. What do I expect from Griffin? This sounds crazy, even to me, and I'm living it. "I just don't know if I'm ready to …"

"Accept that you're her?"

My eyes open to a serious Griffin. What does he mean? "You think I'm her?"

His head shakes side to side a half dozen times. "Fuck, Swayz. No. Why would I? But hell if I know what to make of this. It's an intriguing book. It's a nail-biter movie. But acknowledging it as real life—your life … I just … I don't know if I can do that. I'd be lying if I said it doesn't worry me."

"Worry you how?"

He eases his head back against the headrest, gaze pointed up. "Hypothetically, you're her. She's you. And that's a *big-ass* hypothetical. What does that mean for you? For us? For everyone? I mean … does this Morgan Daisy Gallagher have family? If Doug Mann really murdered her, shouldn't they be told? But by who? Their reincarnated daughter who happens to be the nanny for—"

His head jerks straight again, brow pulled tight. "Nate and her were friends? Or were they more than friends? Who does he really see when he looks at you?"

The girl he loved as much as the woman who died giving birth to his child.

"A ghost."

And they were more than friends. Nate left me hanging with their story. I don't know what happened after they broke up. Did she die? Is that how things ended with them? A ridiculous clashing of egos? A modern day *Pride and Prejudice*?

"How old was she when she died?" he asks.

When Doug Mann murdered her.

"Fifteen."

"Was he fifteen too?"

I nod. Why are the words stuck inside? Griffin is the man I love. My friend. My lover. My future husband. Yet, I can't find the right way to explain the emotional connection I have to Nate and Morgan.

To a past I can't fully remember.

To a present with its claws curled into my heart.

To a future more terrifying than my worst nightmares.

To an unknown that could ruin my existence as I know it.

"Was he in love with her?"

"Does it matter?"

Griffin rests his elbow by the window and massages his temples. "Yes, it matters. I want to know if he's looking at you like a buddy or the girl he lost his virginity to."

"They didn't have sex."

He grunts sarcasm. "I fucking love that you know that. He hired you to watch his daughter, not discuss his sex life. What else do the two of you discuss?"

"Griffin …"

Rubbing his hand over his mouth, he shakes his head, but he won't look at me.

"You're not this guy. You don't get jealous. I've done nothing wrong. It's not my fault these memories and images are in my head. My relationship with Nate is complicated, but it's not intimate."

"To you or to him?"

"I just said—"

Griffin shoves open the door and tears out of the vehicle like it's suffocating him. I jump out and chase after him as he paces the empty lot, head down, hands laced behind his neck.

"I'm marrying you. You. You. You." As soon as I get in front of him, he pivots and stalks the other way.

"Well, who the hell am I marrying?" He whips around, bending forward to get in my face. "Swayze? Morgan Daisy Gallagher?"

"Me." My voice cracks as I blink back the tears.

"And who are you?"

"Swayze."

The tension in his face eases a bit. "Are you sure?"

I push all the anxiety, all the fear, and all the confusion down into a dark hole I think is my soul. And I breathe in as much courage as I can muster, tipping my chin up. "Yes."

He grabs my face and rests his forehead against mine. Without a confession, I feel his guilt. Without a single word, I feel his love. Let this be one more day where I'm granted the miracle of not losing Griffin.

"YOU'RE QUIET."

I tickle Morgan's feet as she kicks and coos on the living room floor while Nate packs his lunch. I took one day off for the funeral. Maybe I should have taken two.

"Just waiting for you to leave, Professor. That's when Morgan and I get the party started—bounce house, ponies, clowns, a DJ, cotton candy."

He glances up with a smirk on his face. I fall short of matching it.

"Do you want to talk about it?"

It? This is the first he's attempted to have a conversation beyond Morgan since Erica died—not that we've had that many opportunities.

"You'll have to be more specific."

"Your friend's death. Why Griffin asked you about Daisy? Or that diamond ring on your left hand."

The ring. I glance at it. "Erica's dead. The guy who killed her still lives in the apartment across from hers. They're calling it an accident. She slipped, hit her head, and drowned. I don't believe it. Seriously, how many people slip in the bathtub, get knocked out, and drown?"

I frown, looking at my ring. "And Griffin proposed to me. I said yes."

Nate returns a cautious nod. "If what you believe about this man is true … I don't think you should be living in that building."

"I'm not. I moved in with Griffin."

He nods again. "Should I say congratulations?"

I laugh. "Only if you want to."

There's a pregnant pause.

"I'm surprised you don't want to talk about Daisy. You

always want to talk about her."

I guess he's not going to congratulate me.

"I do want to talk about her." He has no idea how badly I want to talk about Daisy and her death. "But you have five minutes before you need to be out the door. Five minutes won't be enough time."

"Can you stay when I get home? I'll bring dinner."

"I don't think Griffin wants me having dinner with you."

"He doesn't trust you?"

"Try again."

Nate grins. "Me? Did I do something to lose his trust?"

"Yes. You suggested I'm Daisy."

"Ah, so now I'm crazy in his mind?"

"That's not quite it either."

"Then what?"

"Go to work, Professor. I don't want to talk about Griffin with you."

He moves toward me. I hate how he moves toward me, or maybe it's the way he looks at me when he's doing it. It's familiar—too familiar. And comfortable. And … unnerving. Completely unnerving.

He lowers onto his hands and knees. "Have a good day," he says, kissing Morgan on the cheek. She kicks and rewards him with a grin. When he lifts his head, he stops just inches from my face.

Way. Too. Close.

"Congratulations," he murmurs. "I'm glad you found a real boyfriend."

My lungs collapse.

Daisy …

"Fine. I'll be your girlfriend, but only until I find a real boy-

friend."

"A real boyfriend?"

"Yes. A real boyfriend. One who brings me flowers and choco-late and opens doors for me like my dad opens doors for my mom. And one who kisses me right here." She pointed to a spot on her neck just below her ear. *"My dad kisses my mom there, and it always makes her giggle."*

Nate's gaze shifts to my neck, right below my ear. I swear to God I will shatter if he kisses me there. But not just because it's wrong. I'll shatter because I know I won't stop him. It's not about wanting him or loving him. Griffin is the love of my life. There's just this indescribable need I have to know what Nate's lips feel like against my neck.

Will it feel as familiar as the other times we've touched?

Will it bring more memories to life?

Will I feel what Daisy felt when he kissed her under her ear?

Will I hate myself for letting him do it? For needing to *know?* For risking everything?

"Breathe, Swayze."

I attempt to stifle my gasp—my reaction to his proximity. Nate grins like the boy I used to know as he lumbers to stand-ing.

Like the boy I used to know ...

"Be good, girls." He winks and walks away before making sure I have a pulse. Not very responsible of him.

MORGAN AND I spend the day in Nate's bedroom, taking complete liberty of his offer to let me snoop. I'm certain I surpassed snooping hours ago, about the same time I shut off all thoughts of the camera watching me. Flashes of Erica and Daisy haunt me. I can't let this go.

Something takes over inside, and I tear apart his room and closet, looking for anything to fill in the gaps. When every drawer is pulled from the dresser and dumped out onto the floor, revealing no new clues, I move on to his office. I'm not sure who this woman is inside of me, this possessed demon rummaging through everything, leaving a mess in my wake.

Nothing.

When Morgan's patience ends, I get her a bottle and plant my ass amongst the sea of scattered photos on Nate's bed. I need answers, but they're not here.

"Hey."

I snap my head up as Morgan drifts off to sleep with a tiny bit of milk left in her bottle.

Nate surveys the ransacked room. Wait until he sees his office. "Find what you were looking for?" he says slowly like *put the gun down.*

I shake my head, feeling defeated. Numb.

"Why don't I lay her down? Then maybe I can help you."

I nod, letting the bottle fall from my grip as he takes Morgan from me. A few minutes later he returns, making another inspection of the disaster.

"I need to know how Daisy died," I say in an agonizing whisper.

Nate gathers up as many photos from the bed as he can at once, sets them on the nightstand, and eases onto the bed, resting his head on the pillow. He stares at the ceiling.

"Daisy's mom called my house, wondering if she was with me. I hadn't seen her in over a week."

"Sorry, Mrs. Gallagher, she's not here. I don't know if she told you but ... we kinda broke up. It's my fault. I need to apologize."

"Sweetie, I know. She was very emotional about it."

I died inside. I'd hurt Daisy because of my stupid pride.

"But right now we just need to find her," her mom said.

I glanced at the microwave clock. It was almost nine o'clock at night. I listed off every friend she had, but they'd tried everyone.

"We're very worried. Do you have any idea where she'd be? A secret hideout? A favorite restaurant? A ... new boyfriend?"

I flinched. A real boyfriend.

No. No way. Not in a week. We were only fifteen, but she loved me.

"There is this place we used to go, but I made her promise to not go back."

"Where, Nate? I'm going out of my mind. My next call will be the police."

"Come get me and I'll show you how to get there."

Mr. and Mrs. Gallagher drove me to the abandoned property that was not really abandoned. I didn't mention it at first.

"Who lives here?" her dad asked as we pulled in the driveway.

"No one. Or so we thought until ..."

"Until?" Her mom turned in her seat, pinning me with a firm look.

"Last week Morgan told me she met the son of the owners. His parents are both dead, so he came back to take care of some things. I made her promise to never come back here ... especially alone."

Her dad flew out of the car without even killing the ignition. He knocked on the door and rang the doorbell, but no one answered. He flipped on a flashlight, aiming the beam into the woods behind the house.

"What's back there?"

"A tree house and a lake."

We checked out the tree house and the area of the lake around the dock, but by that time it was too dark to see much.

If I wouldn't have been such a jerk, we wouldn't have broken up and Daisy would have been with me that night. The Gallaghers took me home. I didn't want them to leave me. I wanted to stay with them and help look for Daisy, but they insisted there wasn't any more I could do.

I didn't fall asleep until the early hours of the morning. Concern for Daisy suffocated my conscience and heart. But eventually, I surrendered to my tired eyes.

"Nate?"

I jumped awake, startled by my dad's voice and his hand on my head.

"Daisy … did the Gallaghers call?" I bolted up straight, rubbing my eyes with the heels of my hands.

My dad frowned the same frown he gave me when he told me my mom had left us for the first time. Actually, this frown was worse. So much worse.

"Mr. Gallagher just called." He rested his hand on my shoulder and squeezed it. "They found her."

"Where?" I scooted out of bed, shoving my legs into my jeans and tugging on a dirty shirt. "I need to see her. I was so stupid, Dad. I messed up. I have to apologize. Her mom said she was very emotional after we broke up." My feet fought with my shoes as I tried to get them on without untying them. "I bet I made her cry. I'm such an idiot."

My dad grabbed my arm, squeezing it tighter than he did my shoulder. I eyed his hand with confusion before shifting my gaze to meet his. I don't remember what he said. I just remember how it felt to have my world end—my heart ripped from my chest. My soul shattered.

Nothing would ever hurt this bad … nothing.

Daisy's body.

Dead.

Drowned in the lake.

An accident.

Old abandoned property.

Tangled in the rope under the dock.

My dad's expression grew more painfully sympathetic as I shook my head in denial. Fifteen-year-old girls don't die like that. Daisy would never go to the lake by herself. It was a mistake. Not her body. No ... no ... NO!

Nate's words rip from his chest—strangled and raw.

I bat the tears away from my eyes while his gaze remains fixed to the ceiling—the past.

"She was murdered," I whisper.

His head rolls side to side on the pillow. "No. She drowned. It was an accident. They said she must have fallen out of the canoe while trying to tie it to the dock. She hit her head on the post and got tangled in the rope. I don't know why she was there. She knew better."

"Nate ..." I can't stop the tears.

He glances at me and snaps his body to sitting, grabbing my head with urgency, eyes wide and wild. "You remember ..." he whispers, wiping my tears with his thumbs.

Rubbing my quivering lips together, I shake my head. "She was murdered."

His brows pull together. "No. Why are you saying this?"

"Doug Mann ..."

He continues to shake his head, gripping mine more firmly. "How do you know that name?"

I swallow past the swelling pain in my throat. "He was the son. Wasn't he?"

Nate's gaze flits along my face for a few seconds. "Yes. Jesus … tell me what's going on? Where did you hear his name? What do you remember? Where is this coming from?"

I wasn't her. I wasn't her. I wasn't her. God … whose memories are these, if they're not Nate's?

I blink out more tears. "I'm scared." All these years, my need to feel safe … the harbor I found in Griffin … *This* is it. This is the fear that's chased me even when I couldn't see it— but I've always felt it.

A sob breaks from my chest.

Nate pulls me into his arms. "Don't be scared. I won't let anything happen to you ever again."

I'm not her. Nate … no …

He can't protect me. I'm not his to protect, but my body doesn't know that as I cling to the familiar home of his embrace. I've been here many times before.

Oh my god …

I *have* been here many times before. Not this body … but somewhere in my mind the memory has transcended time, breeding new life every time Nate touches me. Whatever this is … it's woven into a part of me I cannot explain—a part of me I can no longer deny.

Who am I?

A ghost?

An unfinished life?

A fractured soul?

Everything hurts. I've spent my life trying to find myself. Desperate for a sense of normalcy. I found it with Griffin. I found everything with him.

Until now …

I claw at Nate's shirt, desperate to feel safe.

"Shh …" He pulls me closer, until my arms are wrapped around his body, face buried into his neck.

I can't let go—can't pull away. I'm a misfit puzzle, and some of my pieces fit with Nate. Only he can fill in the gaps and make those parts of me feel whole.

Whole. Can I ever be whole when I don't know who I am?

This isn't Griffin's touch. This isn't my father's touch. But … it's just as familiar. It makes me feel safe and loved. Can I have this and let it simply be Nate?

"Do you remember?" he whispers, resting his cheek on the top of my head.

"No … yes … just …"

Just the man who killed her. Me … did he kill me?

Nate starts to pull away, but my fingers curl into his shirt and my arms tighten around his body.

Warm lips press to the top of my head. Strong hands embrace me, scooting me closer until I'm on his lap—straddling him, hugging him, and clinging to a past I still don't understand.

He wants answers I can't give. He needs recognition, but it's lost in the depths of my mind that may never see the light of this life.

"I see Daisy, but you weren't there. I've never seen her in my head before. She wasn't me … she was just … her. Scared."

Scared. Scared like me. Desperate to feel safe and protected.

"Why was she scared?"

Because she knew she was going to die.

I blink and more tears break free. This isn't closure for Nate, this is torture. She hit her head, passed out, and drowned. Maybe she never woke up—never suffered. He must tell himself that every day to make each breath he takes without her feel tolerable.

He blames himself for her death. What's in my head will destroy him. I won't break him again. Morgan needs her father, and Nate deserves a life filled with happiness. Not regret.

I pull back, resting my hands flat on his chest. He catches my tears with his thumbs.

This isn't right. I can't bring myself to tell him, so I back my way out.

"She looked scared." I shake my head. "I-I think I must have thought she was scared of someone, but it could have been the darkness, being alone, knowing she wasn't supposed to be there by herself."

Confusion mars his face. "How do you know Doug Mann's name?"

"I …" I shake my head. "I … looked it up. Who um … owned the house." I slide off his lap and stand, wiping my eyes and running my hands through my hair. "I have to go. I'm sorry about the mess. I'll clean it up first thing in the morning."

"Swayze …"

I bolt down the hall, grab my bag, and jog toward the door.

"Swayze?"

"Goodnight." I shut the door behind me and sprint to my car, fumbling with my key to get it started.

From the front door, Nate studies me, dragging a frustrated hand through his wavy hair.

"I'm sorry," I whisper, shoving my car into reverse.

CHAPTER THREE

I CAN'T STOP shaking. This nightmare won't end, even with my eyes wide open. I need to be Swayze. I need to forget the images in my mind. I *need* … my grocery store guy.

"Hey, Swayz. How was your day?" Griffin looks up from the motorcycle. I think it belongs to our new neighbor, but I don't know for sure, and I don't care.

My hands ball into fists to stop the shaking, but it doesn't help. It feels like my entire existence wants to unravel. With every breath, my lungs wage war against the pounding of my heart.

"Swayz?" Griffin's gaze tracks me as I brush past him.

I hit the down button on the garage door.

Griffin wipes his hands on a grease-stained towel as he climbs to his feet. "Baby, what's going on?"

Breathe. Breathe. Breathe.

Forget. Let go. Be Swayze.

This life. This is my life. This has to be my life. I can't *live* without this life.

I flip off the lights, leaving only a dim splash of illumination from the streetlight filtering in from the high window off to my right.

"Swayz … what's going—"

I crash into him, kissing him like I need his breath to fill my lungs. My hands fist his shirt.

He tries to pull away. "What's going on?"

I lift onto my toes to kiss him again.

He grabs my shoulders to stop me. "Swayze, what's wrong?"

I suck in a shaky breath, but it doesn't stop the tears. "I need *you* … if you love me … you'll give me this without question."

His brow knits tightly. "I'm a mess." He is. He's covered in sweat and grease.

My words fight past the pain, coming out as a strangled whisper. "So am I …"

"Swayz …" He shakes his head slowly.

Even if he can't understand, he can feel. And right now I know he feels my pain.

My hand slides along his stubble-covered jaw and over a black smudge until my fingers curl around his bandana, pulling it off to reveal his newly-shaven head. "Make me forget that anything exists beyond these four walls."

I let his gaze wash over me, like a savior baptizing me, cleansing my sins and restoring my faith. His love is my religion.

Griffin releases my shoulders and clutches the hem of my shirt, peeling it over my head. I do the same to him. I remove my bra, and he palms my head, taking my mouth with hunger. This man kisses me like the ocean claims the shore, knocking me back until I surrender, pulling me into blinding depths, swallowing me whole. And just like that … the world disappears.

Four walls.

Two bodies.

One love.

We lose all that doesn't matter—our clothes, yesterday's memories, tomorrow's plans. On a dirty drop cloth, over a cold floor, surrounded by musky sweat and grease ... We embrace each other and these stolen minutes. The last two people on Earth.

His lips move down my body as I arch my back, closing my eyes.

Our fingers thread together, clenching, claiming, holding on to this moment.

He sits up, pulling me onto him, nose to nose as he whispers, "I'm never letting you go."

Four walls and this man—*nothing* else matters.

My hips rock into his, feeling him deep inside of me. "I love you now ..." I close my eyes and move with his body. Kissing my way up his neck, I stop at his ear, "I will love you always." My eyes squeeze shut, forcing out a few residual tears. "Please don't ever forget it."

We cling to each other. Maybe if we're strong enough, we can make it through the storm without being ripped apart, stranded—completely alone.

God ... I hope we're strong enough.

"GOOD MORNING." GRIFFIN hands me a cup of coffee as I drop my tired ass onto the kitchen chair.

I smile—the shy kind that's afraid to confront what happened over the past ten hours. Last night rivaled the make-up sex we had after Griffin's birthday. He didn't want to talk then. He wanted to *take*. Looking back, I think he wanted to prove that nothing mattered outside of us.

Last night I begged for silence and the physical reassurance that I'm still that woman he fell in love with. I'm still that woman enraptured in all things Griffin Calloway. Last night I needed to lose myself in *us*, overwhelmed with the need to shut out everything beyond our four walls.

Today I will return to Nate's house with its haunting memories of me clinging to him, the familiarity of his embrace, and the most haunting part of all … I think Nate may be right.

I'm Daisy.

Griffin inspects me in silence as he sips his green protein drink.

My lungs reach for a breath of courage. I owe him an explanation. He gave me everything last night, without question. "If I walk away from this job…" I slowly trace the pad of my finger over the rim of my coffee mug "…it won't change the memories I have of the past."

His expression hardens ever so slightly. Silent and stoic.

"I don't want you to get mad at me. But I don't want to lie to you either. This walking-on-eggshells thing won't work forever. You ask me about my day, and…" I shake my head, shake off the pain that's suffocating me "…I know it's not small talk. You *really* want to know about my day—about me."

I reach across the table, resting my hand on his. He stares at our hands with a blank look.

"And I love you so much for that. But this other person in my head keeps stealing minutes from my day, making it her day. So when you ask me that question, I feel like the truth will pull us apart, but so will a lie. So …" I shrug. "It hurts—" Tears burn my eyes, but I don't give them life. "The thought of losing you is unbearable."

His gaze crawls along the table between us, making its way

to meet mine. I see my whole world in his eyes, but when I close mine, I see many worlds. Immutable images. I feel deep love and loss. And I hear voices that won't be silenced.

"Right now … who are you?" he asks.

I ease out of my chair and slide my leg over his lap, putting us face to face. "I'm Swayze."

And I am. Right now. With him. I'm Swayze Samuels. Daughter to Krista. Fiancée to Griffin. Nanny to Morgan. And employee to Professor Nathaniel Hunt.

The line is there. I can see it. But I fear that time will blur it.

"I love *you*." He brushes his lips over mine.

Swayze. He loves the girl he saved in the grocery store. That's who he wants to marry. I want to be her. She has the perfect man. A future filled with promise. A loving family. Health. Youth. Endless possibilities.

"She loves you too." I softly kiss his top lip and then his bottom lip.

Griffin shakes his head, fingers curling into my hips. "Don't say that. Don't talk in some fucking third person like a schizophrenic."

I frame his face to stop his head shaking. "*I* love you. *I'm* going to marry you." These words are for him, but they're also for me.

If I lost an arm, I'd still be me. If I shaved my head, I'd still be me. If I lost all memories, I'd still be me. I need to carry this one absolute truth with me at all times.

"I have to get to work. Let's go out for dinner tonight and plan a wedding."

After a few blinks, Griffin surrenders something resembling a smile. "Good idea. I don't want a long engagement." He nuzzles his face into my neck.

I hug him. This is the only embrace I want comforting me for the rest of my life.

I PULL INTO Nate's driveway a few minutes early and call the detective working on Erica's case. He tells me there's too much inconclusive evidence to question Doug Mann any further. There was no sign of foul play. It was an accident. Case closed.

She slipped and hit her head while getting into the bathtub and she drowned.

Daisy drowned. Daisy's death was an accident.

Except … my memories tell a different story.

I take a deep breath to calm my anger before opening the door to Nate's house. "Good morning."

"Shh … in my office."

I peek around the corner. "She's still asleep?"

Nate glances up as he slips his laptop into his messenger bag. "Yes. She was up earlier. For whatever reason, she wanted to smile and giggle at 4:00 a.m." He fists a hand over his mouth to hide his yawn. "I'm going to feel it later today."

I offer him a hint of a smile, trying to move past last night and everything the detective just told me.

"Did you sleep well?" Nate saunters toward me.

I turn and lead the way to the kitchen. "Well enough." Not that well. Sex. I had endless sex with Griffin until my mind let go of what happened here, with *you*, Nate.

"Coffee?" He holds up the pot before filling his cup.

"Just had some, but thank you."

He pours it and brings the cup to his mouth, eyeing me

with an unreadable expression. "You seem distracted."

An understatement.

"Can I ask you something?"

Nate takes a sip and rubs his lips together. "You can ask me anything."

"If I admit that I'm Daisy, can we forget about it?"

His eyebrows shoot up his forehead, brushing his wayward curls. "You believe it?"

I shrug. "For lack of any other explanation ... yes."

His chin dips into a contemplative nod. "You didn't just wake up this morning with recognition of her life?"

"No."

He fails at masking his disappointment.

"I feel like you want me to admit that I'm her. The books in your nightstand confirm it."

There's not an ounce of shock on his face. He knows I've been snooping.

"I think there's a chance that you're right. And I'm not sure what the protocol is for this, but no matter what memories I have from another life, it doesn't change the fact that I'm Swayze Samuels in this life."

"So you want to forget about *everything*?"

I grunt a painful laugh. "I don't think I have the option to forget anything. Unless they invent an off switch for the brain. I just don't want to talk about it anymore. I'll try to keep all of my comments relevant to things I would know about you in this life, and you'll stop looking at me like ..."

"Like?" He slips an apple and protein bar into the back pocket of his bag.

"Like ... I don't know. Like anything other than the twenty-one-year-old nanny that I am."

"You want us to pretend."

"No … yes. When you say it that way it sounds ridiculous. You know what I mean."

His teeth rake along his lower lip several times while he eyes me. "This is causing problems between you and Griffin?"

My gaze drops to my feet. "Sometimes. I don't want to lose him. It's not fair to ask him to share me with another life. It's insane to ask him to understand. And I'm tired of feeling ripped down the middle."

"Okay."

My head snaps up. "Okay?"

Nate nods. "We won't talk of it again. Your happiness comes first."

"Don't say that. An employer wouldn't say that."

He chuckles. "I disagree. A good employer would want a happy employee."

"Happy? Yes. As in, maybe leave a little more food in the house. Or trusting me enough to not need constant surveillance. That would make me happy. Happi*ness* implies more. It implies you have concern for my future beyond this job. I don't want you to be invested in my *happiness*."

Nate flinches. It's slight, but I don't miss it. He slides the strap to his bag over his shoulder and snatches his coffee. "I'll stop by the grocery store on the way home. Text me with your list of food." His tone is a little abrasive. "If you were my friend Daisy, I'd shut off the cameras. I know Daisy. I trust her implicitly. Swayze is a twenty-one-year-old nanny whom I've not known long enough to warrant such implicit trust. The cameras stay on. Have a good day, Swayze."

Ouch.

I bite my tongue. He's respecting my wish. I have to let it

go. I just didn't imagine it feeling like this.

"Good day, Professor Hunt."

My words make him pause at the back door. I wait for him to turn back toward me. I wait to see the pain on his face. He doesn't turn. He doesn't show me his reaction. And that's for the best.

CHAPTER FOUR

WEEKS PASS WITHOUT mention of Daisy. Each night I leave Professor Hunt's house with a lukewarm goodbye and hurry home to my fiancé. We immerse ourselves in wedding planning and dinners with his family and my mom. I find a rhythm to my life again.

I wish I could say I don't think of Daisy, or Erica, or the free man who murdered them. I wish I could say I don't miss the friendship I had with Nate. I wish I could say everything in life is mind over matter.

I wish …

"What are your plans for Thanksgiving?" I ask Nate as he goes through his morning routine in the kitchen while Morgan rolls around on the floor, working her way up to all fours only to flop back down to her tummy and take off rolling again.

"The usual gluttony," he replies without making the slightest glance in my direction.

"Griffin and his dad are smoking a turkey. I'm in charge of the mashed potatoes."

He nods once, keeping his gaze on his busy hands. I miss him. Even though I see him five out of seven days, I still miss him. And the worst fucking part … I still carry that picture of him in my pocket. It's my dirty little secret.

It's flat-out crazy because I can't explain my need to have it near me or my need to stare at it for long minutes when I'm alone or out of the camera's view.

"Are your parents coming to your house or are you going to their house?"

"Not sure." He brushes past me with no visual acknowledgment as he lowers to the floor and kisses Morgan goodbye. "Love you, baby doll. Have a good day."

I stare him down, silently begging for him to look at me, but he doesn't. This shouldn't hurt, but it does.

"Hey ..." I jump up and chase after him.

He stops at the door. "Yeah?"

That's all I wanted, just to have him look at me.

"Hey what?"

I shake my head, feeling stupid for my desperation. "Um ..." I wanted him to look at me and now I can't keep my gaze locked to his. It's too matter-of-fact. Neutral. Impersonal.

It's exactly what I thought I wanted.

"I was thinking of going through Morgan's clothes. She's outgrown a lot of them. Do you want them put in bags to sell or donate or ..." I bite my lips together for a few seconds. "Do you want to save them in case you have ..."

Gulp. Choke. I'm dying. All I wanted was for him to look at me and it's careened into a train wreck.

"Have more children?"

I shrug.

"I pay you to watch Morgan. I'll deal with her clothes and their fate."

I nod.

"Anything else?"

"No," I murmur.

"Okay." He opens the door.

I grip his arm. I have no idea why. My brain has a two-second delay.

Nate stares at my hold on him a few seconds before shooting me the look. The why-the-hell-are-you-touching-me look. I crawled onto his lap and cried my eyes out. He promised to never let anything bad happen to me. And now we're here in this cold existence.

Yank your arm out of my hold, Nate. Reprimand me for crossing a line. Tell me you're just obeying my wishes. Do anything. Say anything. But don't just look at me, frozen in place, submitting to my touch.

I suck in one breath after another, each time hoping the right words will spill from my mouth, but every inhale dies in a wasted exhale of nothingness. Right now my feelings don't have words, so I release him.

After a few more seconds of silence, I turn and go back to Morgan. The *thunk* of the door sounds behind me.

THE NEXT FEW days I spend all of Morgan's nap time staring at the photo of Nate. Sometimes I keep it in my book instead of in my pocket. If he's monitoring the video feed, all he sees is the book, not the photo I keep shifting from page to page like a bookmark.

This heightened fucked-up-ness spurs me to make an appointment with Dr. Greyson.

"IT'S BEEN AWHILE," I state the obvious before Dr. Greyson gets the chance.

"I'm here when you need me." He leans back, hands folded in his lap.

"Thank you. Can I just throw everything out on the table and let you figure out how to piece it all together?"

A tiny grin graces his face. "I can't promise to piece anything together, but I'm here to listen and help in any way I can."

I sigh, readying myself for the big spill. "I'm engaged to Griffin." I hold up my hand so he can see my ring.

"Congratulations."

"Thanks. I love him. I'm happy with him. He's my dream come true. I love his family. I love that his family loves me and even my mom. Our moms have lunch together. They're genuine friends. We're planning a spring wedding. I want a hundred babies with Griffin."

Dr. Greyson lifts a single brow.

"Okay, maybe like four … but you get what I mean. My relationship with my mom has greatly improved. She's living again, not just grieving my father's death. And she's even started taking photos again."

I pause to catch my breath.

"It sounds like things are going well for you."

"I know, right? It's the perfect life. What more could I possibly want or need?"

He nods. "I sense there's more. Maybe the true reason for your visit?"

"It's Nathaniel Hunt. I know this feels like a conflict of interest. I'm not sure he even still sees you. I haven't asked. But here's the issue: He thinks I'm the reincarnation of his childhood friend. The things I told you I know about him? He thinks it's because I'm his friend Daisy. I didn't believe this for the longest time because I didn't remember her, only him. How could I be her and not remember her? It makes no sense."

Dr. Grayson leans forward and steeples his fingers. Things are serious since we're already at steepled fingers.

"The problem is … I've had these memories or flashbacks of her. And I say *her* because I still don't connect her to me. But the only logical explanation for these memories and my knowledge of this time before I—Swayze—was born is that I'm her. So …" I sigh. "I honestly believe I'm her."

He narrows his eyes a bit, making a slight shift of his head to the side.

"Now, before you feel obligated to solve the reincarnation mystery, I have to tell you that's not exactly why I'm here. I've decided to accept that I'm her. But I don't want to be her because I like my life as Swayze. So I got Nate to agree that we wouldn't talk of her again. And I don't talk about her anymore with my fiancé either. But …" I reach back and rub my neck with both hands.

"You can't control your thoughts and they keep going back to her and the memories you have."

"Yeah." I cringe. "But it's not just that. I can ignore memories, push them aside. It's the feelings. Nate and I grew close over this. I think in some ways we were Nate and Daisy again. Not romantically."

I feel like this isn't entirely true. But it's not entirely false either. It's … complicated.

"Friends," I say. "Very familiar friends. But that complicated my life with Griffin, so I asked Nate to forget about the past. Daisy. My memories. I asked him to treat me like an employee. Period."

"And how is he doing with that?"

"Great. That's the problem. He's giving me exactly what I wanted, and it was good for a while, but now it doesn't feel so good. The thing is ... I miss him. Things feel cold and very robotic between us."

"What do you miss?"

"His smile. When I met him he was this broken man who lost his wife. But over time he smiled and joked. It was nice. Now his smiles seem forced, and he hardly looks at me. It's a simple *good morning* and *good night*."

"Are you worried he's not happy now?"

"Is he?" I know he can't answer that, but I'd love to know.

Dr. Greyson retrieves his famous tin of mints. "Does Swayze miss him or does the part of you that feels like his childhood friend miss him?"

"I don't know. I have trouble separating the two when I'm around him."

He opens his side drawer. "I'm going to give you the name of a colleague of mine. I'd like you to pay her a visit. I'll let her know to expect your call. She's well-trained and quite knowledgeable about the theories of past lives."

I take the business card from him.

Professor Hazel Albright

I squint at the card for a few seconds, fighting for the connection. I've heard her name before.

"She's written books on this topic."

My gaze shoots up to his. That's where I've seen her name. Nate has her book in his nightstand.

"She's at the university?"

"Yes. She's a professor there, but she takes on a few cases of particular interest."

"And by particular interest, you mean reincarnation."

"By particular interest I mean rare cases referred to her by trusted colleagues."

I nod, staring at her card. I wonder if Nate knows her? Standing, I slip the business card into my purse. "Do you believe in reincarnation?"

"My beliefs don't matter. They're just that … beliefs."

My lips twist. "I didn't believe in it. I still can't really wrap my head around it, but if I don't choose to accept it as the answer, then I'm just a crazy person. I don't want to be a crazy person."

Dr. Greyson stands, escorting me to the door. "Swayze, you're not crazy."

I chuckle. "Will you write that on my chart so I have it in a permanent medical record?"

He grins because he doesn't know about Erica and Doug Mann and the Daisy connection. *That* might make him second-guess my sanity.

CHAPTER FIVE
Nathaniel

E VERY EVENING I give myself a pep talk before walking into the house. I have a nanny. Her name is Swayze Samuels. She's just a nanny. Morgan's attached to her, so while I should look for a new nanny, I feel like Swayze is best for my daughter—not for me.

"Dashing through the snow …"

My head jerks back as I open the door to the greeting of Christmas music. It's two weeks until Thanksgiving. Why is there Christmas music playing?

The door chime makes Swayze jump as usual. She spins around, hugging Morgan to her. I hate that her smile fades when she sees me. I hate that I can't get the fucking nerve to share my own smile.

"A little early for Christmas music." I set my bag on the chair, keeping my eyes on Morgan while I wash my hands.

"Is it ever too early for Christmas music?"

"Yes." I steal Morgan from her. "Hey, baby doll. I missed you today."

Swayze holds her spot next to me. Usually she's halfway out the door by now.

"Thank you, Swayze. Drive safely," I say as if I'm talking to Morgan because I don't like looking at Swayze. Or maybe I don't like the way she looks at me like I've done something wrong.

"Did uh …" Her words lack any sort of confidence. "Did you have a good day?"

I glance over at her and sit on the sofa, letting Morgan's strong legs push off mine in her constant desire to bounce. "It was fine. Thank you. Did you have a good day?"

"We did." She hugs herself, rubbing her lips together and shifting her weight from one leg to the other.

"Okay. Well … glad to hear it."

"Doing anything exciting this weekend?"

"Just the usual." Why is she stalling? "You?"

"My birthday is Sunday, so we're having a family dinner at Griffin's parents' house."

"I didn't know. Happy early birthday. Twenty-two." I shake my head. "Enjoy your youth."

She nods, working the hell out of her lips. Her mind must be racing. I can see it in her tight brow. I can predict where this is going, but she's conflicted about breaking her own rules. I'm not going to help her out, and maybe that makes me a dick, but I'm so lost right now I refuse to make any assumptions with her.

"You're not *that* old. I think a lot of people would say any-one in their thirties still retains a lot of youth."

I grin at my smiling baby. "Hmm … maybe so."

"So …" She rocks back and forth on her heels. "Have a good one."

"You too."

Halfway to the door she stops and turns. "Jeez, would it kill you to share a little? I know what I said about keeping things professional, but how is it that when I mention my birthday is Sunday you have no natural instinct to say, 'Oh, really? My birthday is tomorrow.'"

Morgan's chubby hands reach for my face. I kiss her fingers. "I didn't know your birthday is Sunday until you mentioned it, but I assumed you might know that my birthday is tomorrow. Sorry. I get a little confused as to when we're being honest and when we're supposed to pretend. I went for the honest assumption, but clearly you wanted me to pretend. So, wow! My birthday is tomorrow. How crazy is it that our birthdays are just a day apart?"

Her hands land on her hips. "Now you're mocking me?"

Easing Morgan to sit on my lap, I bounce my knee a little. "I'd never do that. Thank you for watching Morgan. Drive safely. Have a nice weekend and a happy birthday." After a few seconds of her not moving, I glance in her direction. The pained expression she has kills me. It's not my intention to hurt her, just the opposite. My attempt at respecting her wishes by giving her whatever she thinks she needs or wants is to keep from hurting her.

But right now I get the sense that she doesn't know what she wants or needs. I lay Morgan onto her new play mat, with padded sides that keep her contained, and make my way to the lost girl standing idle like something frozen in time.

Swayze stares at my chest, unblinking. I want to pull her into my arms and make promises that aren't mine to make.

"What's your favorite cake flavor?" I murmur, hoping my reverence conveys my sincerity.

"Chocolate." She keeps her gaze locked to my chest.

"What's the best birthday present anyone has ever given you?"

She shrugs. "Nothing stands out."

"Well, that's sad."

Her head eases up until I have her full attention. "I miss you."

I flinch at the pain in her voice because I don't know how to make it go away.

"I love Griffin. I'm marrying him. I love his family. And they love me. But ..." Her jaw works side to side a few times. "I miss you. And I don't know why."

My fingers draw into fists, fighting the urge to touch her. She's not mine to touch.

"I'm here." I search for a smile that's reassuring, probably a million miles from hitting the mark because I miss her too. "As your employer. As your friend. As whomever you need me to be."

She nods slowly, confusion still embedded in her forehead. "I need you to be..." eyes closed, she shakes her head "...an answer."

Don't touch her. Don't. Fucking. Touch. Her.

"What's the question?"

Blinking a few times, her shoulders lift into a subtle shrug. "I'm not sure yet. But maybe I'll know soon."

I can't decipher that cryptic statement, so I force myself to trust that everything will work out in time. If there's some divine or cosmic reason for all of this, it will be revealed.

Nothing hurried.

Surrendering to patience.

Ignoring time.

Living for the unknown.

Embracing the unexpected.

"I'm sorry," she whispers, letting her gaze drift to the floor.

"For what?"

"For waking the dead."

Morgan fusses. I glance back at her, rubbing the back of my neck. "You didn't wake the dead. You comforted the living."

Biting her lips together, she nods. It's more of an acknowledgment nod instead of one that says she understands. We surpassed logic and any sort of true understanding the day she confronted me in the waiting room of Dr. Greyson's office. My best friend is a twenty-one-year-old woman. There's no logic to be had.

"Have a nice birthday. Make your wish big. Blow out all your candles. You deserve ..." My thoughts drift into the past. "You deserve a long, wonderful life."

"Long," she echoes me.

"Wonderful." I smile.

"Goodnight ..." Her mouth opens to say more, brow wrinkled.

Goodnight, Professor? Goodnight, Nate? Who am I to her?

After a little sigh, she relinquishes a sad smile. "Goodnight. Happy Birthday to you too."

I nod, watching her walk to the door. She doesn't look back. As much as it pains me, maybe she should never look back.

CHAPTER SIX

I WISH FOR the police to find the right evidence to toss Doug Mann's murderous ass in prison for the rest of his life. Then I blow out all my candles at once.

Wish granted. Right?

"Happy Birthday." Griffin kisses my neck and whispers in my ear, "Did you wish for your grocery store guy to let you blow his candle later?" He bites my earlobe while his family looks on in adoration.

I giggle, elbowing him in the ribs.

"Whispering sweet nothings to my daughter?" My mom smiles like she really believes it.

"Absolutely, Krista." Griffin winks.

"Are we on for dress shopping Tuesday? They're open until nine. So as long as your boss doesn't run late, we should have plenty of time to try things on."

I return a tight smile to my mom. "Actually, I have an appointment Tuesday night."

"An evening appointment?" She eyes me with suspicion.

Griffin's gaze cuts to me from the other side of the kitchen where he's busy helping Sherri serve the cake and ice cream. "What appointment, Swayz?"

"Therapist."

"You said Dr. Greyson didn't think he needed to see you anymore," Griffin says.

I did say that. "Yeah, didn't I mention that he also recommended I see this psychiatrist who works at the university? He thought she might connect with me better because …" I mumble the final words, hoping the race to get cake will distract everyone from my story that doesn't need to be told.

"Because she's a woman?" Mom asks.

Because I'm reincarnated and she's written books about it. "I guess she's experienced similar things that I have experienced."

"Did she have a friend die suddenly too?" Sherri gives me a sad smile.

Griffin, however, refuses to stop eyeing me with clear distrust. He knows my therapy is about Daisy. Not my dad. Not dealing with Erica's death. So I avoid eye contact with him.

"I'm not entirely sure. Dr. Greyson didn't go into a lot of detail. He just thought we'd be a better fit for whatever reason. I trust him, so I didn't ask that many questions. I guess I'll find out more when I see her Tuesday."

"Want me to come with you?" Griffin asks, forcing me to look at him. "I don't like the idea of you walking around that campus alone at night."

He has a valid point that I can't argue in front of our family. "I have a can of pepper spray."

"Swayze, I'd rather Griffin be with you." My mom gives me the usual motherly don't-be-stupid look.

"You're going to be bored."

Griffin strips me of my lies and maybe even my clothes with his narrowed stare and twisted lips. I squirm a bit.

"I'll have just one scoop of ice cream." I go for the distraction.

"One scoop, huh?" He drops the ice cream scoop.

Why did he do that?

"Griff!" I squeal when he scoops me up instead of the ice cream, tossing me over his shoulder.

"One …" He smacks my ass. "Two …" Another spanking.

Our family looks on from the living room with amusement as Griffin hauls me up the stairs.

"Nothing inappropriate. Children in the house," Sherri yells.

"Griffin! Put me down."

Smack. Smack. Smack.

It's beginning to sting. A guy with his strength and large hands cannot smack a delicate ass like mine, twenty-two times, without impairing my ability to sit for several days.

"Twenty-two." He tosses me onto the bed in his old room.

I rub my backside. "What's gotten into you?" My smile fades when he shuts the door and leans back against it, jaw clenched, arms crossed over his chest like he left his sense of humor out in the hallway.

"A new shrink? What the fuck, Swayze? I thought you were fine. You've been assuring me you're fine for quite some time. What made you go see Dr. Greyson again, and what the hell is going on that he felt the need to refer you to someone else?"

My head whips back. "Sorry. Did I catch you off guard like you dragging me up here to lecture me on *my birthday?*"

He pushes a quick breath out of his nose. "Really? You want to talk birthdays with me?"

"Low blow."

"No. Low blow is lying to me."

I fist the blanket on his bed. "I'm not lying to you."

"Omission of the whole truth is lying. You led me to believe that you were done with therapy."

"Is me being done with therapy a condition of our relationship? Our engagement?"

He answers with a look that makes a hairline fracture in my heart. I like the you-are-my-whole-world look. This bears an uncanny resemblance to the you-forgot-my-birthday look. Not my favorite look.

"What are you going to talk about with this new therapist?"

How I'm on the verge of losing everything that matters, and I can't seem to stop the self-destruction.

"How abusive my boyfriend is to me." Regret backhands me so fast it feels like I just hit a car head on. And the deafening silence that falls between us confirms the fatalities.

I can't look at him another second. The pain in his eyes makes it impossible to breathe. Griffin would never hurt me. Ever. It was a poorly delivered joke laced with more revenge than sarcasm.

This toxic thing called fear keeps driving a wedge between us. *I* keep driving a wedge between us. The harder I try to hold onto him, the further away he slips.

Daisy is not a gift. She's a fucking curse.

Griffin turns and opens the door.

"No!" I bolt after him, shoving the door shut again, grabbing his shirt and tugging at it until he looks at me. "It was a joke. A terrible, morbid, ill-timed joke. I'm sorry. I'm scared. I'm desperate. I'm ..."

My heart can't keep up with my emotions. It's a pulsing siren in my chest, warning me to shut up. And it hurts so much more than the playful bite of his hand on my ass.

He's a concrete wall, no matter how much I try to shake him.

"She's inside of me."

Now he gives me his full attention.

"Or…" I shake my head, pinching my eyes shut "…I'm her. But I don't think I totally am. I can't figure it out. And I can't let it go because these memories stay with me no matter where I go. They're in my head, and as time passes, they only get stronger and more vivid. It's not just Nate. He may have been some trigger for this, but she's there, Griff. She won't go away."

He blinks.

I wait.

Another blink.

I'm dying here.

It's like a young child telling her parents there is an alien in the closet that only she can see. But she's not crazy. It's really there, even if there is no proof of aliens.

"You need a different job," he says. It's flat and matter-of-fact.

I don't want him to be angry with me, but I'd feel better if his words were infused with some sort of emotion.

"I can't quit my job."

"You can." He bites his lips together, eyes wide, and head cocked to the side as if he's daring me to argue with him.

"Let's go. I'm the guest of honor, *not* that I deserve to have a special birthday. We both know I'm the worst human that ever lived. In fact, we can say our goodbyes and go home. You can drop me off at the curb as you back out of the driveway. Whatever." I grab the doorknob, but Griffin doesn't budge from the door.

His gaze bores a hole into my head, but I refuse to look at him.

"Hitler was worse," he says.

It's funny. But it's not.

It's heartbreaking. But it shouldn't be.

"Don't be insecure. That's not the woman I met in the grocery store."

I nod slowly, not really agreeing to anything other than the universe whispering, "You're screwed."

Insecure. Ha! I'm not sure it's fair to expect me to be anything *but* insecure. There's a whole other world—a whole other time—in my head. It's like taking someone halfway around the world and dropping them off in a desert without food or water and bidding them farewell with a "Bye. Don't be insecure."

Nothing makes a person feel more insecure than the unknown. This isn't mind over matter. I can't run around with my fingers in my ears, yelling "La la la ... I can't hear you, Daisy." But I'll save that argument for another day.

"I'll do my best to be who you want me to be."

"You're making me feel like a dick." He frowns.

I shrug, giving him a tight-lipped smile. "Well, you're big, sometimes overbearing, and completely unbendable when you get worked up. I think that's a dictionary definition of a dick. Now ... are you done ruining my birthday? Are we *even* since I'm a step away from Hitler and no longer the woman from the grocery store? Which is funny because I don't know how I led you to believe I was anything short of a disaster that day."

Griffin scrapes his teeth over the corner of his lower lip, inspecting me through squinted eyes. "Do you want to marry me?"

It's hard to catch my breath under the weight of his words. A chill slithers to my core as I gaze at him unblinkingly. "How can you ask me that?"

He lifts his hands up and lets them fall to his sides, releasing a heavy sigh.

Why doesn't he answer me? Is the lump in his throat as thick as the one swelling in mine? Or does he have nothing to say?

"Move." My pulse stutters like my voice, choking on hurt and anger.

His head turns away from me with a slack expression and vacant eyes. After a few long seconds, he steps aside. My shaky hand fumbles with the doorknob before it opens. I race halfway down the stairs and stop. Biting my quivering lips together, I bend over to catch my breath and swallow back the sob that wants to escape.

Breathe. Breathe. Breathe.

"Pull it together," I whisper to myself. Taking a deep breath, I blink a few times to gather some composure.

"Your ice cream has melted." Sophie hands me my bowl of cake and melted ice cream."

"I don't mind." I force a smile. It feels like a believable one, but my mom's pursed lips and raised brows tell me I'm not selling it as well as I think I am.

"Where's Griffin?" Sherri asks as I shovel down the soggy cake—anything to keep my chin from trembling and distract the rest of my body from doing what it wants to do—curl up in a ball and cry.

"Right here," he says from behind me.

I take another bite of cake, avoiding my mom's scrutinizing gaze. Griffin brushes past me with his bowl of cake and ice cream. A rare splurge for him. He plops down on the sofa, giving Hayley a playful nudge. She grins, nudging him back.

Through the corner of my eye, I watch my mom's gaze bounce between Griffin on the sofa—ignoring me—and me leaning against the wall because I don't want to sit next to anyone and have to form actual words.

"Swayze, you have a message." Sophie holds up my phone that's on the coffee table. "Aw … it's Morgan." She smiles at the screen.

"Let me see." Hayley snatches the phone from her. "It's a happy birthday message. She's so cute." She tips the screen toward Griffin.

His lips pull into a tight grin.

After the phone gets passed around the room, Sherri hands it to me. It's a photo of a smiley Morgan with a sticky note on her tummy that says "Happy birthday, Swayze." I don't stare at it too long, and I don't react to it because I know Griffin's eyes are on me. Instead, I slip the phone in my pocket and finish the last few spoonfuls of chocolate and vanilla cake soup.

"We should have invited them to your party." Sherri says like a verbal facepalm.

Yeah, that would have been a great idea. Just me, my fiancé, my boyfriend from another life, and his daughter named after me from that other life.

"I think he had plans this weekend. His birthday was yesterday."

"I hope he had plans, otherwise we could have celebrated both birthdays. We've been wanting to meet the sexy professor." Sherri shoots my mom a suggestive grin, but Griffin looks ready to bust out of his clothes like the Hulk.

She has no idea her son is not a Professor Hunt fan, and he has no idea she's making the sexy comment for my mom's benefit, not mine.

"Sexy Professor?" Scott pinches Sherri's leg.

She shoos him away. "For Krista. I'm happily married."

He nuzzles her neck. "Better be."

I love the alpha side to the Calloway men, except when mine makes me feel unwanted on my birthday.

"Sit, Swayze." Hayley stands. "I'm skipping out early to go to a movie with Maycee." She takes my empty bowl and hugs me. "Happy birthday, Sis."

Sis ... Don't cry.

"Sit." She jerks her head toward the empty spot on the sofa next to the Hulk.

Sherri and Scott chat with my mom about the Alaskan cruise they have planned for their anniversary next summer. Sophie and Chloe flip through the channels on the TV. I make the uncomfortable journey to the sofa and ease onto it, leaning toward the arm so my body doesn't touch Griffin's.

He taps his spoon against his empty bowl, releasing what I know are nerves or built up anger over our argument and probably the birthday text too. Sherri frowns, leaning forward and taking the bowl from him, setting it next to hers on the coffee table while rolling her eyes at him.

"Scoot over." Sophie kicks her feet at Griffin as she tries to sprawl out on the other side of him.

He scoots toward me, forcing our bodies to touch. I stiffen, hugging my arms to myself. My mom's brow wrinkles as she observes us, probably not paying any attention to Sherri and Scott's verbal itinerary.

I have to either surrender with the yes-we're-fighting-I'll-tell-you-about-it-later look or I need to make a move that says we're fine. But I can't deal with another second of her scrutiny. Just as I decide to give her the look, Sherri glances at me as if she realizes my mom is distracted by something.

I'm not prepared to give Sherri that look, even if I think

she'd understand, so I swallow every last bit of my stupid pride and ease my head against Griffin's shoulder. If it looks half as awkward as it feels, I'm screwed.

He tenses. I guess he's not in the mood to play along. Mom flinches, seeing the obvious rejection he's giving me, but the gesture seems to be enough for Sherri to offer me a warm smile before returning her attention to Scott. Griffin's hands remain folded in his lap. I feel like a fly on the backside of a horse. Any minute he could whip his tail and shoo me away.

My mom shoots a sympathetic look that I don't need and returns her attention to Sherri as if to let me off the hook. I lift my head from his shoulder, releasing a slow breath while fiddling with my engagement ring, turning it in circles. Maybe I should slip it off, hand it to him, and leave.

What if he asked me if I still wanted to marry him because deep down he's asking himself if he still wants to marry me? What if he wants me to go first, giving him an easy out?

"Have you two made honeymoon plans yet?" Sherri asks.

I gulp down a large pool of saliva.

Griffin fists his hand to his mouth, coughing while shaking his head several times. Nice response.

No.

No honeymoon plans.

There has to be a wedding first.

"Well, don't wait too long. The earlier you book, the better deal you'll get. Like your dad and I got a great deal on our trip to Alaska."

Griffin nods. I'm not sure if he's smiling at all. I refuse to turn my head that far to see his whole face.

Sherri gives us a twisted smile. "You two look bored. Go. I'm sure you have things you'd rather be doing." She gives us a suggestive wink.

I look for that pathetic excuse of a smile again.

"Thanks for dinner, Mom." Griffin stands, leaving me to sink back into the corner of the old sofa. "Goodnight, Krista."

Bravo. He's playing the part. But am I supposed to go with him? I stand. All of my stuff is at his house. I have nowhere else to go, but I'm sure my mom would take me in.

"Yes, thank you for dinner. It was really good." I hug Sherri and Scott.

My mom stands, waiting for her hug. "Call me. I'm here for you, sweetie," she whispers in my ear when we embrace.

I nod since words are trapped behind the ball of emotion lodged in my throat. They all wish me a final happy birthday as I slip on my coat and follow Griffin out the front door.

Yep. Happy birthday to me.

"I want to marry you, you stupid grocery store guy." I stand a few feet from the front of his truck.

He stops at his door with his back to me.

"But I don't have to. It won't change my love for you. So maybe you find a girl who isn't so fucked-up in the head. I'll still love you. Maybe you marry her and have three wonderful children. I'll still love you. If *you* no longer want to marry me … I'll still love you. I'll still love your family. I'll still love the memories of who we were and the dream of what could have been. And I'll wish you nothing but utter bliss and the most beautiful happiness because …"

Because you deserve something better than who I am at this point in my life—a lost soul sharing space with memories from another time.

"Get in," he says, opening his door.

On a defeated sigh, my shoulders slump as I climb into his truck.

CHAPTER SEVEN

D R. ALBRIGHT'S OFFICE is filled with three solid walls of books and one wall with a small window. It's the same size office as Nate's office, but it feels half the size because she's clearly a collector. So many books.

"Please have a seat, Swayze." She smiles.

My gaze drifts from the floor-to-ceiling bookshelves and lands on her pale face that holds a pleasant, comforting smile. I ease into the chair.

"Tea?" She pours water into a teacup.

"No, thank you." I return a smile as sweet as the two packets of sugar she adds to her tea. "My boss works here at the university." I want to know if she knows Nate or if her book in his nightstand is just a coincidence.

"Is that so?" She keeps her gaze on the spoon and teacup.

"Nathaniel Hunt."

Dr. Albright nods. "He was a student of mine."

I wait for her to elaborate. She doesn't.

"Dr. Greyson sent me your files. I've read through his notes, but they're rubbish. I want *you* to tell me about … you." She looks up, grinning while bringing the teacup to her lips.

"I won't ease into this because I don't think I have to with you."

She sets her teacup down, giving me her full attention.

"I'm pretty certain I'm the reincarnation of Nathaniel

Hunt's childhood friend who was murdered."

Dr. Albright's brows shoot up her forehead. "Murdered?"

I nod. "He doesn't know this. No one does except my boy-friend—fiancé." It's sad I don't know what Griffin is at the moment. We've spoken a handful of words since the ride home on my birthday. An ocean could fit between us in bed, but in the middle of the night his arms find their way around me. By the time I wake up, his arms are gone and so is he.

She nods. "Go on."

I tell her everything, starting with the day I saw Nate in Dr. Greyson's office. I tell her about the book of hers I found in Nate's nightstand. I tell her about Doug Mann and Erica. I tell her about the first time the visions in my head were from Daisy's point of view without Nate—the memories of her death. *My death?*

She listens without interrupting or showing any emotion beyond a few nods. No smiles. No flinching. No frowns.

My hand rubs over my front pocket a few times. I want her help, and I'm willing to give her anything to get it, so I slip the photo of Nate out of my pocket. It's bowed from spending so much time molded to my body.

"I took this from Nate." I slide it on her desk.

Her lips pull into a soft smile. "That's the student I re-member. He's always been incredibly handsome. The hair …" She glances up.

I nod. The hair. Nate has the most beautiful hair. Those curls beg for a woman's fingers to—

"You're blushing."

My head jerks up from the photo on the desk to meet her bright eyes.

"What were you just thinking while looking at it?"

"Um …" I clear my throat.

"It's just between the two of us. Woman to woman … what were you thinking?"

My lower lip curls inward as I nibble at some dry skin on it, eyes filling with emotion—shame. "I was thinking his hair begs for a woman's fingers to comb it, fist it, tug it."

Yeah, I'm blushing. My neck and cheeks burn.

"But I'm engaged to a man I love more than anything. I shouldn't have these thoughts. I shouldn't have this picture with me." My finger dabs the corner of my eye to catch the stray tear that tries to escape.

"It's not just that. I originally took it because this is a Nate I never got to see. And his expression in this photo haunts me. I don't know why I can't stop looking at it. It's like I'm waiting for him to tell me his life's story." I laugh. "It's so messed-up."

"Give me your wish list." She takes another sip of tea. It's her third cup.

"My wish list?"

"Yes. If I gave you a piece of paper and told you to write down five things you wish for, what would they be?"

"Like a new car?"

She shrugs. "Any wish for the future. We can't change the past."

"I wish Griffin understood what I'm going through. I wish the police would arrest Doug Mann. I wish I could stop staring at this stupid photo. I wish I could find a different job and not miss Nate and Morgan. I wish …"

Swallowing hard, I shake my head.

"Finish."

"I wish Daisy never died."

"We can't change the past. Try again."

My jaw clenches as I rub my hands over my jeans again and again.

"I wish I knew everything or nothing instead of this fragmented memory that's driving me crazy."

Dr. Albright scribbles on a piece of paper. I lean forward. It's the list of my wishes.

"Dr. Greyson rarely refers people to me. It's usually the other way around. The main reason is because I'm a full-time professor. He sent you to me because I'm a bit of an oddity in our profession. I have memories of past lives. I believe in reincarnation. My theories are widely disputed and hugely unpopular in the psychiatric community."

"Are your memories fragmented like mine?"

"Some are. Others are quite detailed. I don't think two souls are ever the same. I don't think you're the Daisy Nathaniel remembers. I think souls are woven from many lifetimes. Think of it like ancestry. I'm not all German, but I'm part German. Memories are the hard part to figure out. I like to think of them like dominant and recessive genes. Most souls live in harmony when they move on. I call those little interwoven soul fibers the recessive souls. They're not expressed. But sometimes we encounter dominant threads that are expressed through memory."

She chuckles. "Some people believe those are the stubborn souls that want to finish their stories. That's a little too simplistic and fictional for me."

"Why do you say that?"

"I'm in awe of life—both physical and spiritual. I'm certain I've read more books than anyone who has walked the grounds of this campus since it originated. Yet, I'm just as certain that I've barely scratched the surface of the bigger picture. The question that no one can truly answer ..."

I nod slowly. "Why are we here?"

"Precisely." She winks, leaning back in her chair, rocking gently. "Why are we here? What is the meaning of life? What is my purpose? Are humans supposed to mate for life? Is there a god?"

It's official. I'm overwhelmed. I feel very small at the moment.

"I turned twenty-two on Sunday. And I hate it when people treat me like I'm young and stupid. But if I'm being honest ... I feel very young and stupid. I don't sit around contemplating the meaning of life. I like good movies, wine and chocolate, time with my fiancé, mystery and romance novels. A beach? I'm there. A sale on cute leggings? I'll buy ten pairs. Adjusting to adulthood and having a degree is overwhelming enough. But past lives? Souls? Dominant and recessive expressions of ... whatever? No."

I shake my head a half dozen times. "That's not what I want to think about at this time in my life. But I also don't want to deal with the guilt that comes from knowing who killed my friend and not being able to do anything about it."

"I understand. I truly do. Let's talk again next week. In the meantime, I want you to think about a few things. We can try hypnosis to either repress unfavorable memories or bring forth missing pieces. It's not a guarantee, and it doesn't come without risks. Also, I want you to consider telling Nathaniel about your memories of Daisy's death. I know you think it could hurt him and compound the guilt he already feels, but it could also lead to opening up new evidence that could put Doug Mann behind bars. Nathaniel would want that, no matter what the emotional cost is to him. I'm certain of it."

I slip on my jacket. "And what do I do with my fiancé? I'm so afraid of losing him through all of this."

"Be honest with him. You want to marry a man who loves *and* accepts you. Daisy is part of you. She's not going anywhere."

Not the answer I want to hear. I smile anyway. "Thank you."

CHAPTER EIGHT

"GOOD MORNING," I say to Nate, not feeling so good about the morning or the past three days.

"Hey. She's been changed and fed. The coffee is hot. There's leftover Thai in the fridge. Help yourself."

Morgan coos when I take her from Nate. I kiss her rosy cheek. She giggles. I love her.

"I'm not used to being the chipper one. Everything okay?"

I hug Morgan to me and lean against the island. "Griffin's not speaking to me. Or he's avoiding me. It feels the same either way. Dr. Greyson passed me off to someone else. And I have something to tell you, but there's no time, so it will have to wait until later. Or another day. Another week ... Whatever."

"I'm sorry you're having problems with Griffin. Dr. Greyson wouldn't pass you off to someone else unless he thought it was in your best interest. And just tell me whatever it is you need to tell me." He hikes the strap of his messenger bag onto his shoulder while sipping his coffee.

"Oh ..." I dig into my pocket and toss his photo onto the counter. "And I stole this photo because I like to look at it. Why? I don't know. It's wrong. It's messed-up beyond words. You should fire me and get a restraining order."

I crumble inside like an imploding building.

Nate sets his cup on the counter and picks up the photo,

bringing it closer to his face, eyes narrowing a fraction. "My first trip to the West Coast. I went with a buddy. He took the shot." He sets it back on the counter. "Keep it."

My head juts back. "What? No. Why would I keep it?"

"For the same reason you took it in the first place." He shrugs.

"No way. It's so wrong."

"Why? Are you fantasizing about that guy?" He chuckles like it's insane.

That guy?

"Yes. NO! I mean no. God no!" I shake my head and hug Morgan tighter, refocusing my attention from the photo to her.

Nate reaches into his pocket and pulls out his wallet, trying to fish something out with his big paws. "I've carried this around for over twenty years. Does this make you feel better?" He holds out a black and white picture of Daisy. "Her friend did her hair, makeup ... even fake nails. Emily liked photography and said Daisy should be a model. She took a bunch of photos. I knew nothing about this until after Daisy died. Emily gave me this one after the funeral. I used to look at it every day. But now ..."

My gaze lifts to his.

He shrugs, giving me this look. What look? I'm not sure. But the longer he keeps it plastered to his face, the more certain I feel that it's the I-don't-look-at-it-anymore-because-you're-right-here look.

I don't like this look one single bit.

When I break the stare-off, he slips the photo back into his wallet. "I have to go. But just remember ... Daisy and I were friends first and foremost."

"So you think we should be friends?"

Grabbing his cup, he saunters to the back door. "Why not?"

"Why not?" I say to Morgan after the door shuts behind Nate. "Because I can't be friends with men who I've had sex with in my dreams."

Then, because I'm hell-bent on ruining my life before I hit twenty-five, I grab the photo off the counter and slide it back in my pocket.

GRIFFIN HAS DONE a stupendous job of working late every night since my birthday and sneaking in after I'm asleep, only to be out the door before I wake up.

No calls.

No texts.

No love notes on the nightstand.

Tonight I eat dinner alone, leaving him a taco salad in the fridge in case he wants it when he comes inside later. But I miss him. I think he's waiting for me to bridge this gap between us with an apology for being *me*. Dr. Albright is right. Daisy is an irremovable part of me. I can't let her go any more than I can leave my foot at home for the day.

Maybe I can negotiate a truce for now. I grab my sweatshirt and head out to the garage. The door is shut since it's cooler outside, so I go through the access door at the back. A woman with long black hair, leather chaps, and the tightest shirt I have ever seen, glances at me from *my* bucket next to Griffin.

She smiles.

Griffin sits back on his heels and looks over his shoulder, eyeing me for a few seconds with no smile. "Need something?"

My bucket. I need my bucket. *Why is this woman sitting on my bucket!*

"I made taco salad." *And that's my bucket.*

"Put it in the fridge." He turns back toward the motorcycle.

No "thank you." No introduction.

"I'm Apple."

I squint. "Excuse me?"

The bucket thief runs her fingers (which have rings on every single one) through her eternally long hair. "My name's Apple. Thanks for loaning your guy to me for the night. Something's knocking with my girl, and I leave for Cali tomorrow."

Fritter. Pie. Crisp. Dumpling. Turnover. Jelly. Who names their child *Apple*!

I sigh with a soft smile. I know this answer—the same generation of stoned hippies who named their kid Swayze. Do I say *hi* or *my condolences*?

Neither.

I say *Bitch, get off my bucket, and I don't loan my guy to anyone.* Okay, I don't say that either.

"I'm Swayze. And you can come inside and wait if you don't want to sit out here on that uncomfortable bucket while he works on your bike."

"Are you kidding?" She eyes Griff, nudging the toe of her boot against his leg. And he gives her a smile. A fucking smile! Like they're sharing some secret message. "I used to watch Griff all the time. It's mesmerizing. I could watch him all day."

I'm fond of blue, but all I can see right now is red.

She pulls a stick of gum out of her pocket and rips half of it off with her teeth and holds the other half up to Griffin's mouth.

Blazing RED!

I'm ready to pound her into applesauce and drag him by his nuts into the house. The only thing that stops me (other than the fact that she looks like she could kick my ass) is Griffin's headshake as she tempts him with her gum.

"Your loss. It's spearmint, your favorite." She grins at him, shoving the other half into her mouth before glancing back over at me like she forgot I'm here. "Man, I never imagined Griff settling down with a sweet girl like you. Good for you, babe." She nudges his leg again.

Babe … BABE!?!

My right eye twitches as I try to hear past the pounding in my ears. He doesn't acknowledge her flirting, but he doesn't tell her to stop either. And he's not telling her to get off my bucket. But even worse … I can tell this is a woman who has had sex with *my* man and therefore I hate her. And I hate him right now too.

Twenty-two was supposed to be my year of maturity. Epic fail. Maybe twenty-three will be my year.

I clear my throat. Griff looks over his shoulder again.

Crossing my arms over my chest, I bite my lips together for a few seconds to even out my breath. "How much longer will you be?"

He shrugs. "I don't know. Do you need something?"

Apple pulls her gum out in a long string, then twists it around her tongue. My gaze ping-pongs between the two of them. I suppose she does look more like the kind of woman who would be with a guy like Griffin. She's sexy and flirty. Clearly she's confident. And she has tattoos and rides a motorcycle.

It feels like two against one, so I shake my head. "No," I murmur, turn, and go back inside the house.

"Hold it together." I give myself another pep talk as I plop down on the sofa, sucking in a shaky breath. I want to cry and kill something at the same time. Stupid runaway mind. I hate that my brain allowed Nate into it in such an intimate way, but I don't want in his bed, no matter what crazy things worm their way into my head.

Can Griffin say the same thing about Apple? Does he see her and think of me as this huge mistake? I hate that my list for wanting to be with him goes on to infinity, but I can't imagine that his list would require more than an index card. Where did I lose my self-esteem? Did I ever really have it?

Confident women are attractive. Griffin's confident and I find it incredibly sexy. What must he think of this person I've become ... fumbling around for my sense of true self? I can't find my footing in this life.

Knock. Knock.

Before I can get to the back door, Apple opens it, peeking her head inside.

"Hey, Griff said there's beer in the fridge. He only has water in the one in the garage."

"Oh ..." I give her a tight smile as I open the fridge door and grab a bottle from the back that we keep for his parents when they come by. "Here." I hand her the bottle.

She gives me a cringe kind of smile. "One for Griff too."

"He doesn't usually drink."

She shrugs, biting her plump lower lip. "I asked if he wanted one too, and he said 'sure.'"

I swallow my anger and open the fridge door again, but the anger won't go down. It sits in my throat, choking me. "You know what …" I slam the door shut. "Tell Griff if he wants a beer he can come inside and get it himself."

Apple's pencil-thin brows draw up to peaks. "O—K." She backs out, easing the door shut behind her.

He won't come inside. They'll probably share the bottle I gave Apple. I'm never kissing him again. I will not touch his mouth after he's wrapped his lips around the same bottle that she's had hers.

I rub my temples for a few seconds before uncorking a bottle of red wine and pouring a generous glass.

"To Apple." I raise my glass toward the door. "The woman I will never be." Moving my glass to the bottle of wine, I clink it. "And to you, my bitter Merlot, the first bottle of wine I will drink in its entirety out of sheer jealousy."

I gulp down half the glass, expediting the alcohol to my bloodstream, desperate to slow the circus in my brain and numb the pain in my heart.

An hour or two—who knows—later, I no longer see anything red, except the last few drops of wine in my glass. I didn't quite drink the whole bottle, but I feel … well, I feel nothing. Maybe a little sad that my fiancé is probably sharing a beer in the garage with his ex-lover named Apple. Unless the beer is gone, then they're probably sharing other things.

"Well, there's only one way to find out," I mumble, standing while the room spins a couple of times. I amble outside to the garage, easing the door open just enough to see them before they notice me. He's putting away his tools while she leans against his workbench just inches from him, resting her hands on it so her chest is shoved out.

Stupid big tits.

"You should come out to California with me sometime.

Creed and Kessler would love to see you. One last hurrah before you get hitched to the beer police. What do you say?"

He closes the top drawer to his tool chest. "Don't call her that."

Apple smirks. "You know I'm kidding. She's just not at all what I imagined you settling for."

"Who said I'm settling?" He grabs a towel and works at the grease on his hands.

I hold my breath.

"Is she pregnant?"

"Fuck you." He shakes his head, eyes still focused on his hands.

"Again … kidding. You used to like my humor … and other things."

I could core that fucking Apple. I don't know what I mean by that, but damn … it just popped into my head. I blame it on the Merlot.

"Just think about making the trip sometime. Okay?"

He doesn't say anything, but his head bobs into a slight nod.

Yes? He's going to think about it?

I swallow back the bile that works its way up my throat.

Apple presses two fingers to her lips and then presses those fingers to Griffin's cheek. "Thanks for fixing my girl."

"Be careful on your trip." He looks up.

She smiles.

A slight smile curls his lips.

My heart breaks.

The knot in my stomach tightens, intensifying my nausea.

Before I can close the door, he turns. I let it click shut and run into the house. He saw me. I know he did. Eavesdropping, insecure, crazy Swayze.

I don't stop until I get to the bathroom, bending over the toilet. Nothing comes up. Damn! I can't even succeed at a good vomit tonight. After a few seconds, I wash my face with cold water and scrub my teeth quickly. Shooting across the hall, I strip down and slip on a nightshirt before hitting the light switch and hopping into bed.

Pulling the covers up to hide my face, I pinch my eyes shut and let my buzz take over the rest. But I can't stop thinking about what I heard and what I saw. I can't stop replaying her touching her kissed fingers to his cheek and him nodding to her invitation.

We were perfect. We were us. What happened? When did the jealousy and resentment build this wall between us? And why do I feel like it keeps getting bigger instead of smaller?

The back door closes. I freeze and hold my breath. His footsteps get closer and the bathroom door clicks shut. A few seconds later the shower sounds. I release my breath, focusing on controlling it, calming it before he comes out.

I stay really still again when the shower shuts off. A minute or two later the door opens. His bare feet pad along the wood floor to the other side of the bed. It dips as he sits on the edge. There's the tap of him setting his phone on the nightstand, followed by more shaking of the bed and rustling of the covers.

I will not cry. The closer he is to me, the more this hurts.

I don't blink.

I don't swallow.

I don't breathe.

My body stiffens when his arm hooks my waist, pulling me across the bed and into his embrace.

I blink. Fuck the stupid tears. Here they come.

You suck, Swayze.

I swallow and choke on a sob.

But I still can't breathe because I feel like a fool in love with this guy, who is my opposite in so many ways. Tonight has been another reminder of how I don't fit into his world. Sometimes it feels like more than that … it's this awful feeling I've had my whole life that I don't fit in anywhere.

I'm different. Not good different. Not necessarily bad different. Just … different. Puzzle piece 1001 in a 1000-piece puzzle.

"Tell me about your day, Swayz," he whispers in my ear.

I laugh past the sob that wants to escape. If I wanted a guy who got down on his knees—hands folded at his chest—to apologize, I wouldn't be engaged to Griffin Calloway. This is his apology. It's slow and easy, but I have no doubt that he will own every piece of me again by the time he's done.

"Shitty. This guy I love … he's been ignoring me. And tonight he kinda broke my heart. He let another woman sit on my bucket. And he let her touch him."

His grip on me tightens as he kisses the back of my head. There he goes, gathering up the pieces of me and tucking them away next to his heart. I let him because that's where they belong.

"I should take him out back and beat him a breath from his life for hurting you."

"No. I love him too much. Even if he's falling out of love with me." The last few words break as they fall from my lips.

"Swayz …" He turns me in his arms.

CHAPTER NINE
Griffin

I WASN'T LOOKING for someone who shared my love of motorcycles, NASCAR, tattoos, or working out. Honestly, I wasn't looking for anyone at all. My life was good.

Good job.

Good family.

Good friends.

I worked hard and purchased a house just after my twenty-third birthday. It's not huge, but I don't need much.

Then one day I got behind this blonde in line at the grocery store. Her hair was tangled in a pile on top of her head, falling out of her hairband in all directions. She riffled through her beach-sized handbag in a frantic search for her wallet as the lady at the register frowned in annoyance.

She was a chaotic mess to my diligent organization. I know she struggles with her averageness, but I think of her as not too anything; Swayze is my just right. My own tale of Goldilocks.

I didn't find her. She didn't find me. We found each other. It was effortless. It was perfect.

It still is.

The good. The bad. The sea of ugly in between—as long as it's us, it will always be perfect.

"I'm sorry for breaking you today." I hug her to me as silent sobs rack her body, hands covering her face. I embrace her vulnerability because she doesn't show it to everyone. She trusts me to protect her, yet I let her down. Tonight I should have guarded her heart.

Her bucket. I let someone sit on her bucket and that mattered to her. I hate that I hurt her, but there's an odd pride that it gives me to know that something as simplistic as an overturned bucket in my garage means so much to her.

I pull her hands away from her face, exposing her tear-stained cheeks and quivering chin. "You're it for me. Do you know this? There's no one else. I asked one girl to marry me, and I will never ask another. I want to marry *you*. I want to hold *you*. I want to have a family with *you*. I want *your* hands to fondle my old gray balls."

She chokes out a laugh.

I frame her face, waiting for the perfect shade of blue to look at me. And when those eyes meet mine, I grin. "I want every smile. Every giggle. All the tears. I want to fight with you just to make up with you."

Her mouth pulls into a smile. I take it because I want every single one.

"Did you wash your left cheek really good?"

I chuckle. "Yes. I'm pretty sure I removed at least three layers of skin."

"You're not riding with Apple or any other fruity-named girl to California as long as I'm still alive."

I fight my impending grin and nod.

"And if you ever let another woman sit on my bucket—"

I kiss her until her body relaxes, surrendering to me. "Yeah, yeah…" I mumble over her lips "…such a tough girl. I'm sure we're not done duking it out. You're going to piss me off and I'm going to piss you off." I grab the hem of her nightshirt and pull it up her body and over her head.

And for a few seconds I let her take my breath away. Every day I think this could be the day Swayze doesn't render me speechless, but every day she does. I'm not even sure how she does it. She just ... does.

"But at the end of the good days *and* the bad days, let's promise to meet back here, under the covers, in the dark, to lick each other's battle wounds. Deal?"

Her lips press to my chest. "Can it be that simple? Can we come back to our cocoon—inside these four walls—and shut out the pain? The anger? New psychiatrists? Stolen buckets? Forgotten birthdays?"

I want the answer to be yes. Reality is a buzzkill.

"We can try." I slide my leg between hers.

She ghosts her fingers along my naked ass and up my back. Looks like today isn't the day that her touch stops driving me insane with need. Maybe tomorrow. But I doubt it.

"Why do we keep hurting each other?" she whispers.

"Because we're fucking terrified of losing this." I slip my hand down the back of her panties.

When her lips find mine, I squeeze her sexy ass a little harder until she moans into my mouth.

She nips at my lower lip while rubbing herself against my leg that's threaded between hers. "I wanted to kill her." Her playful nips turn into bites like a dog that's no longer playing.

My head jerks back before she draws blood, narrowing my eyes.

"Thanks for loaning me your guy." Her mocking tone rings with very little sarcasm.

She's jealous.

And pissed off.

I may have underestimated the situation.

"And that gum-sharing, toe-nudging, eyelash-batting bull-shit made me want to pull her perfect black hair out of her head and rip off your testicles for letting her sit on my bucket!"

I one hundred percent underestimated the situation.

"Your bucket ..." I say with the ease of coaxing her away from the ledge.

"*My* bucket." She pushes my chest.

I roll to my back, letting her have control, in spite of my testicles questioning what could happen next.

Swayze straddles me like a queen perched on her throne. "*My* guy." Her hair brushes my face as she leans forward, jaw locked, hands pressed to the pillow on either side of my head. Who is this woman? And where the hell has she been?

"Yours." I grin.

"*Mine.*"

I chuckle. "So what are you going to do with me?"

Her lips part and something dark passes over her face, a cloud forming over my view of the sun. And in a blink, all her feistiness and anger vanishes, leaving behind the expressionless face of a ghost.

CHAPTER TEN

Swayze

"SO WHAT ARE you going to do with me?" Nate's voice. Nate's boyish grin.

Long blond hair from above tickling his face as excitement flashes in his blue eyes.

"Swayz?"

"So what are you going to do with me?" That grin ... Like he's always on the verge of snickering about something or like whatever he's looking at makes him happier than anything else in the world.

"Swayz, are you okay?"

I blink.

It's not Nate. Not his face. Not his voice.

The eyes are whisky and the lips are turned down into a frown.

Griffin sits up, taking me with him. He grabs my head and furrows his brow. "Where'd you go?"

I blink again. "No..." I shake my head "...nowhere."

The concern on his face hardens into something not so soft, not so *nice*. "We're in our house, our bed, sharing something pretty fucking personal and you're a million miles away. Dare I say a lifetime away?"

The thin material of my panties is the only thing between his naked body and mine. He's right. I should be here and only here. And if he didn't look so angry right now, I think I'd feel more shame.

"Did you fuck Apple?" Fight or flight. I couldn't keep those words in if I tried.

His jaw slides side to side several times, eyes black as night in this dark room. "You weren't thinking about me fucking anyone. You weren't thinking about me at all."

"You didn't answer my question."

"Right back at ya, Swayz." He lifts me off his lap and gets out of bed, tugging on sweats and a tee.

I stand on my knees, pulling my nightshirt back over my head as rage knocks on my chest, sending fire up my neck until my ears burn. "I don't care if she was some ... fuck buddy of yours. I care that she asked you to go to California with her sometime and you didn't say *no*. I care that you've been blowing me off for days over something I can't control."

He grabs his pillow and storms out of the bedroom without a word. I chase him into the living room.

"Control? Really? You want to use that excuse? Try this ..." He whips the pillow down on the sofa and rests his hands on his hips. "Quit your fucking job. Plan a wedding. Get out and make new friends. Clean up after yourself. Take a cooking class. Send out your resume to every school in the area. Take on more design clients. Hell ..." His shoulders shoot up into an exaggerated shrug. "Spend more time worrying about who's sitting on your bucket. Do absofuckinglutely anything to keep your mind away from this self-destructive obsession of yours."

I take an uneasy step backwards. The truth hurts more than a thousand lies. Lies can be forgiven, but the truth holds no debts.

My truth—I'm losing Griffin to a past I can't change and a future I can't control.

He scrubs a hand over his face on a heavy sigh. "I'm sorry. I—"

"If I quit …" I start to say with nothing left but defeat in my voice and a dull ache in my chest.

He meets my gaze with regret eating up his face, sinking deep into his eyes.

"If I quit my job, if I find a teaching position, if I make friends in a cooking class, if I take on as many extra design jobs as I can fit into my day … if I do all of that and still have these memories…" I swallow the pain in my throat and draw in a breath to chase away the sting in my eyes "…will there be a wedding?"

"Swayz—"

"Just answer me."

"I asked you to marry me. I'm not taking it back. Set a date. I'll be at the altar. Will *Swayze* be there?"

"Swayze is just a name." I hold my arms out to the side. "This is just a body. *I* will be at the altar."

"And who are you?"

After a few long seconds of silence, I stare at my feet and shrug before turning back to the bedroom. "I thought I was the woman you love," I murmur, retreating with my tattered white flag dragging behind me.

The bed creaks as I crawl into my spot, so does the floor at the end of the bed. Griffin removes his clothes, slides under the covers, and pulls them up over our heads.

No words.

No smiles.

Just two tortured souls scared of losing everything.

"But at the end of the good days and the bad days, let's promise to meet back here, under the covers, in the dark, to lick each other's

battle wounds. Deal?"

He slides off my panties as I shrug off my nightshirt. His mouth covers mine, slow but demanding—eyes wide open as if so much as a blink will pop this temporary bubble.

He kisses me until my lungs burn for a breath.

My neck.

My breasts.

The curve of one hip and then the other.

My hands guide his head between my legs, but I don't close my eyes. Not for one second. I love him. I don't want to share this moment with anyone else. Even if I can't see his eyes, the moment his tongue slides inside of me, I know that soulful gaze is looking up at me with lust and adoration.

I know, as he slides two fingers into me and I moan, that those same eyes start to leaden with pleasure. The bed shifts slightly from his pelvis grinding into the mattress as he lets all these emotions fade away.

We pause life.

We mute the voices.

We drown the pain.

I arch my back and twist as my orgasm hits hard. Griffin crawls up my body and sinks into me before I can see straight. With one hand on the bed next to my head and his other hand gripping the headboard, he drives into me like he wants to exorcise the demons from my mind.

But he can't. And after he finds his own release, he collapses on the bed beside me. I wait for him to speak.

He doesn't.

I wait for his arms to pull me into his body.

They don't.

When his breath evens out, I slip out of bed to use the

bathroom.

"What is happening?" I whisper to myself in the mirror before returning to our bed and a sleeping Griffin.

CHAPTER ELEVEN

HAZELNUT.

I grin.

He's here. Griffin doesn't drink coffee, so this aroma luring me to the kitchen is all for me.

"You're here."

Griffin glances up from his phone, taking a sip of his green drink. "Yeah." He looks so sad. Where's my morning smile? Where's the crook of his finger beckoning me to straddle his lap so he can kiss me good morning?

"Thanks for making coffee." I pour it into a mug and sit next to him at the table. This shouldn't hurt. This shouldn't feel awkward.

But it does.

He gives me a polite smile. "You're welcome."

I don't want polite. I want hands in my hair, lips on my mouth, and the kind of grin that dissolves my panties.

"I'll run by the store on the way home tonight. Text me if there's anything you need."

Keeping his gaze on the phone screen, he nods. God! Give me something more than a nod.

I sigh just before taking a sip of my coffee. As the events of last night replay in my mind, guilt and embarrassment give my conscience a sharp elbow. I lost my shit over a bucket, a rejected half a stick of gum, and one of the most ridiculous female names ever.

Okay … I don't regret my feelings about the name Apple, but the rest feels cringe-worthy in the light of day and the silence of two scorned lovers. We're mere inches apart, but it feels like we're not even in the same house.

"Did you work out this morning?"

I know the answer. I'm just that desperate to settle back into us. If he doesn't answer me soon, I'll be forced to mention the cool weather we've had lately.

The *weather.*

If that's not a sign of a doomed relationship, then I don't know what is. My parents were married for twenty-three years, and I don't ever recall them discussing the weather over coffee. I'm sure the occasional storm came up, but not out of desperation.

There aren't any storms that I know of predicted for Madison anytime soon, so I bite my tongue about the nippy forty-degree weather.

"I gotta go." Griffin scoots back in his chair and stands, taking his glass to the sink.

"You should take your truck. It's cold out."

The stupid weather. I give myself an internal eye roll.

He slips on his jacket and bends down, palming the back of my head and brushing his lips next to my ear. "Have a good day."

I fist his jacket as he goes to stand. His gaze sweeps across my face while I fight to translate what's in my heart and eating at the pit of my stomach. My eyebrows draw together. Griffin returns a sad smile, feathering his knuckles over my cheek.

"I love you too," he whispers.

Yeah, that.

I nod in lieu of actual words.

"HELLLOOO?" I slip off my shoes and my coat.

If I didn't know better, I'd say no one was home. The lights are off in the kitchen. There's no aroma of coffee.

"Hello?" I repeat with a softer voice as I sneak down the hallway.

"Bedroom," Nate says in a groggy almost muffled tone.

"Are you decent?"

His door is partially shut.

"Far from it, but come in anyway."

I peek my head around the door. "Whoa! You're still in bed?" Morgan rolls around on the floor surrounded by enough toys to keep her from escaping out into the hall or into the bathroom.

"Sick." He's on his stomach, like he collapsed. One arm hangs off the side of the bed, loosely gripping a toy.

"Sorry to hear that."

"Uh huh," he mumbles into his pillow.

"I take it you still need me? Or do I have the day off?"

A grunt is his only response.

"Sounds like a yes. Come on, Miss Morgan." I pick her up. "Let's get you away from your sick father."

Another grunt as he lets the toy drop from his hand, but he doesn't move his arm back on the bed. He's nothing more than a corpse.

"Can I get you anything?"

"No."

"Alrighty then. Say feel better, Daddy."

We play, eat, change diaper. Rinse and repeat a couple of times before Morgan goes down for a nap. I lay her in her crib, not confident she'll stay asleep since I usually hold her during naps, but she's good for now. I get a glass of water and poke my head in Nate's room.

"Still alive?"

"Unfortunately." He stiffly rolls from his side to his back, squinting open his eyes.

"I brought you some water."

He eases to sitting. I give him a tight grin, keeping my eyes wide and unblinking, focused only on his eyes instead of the flex of his abs and that heart-shaped birthmark.

"Thank you." He takes the glass and drinks the whole thing.

"Body ache? Chills? Fever?"

"Blinding headache and sore throat."

"Bummer. Sorry."

"She asleep?"

Shoving my hands in the back pockets of my jeans, I nod.

"You owe me some story time." He draws in a pained breath, closing his eyes.

"What?"

"I tell you about Daisy. Tell me something. Anything. What color are your bridesmaids' dresses?"

I laugh. "You don't care about the color of my bridesmaids' dresses."

"True. I just want a distraction from the pain. Sit." He tips his head toward the other side of his bed.

After a few seconds of me not responding, he peeks open one eye. "I won't breathe on you."

I prop up two pillows and ease onto the other side of the

bed, leaning back against the headboard. "Griffin thinks I should get a different job."

Nate grunts. "I don't like this story. Pick a different one."

I glance over at him, but his eyes are still closed. "Were you serious about us being friends? I mean … can you be my guy friend? The one I don't have sex with, but you give me advice about guys that only a guy could give?"

Nate chuckles, but it morphs into a moan as he scoots back down under the covers and rubs his forehead. "Yes to the friends part. And I think it's frowned upon to have sex with the nanny. As far as the advice goes, I'll give it, but it will come with a disclaimer. I don't want to be responsible for you making some life-changing decision that goes awry."

"Griffin worked on a motorcycle last night for this woman who I'm pretty sure is someone he had sex with before we were together. Is it weird that he would agree to do that for her?"

"Did she pay him?"

"I don't know. I didn't ask."

"Then I can't say. Next topic?"

"I'm not done talking about Apple."

"Apple?"

"That's her name. Can you believe it? It's worse than Swayze."

"Who said Swayze is a bad name?"

"Anyone who is not a liar, hippie, or fan of the original *Dirty Dancing*."

"Swayze is a cute name."

I roll my eyes. "And Apple is sweet."

"I'm guessing Griffin is in the dog house." He stops rubbing his head and lets his arm drape over his face.

Drawing my knees to my chest, I hug my legs. "No. We're

just kinda …"

What are we? I don't know.

"Kinda?"

I sigh. "Going through a rough patch thanks to your childhood friend."

"Is she giving you trouble?"

I laugh. "That's an understatement."

"He doesn't buy it?" Nate sighs. "Can't blame him. If I were in his shoes, I wouldn't buy it either."

"I find that hard to believe coming from Professor Albright's student."

Nate cracks his eyes open, easing his head to the side, the discomfort etched along his forehead. "How do you know that?"

Rubbing my lips together, I lift my shoulders. "You have her book on reincarnation in your nightstand drawer. And you told me I could snoop, so—"

"That book doesn't tell you I was her student."

"True. She told me."

Nate's lips part. "How do you know Hazel?"

"Dr. Greyson referred me to her."

"Why?"

I give him the are-you-serious look.

He nods slowly, eyes fixed on me but unfocused, like his thoughts have taken him to somewhere a long way from this bed. "Is this what you needed to talk to me about?"

I shake my head. "Not exactly. But that can wait until you're feeling better."

"Just say it." He flinches, trying to sit up.

"Just rest."

"My head hurts too much to rest. Distract me."

Daisy was murdered is not the right distraction. "Come here." I straighten my legs and lay one of the pillows on them.

Nate's gaze shifts between mine and the pillow.

"Head on the pillow, Professor." I grin.

He eases his head onto the pillow.

"Black." I run my fingers through his beautiful hair, smiling when it curls around my fingers. This is just one of the many things I've wanted to feel with Nate. And just as I imagined, it's so familiar.

"Black?" He closes his eyes and releases a soft sigh as I stroke his hair.

"I want black bridesmaids' dresses. I want everything to be simple and elegant. Black dresses and all white flowers, except for my bouquet which will be all red. Sunset wedding. Soft candlelight. Nothing too big, just intimate and … perfect." I close my eyes for a minute, seeing every single detail with complete clarity.

I don't know how I can love the comfort and familiarity of Nate's hair tangled around my fingers but see Griffin standing at the altar with the biggest smile on his face like he can't wait to spend the rest of his life asking about my days.

"Hmm …" He hums with his face relaxing from the painful grimace that he had just minutes ago. "What else?"

My fingernails tease his scalp before gently working through the tangled locks. "I don't know. What else will distract you from the pain?"

"Tell me how it feels."

I chuckle. "Your pain?"

"To be Swayze, but to have these memories of a life before you were ever born."

I let my fingers slide from his bangs to his eyebrows, brushing the pads of my fingers over the slightly curved line, admiring his long eyelashes resting on his cheeks.

It's intimate, but not sexual.

It's familiar, but new.

It's food to my soul—*her* soul.

"It's confusing and painful. Most days it feels like a curse because I can't make total sense of it. I don't know how it fits into my life." I tuck a wayward curl behind his ear. "But other times it feels like something so much bigger than I can imagine. Like I've been gifted this memory and I need to use it somehow."

I grin to myself. He's so relaxed I'm not sure he's still awake.

"It's just too far beyond any kind of odds that I apply for the job as a nanny to your daughter who you named after ..." I trail off, losing my nerve to say the words.

Nate opens his eyes. "Finish," he whispers.

"Me ... from that life." I ghost my hand over his stubble-covered jaw.

He covers my hand with his, closing his eyes again. "Thank you."

"For what?"

He leans into my hand. "For finding me."

CHAPTER TWELVE

I STOP BY my favorite grocery store on the way home; it always makes me smile. What were the chances of finding my husband in the checkout lane? Probably just slightly higher than remembering another life.

"The yellow onions are thirty cents cheaper."

My stomach tightens, sending a rush of cold panic to my brain.

Don't pass out. Don't pass out. Don't pass out.

I glance over my shoulder, following the gaze of the cashier.

"Swayze is it?" Doug Mann grins like something is funny.

My hands fist. I want to physically hurt him—knock out his fake-capped teeth, kick him in the ribs until they break, and then shove a knife into his heart so slowly he howls in pain until he chokes to death on his own blood.

"Thirty-four ninety-eight," the cashier murmurs.

I shove my credit card into the reader, missing it the first three times because of my shaky hands.

"Debit or credit?"

"D-debit." I swallow hard and fist my hand to chase away the nerves that make it hard to type in my PIN.

The cashier hands me my receipt, and I grab my bags.

"See ya around, *Swayze*."

Swayze. He said my name, but my mind heard *Daisy*. I sprint to my car. When I shift the bags to put them all in one hand so I can open the door, one of them breaks, sending an onion and four oranges rolling in all directions.

"Dammit!" I fumble with the rest of the groceries while trying to pick up my runaway produce.

"I always ask them to double bag my stuff." Doug bends down to pick up an orange.

Screw the oranges. I reach for my keys ... my keys ... where are my keys?

"Looking for these? You always manage to drop your keys when you're around me. Why is this?" He dangles them in front of me like he did outside of my apartment.

I reach for them, and he pulls them away at the last second. My knees wobble as I gulp down each breath.

"I'm just messing with you." A psychotic grin slithers up his scarred face, and he holds out my keys again. "We should go out sometime. Have a drink and toast to our lost friend, Erica."

You killed her screams in my head, but I'm so fucking paralyzed with fear, I'm not sure I could find enough voice to yell if he tried to do anything to me. Before he can taunt me anymore, I snatch the keys and get in my car, locking the doors as he stands next to my window like a clown in a horror movie.

Start car.

Shove it in reverse.

Step on the gas.

Crash!

My racing heart explodes and I nearly wet my pants. I hit a car. *Oh my god!* I grimace, glancing in my rearview mirror. When my gaze flicks back to Doug, he waves and walks in the opposite direction.

AN HOUR LATER, I arrive home with a smashed up rear end, tear-stained cheeks, and a copy of the accident report. I told the other driver that a man threatened me, and I was just trying to get away. When I told the officer the same thing, he asked me what the man did to threaten me.

I couldn't explain it.

I had nothing except the ramblings of a crazy woman, or at least that's what it felt like when the officer gave me a less than sympathetic look. I wasn't trying to get out of paying for the damage, I just wanted them to understand.

That's been the reoccurring theme of my life—misunderstood.

"Hey, where have you been? I needed the onion an hour ago. I ran to my mom's to borrow one," Griffin says with his back to me as he shuts off the stove and slides a pot off the burner.

"Sorry." I drop my purse and the other bag of groceries on the floor.

The *thunk* gets his full attention. He squints at the bag on the floor before glancing up at me. I don't know where we stand after last night. Do I have the right to fall into his arms? Will he comfort me or will the mere mention of Doug's name make him think about my messed-up memories?

"What's wrong?" He moves toward me.

I *need* his arms so badly right now, but I can't even move. Every inch of me, including my emotions, feel drained and numb.

Griffin picks up the bag of groceries, inspecting its contents before looking at me again. "You forgot the onion anyway—"

He stops, more confusion distorts his face. "Have you been crying?"

"The bag broke," I say in a monotone voice, unblinking. "And I saw Doug Mann. Then I backed into a lady's car."

"Jesus …" He sets the bag on the table and pulls me into the place I need to be more than anywhere else in the whole world. "Are you okay? Are you hurt? Did he do anything to you?"

I'm safe. In the arms of this man, I'm always safe. He is my lover, my protector, my place in this world where I can lose myself and find myself.

"Swayz?" He puts me at arm's length. "Are. You. Okay?"

I blink several times, nodding, but not meaning yes. I'm not okay. I don't think I'll be okay as long as Doug Mann is free.

"What if I get close to him? What if we catch him before he kills again?"

Griffin shakes his head. "What are you talking about? Get close to him? Are you fucking kidding me?"

"I can't live like this." I take a step back, shaking my head. "I know you can't completely understand, so I'm asking you to trust me. He's a murderer, Griff. He'll do it again. And he has his eyes on me because he knows I know. Living my life looking over my shoulder is no way to live."

Griffin releases a heavy sigh while scratching the back of his neck. "Let's move."

"What? No. Are you crazy?"

"I can look for an opening at another dealership. We can go somewhere where there's more job openings for you. We're young, Swayz. We can go anywhere and do anything we want."

"I'm not running away." My voice escalates. "He could follow us. He's a murderer. A dangerous man. We can't just walk away. What if he takes another life? I can't have that on my conscience. We need to—"

"Swayze!" He laces his hands behind his head while looking up at the ceiling, baring his corded neck. "I'll go over to his apartment right now and end his life, but I will *not* let you put yourself in harm's way. Just ..." He shakes his head with another frustrated sigh. "What did he say to you?"

"He said we should get together for a drink and toast to Erica. Who says that? She wasn't his friend. He was nothing but a creepy neighbor. And he knew my name. I never told him my name!"

"He probably heard me say it the day Erica died and you accused him of being a murderer."

I dig my teeth into my lower lip. "No. What if I misheard him? What if he said Daisy and not Swayze?"

"Fuck ... not this—"

"Yes. THIS! This. This. This! You have to accept this, Griffin. Like it or not, the only explanation for what I know and the memories I have is that I'm her. She's me. The idea of reincarnation might not make sense to you or a whole helluva lot of other people, but it is, in fact, the *only* explanation. This is a bone-deep feeling I have about Doug Mann. I see things in my mind. I hear his voice. I hear *her* voice. The memories of Nate's past. The images I have of seemingly complete strangers ... Gah!"

I throw my arms up in the air. "My whole past! *This* is the reason I knew more than I should have known of very specific things. I knew what *she* knew. All those stupid tests. All those wasted years. No one even thought to consider I brought forth pieces of another life. It's like young prodigies, only I'm not a prodigy. I'm just a girl who was murdered by some sick bastard. My soul wasn't finished."

His jaw relaxes as his gaze clouds over.

I wait. It's a lot to process. Maybe if I keep feeding this to him in manageable doses, he'll come to terms with it and accept me for who I am and who I was.

"Salmon, green beans, and sweet potatoes."

Okay. Maybe I gave him an overdose of it tonight.

He blinks, refocusing on me for a split second before turning back to his dinner preparation.

We eat in silence.

We get ready for bed.

We find the comfort of each other's arms.

We do it all without sharing another word.

I guess sometimes life has to figure itself out.

CHAPTER THIRTEEN

"I SAW YOU pull in. Nice truck." Nate grins.
Slipping off my jacket, I blow a kiss to Morgan rolling around on a blanket with a dozen toys. "Looks like you're feeling better."

He butters a piece of toast. "Better? Yes. Awesome? No. But I don't like missing class."

I grunt a laugh. "I think expecting an *awesome* day is just flat-out greedy. Yesterday was a terrible day. I don't need awesome. I'm good with not terrible. You should be too."

Morgan grins when I get on all fours and nuzzle my nose into her neck.

"If I recall correctly, I was the one groaning in misery yesterday. How did your day go down the drain between leaving my house and going to bed last night?"

Sitting back on my heels, I draw in a big breath. "On my way home, I stopped by the grocery store. The guy who murdered my friend, Erica, was in line behind me. I hurried out to my car and one of my bags broke. Then I dropped my keys. He picked them up and taunted me with them. Then completely flustered, I backed out and hit another car. When I got home, I tried to explain to Griffin why I need to draw Doug in and catch him so he doesn't do to another girl what he did to Erica and Daisy."

Nate freezes midway to taking another bite of toast. Eyes

unblinking.

It came out. *Daisy* just came out of my mouth in a flurry of frustration and raw emotions.

"What did you just say?"

My gaze shifts to Morgan. I tickle the bottom of her feet. "The man who killed Erica is the same man who killed Daisy."

"You don't know what you're talking about," he says with an edge of irritation to his voice.

I laugh. It's not funny. Yet it is incredibly ironic. "You don't have to believe me. It's probably in your best interest if you don't. But I said it and that's all that matters. Dr. Albright said I should tell you." I shrug, keeping my focus on Morgan. "There. Now I've told you. Maybe she'll be proud of me for doing my homework."

"Don't ever say that again. Understood?"

I look up, meeting his hardened expression. "Are you kidding me?" My eyes bulge out of my head. "I realize you feel responsible for not being with Daisy. I get it. In some ways you feel responsible for her death—which you are not. But don't you dare scold me for saying what's in my head. Can you even begin to comprehend what this means to me? When my mind flips on the replay reel and I see Doug and his bloodied face, and I hear his words, it's not some book or movie. It's my life. I'm remembering the end of my life as Daisy Gallagher. I'm on the verge of remembering my death!

"And I'm sorry … I didn't want to share this burden with you, even when Dr. Albright said I should. It just came out. Now you have to decide … what's it going to be, Nate? Are we *friends*? If I forgive you for breaking up with me over your stubborn pride, will you listen to me? I need someone to listen to me. Someone who will believe me. Someone who will help me stop this sick bastard from killing another innocent person."

This new, intimidating, really pissed off looking Nate steps closer. "You're lying to me. So cancel whatever fucking plans you may have tonight because as soon as I get home, you're telling me everything before I let you take one step out of this house."

"Don't swear in front of your daughter," I grit through a tight smile. This is not my fault. I'm not a liar. He's not going to make me feel like I've done something wrong.

The muscles in his jaw twitch a few times. Why have I been making the men in my life so angry lately?

It's NOT my fault!

I pick up Morgan and move her arm like a puppet's. "Bye, Daddy. You're going to be late if you don't stop scowling at my favorite nanny."

"Swayze …" he says my name like he's warning me to keep my tongue in my mouth.

"Professor …"

He leaves.

I hold every emotion inside. If I let him break me in the process of trying to protect himself, we all suffer and Doug remains a free man. I need Nate's help, so I'll take a few verbal punches and scowls of distrust to put an end to this nightmare.

GRIFFIN'S WORKING LATE. I tell him I'm going to an exercise class; he doesn't question it since I have always been sporadic with my gym visits. And it's not a lie. I do have my workout clothes in the truck, I just might not get there until later. Or at all.

> **Professor:** *I'm leaving now. My dad will be there soon to get Morgan. Pack her diaper bag and formula. And DON'T LEAVE.*
>
> **Me:** *I've read this three times and I don't see a 'please.' Surely I'm just missing it????*

He doesn't respond.

Within ten minutes his dad arrives.

"Hello?" He calls from the front door.

I fasten Morgan into her carrier. "Coming." Slinging the diaper bag over my shoulder, I deliver Morgan to her grandpa.

"Hi, you must be Swayze."

I nod at the familiar face. "I'd say you must be Mr. Hunt, but there's no missing the resemblance."

"The hair give it away?"

I hand him the diaper bag and smile. "The eyes."

"Sure." He gives me a playful grin.

"I just fed her and changed her diaper, but everything's in the diaper bag, including extra outfits."

He takes Morgan. "Well, I hope you get your contract renegotiated. Nathaniel speaks highly of you. I'd hate for him to lose such a good nanny."

"My contract ..." I nod slowly. "Yeah."

He points over my shoulder. "I'm taking the other car since there's a car seat base in the back."

"Of course." I step aside and follow him to the back garage door.

"It was nice to meet you, Swayze."

"You too, Mr. Hunt."

"Call me David."

"Okay, David. Do you need help getting her seat in the base?"

"Nope. Nathaniel showed me a while back when he went out with some friends."

The professor has friends. Of course he does. Everyone has friends. But since he hasn't mentioned them to me, it's as if they don't exist.

When he pulls out, I give him one final wave and press the button to the garage door. It stops halfway down and goes back up.

The professor's SUV pulls into its spot. He looks as intimidating as he did when he left this morning. Time didn't soften his anger.

Poor me.

"Where's dinner?"

He shuts the door and pins me with one look that makes my knees shake. "Get inside. No dinner."

I hold my ground. He stops two steps below me, putting us at eye level.

"You need to say the word please. I'm not your employee at the moment."

"Get. Inside."

"Why are you so mad?"

He bulldozes his way past me. I drag my feet behind him into the kitchen.

Tossing his messenger bag on the sofa, he turns. "Who are you?"

I squint. "What do you mean?"

"You're not her. Daisy would never do this. I *don't* appreciate whatever sick and twisted game this is you're playing. You can't just come out of fucking nowhere with this murder accusation. What the hell is wrong with you?"

My jaw unhinges and I try to close it, but it keeps falling open, waiting for words to come out. But they don't. Even my thoughts slow to a stop.

I have absolutely nothing.

"You said you looked up the owner of the house and that's how you knew Doug Mann's name." Nate shakes his head. "And now you're saying your friend was murdered by him. Nothing you say makes sense, which means you're lying. Why the fuck are you lying about this?"

"I …" I swallow hard. "I lived in the same building. Doug Mann lives in an apartment one floor up from the one that was mine. Right across the hall from Erica."

"Then why did you say you looked him up!"

I jump as my stomach roils from the hard punch of his anger. "Because I didn't want to hurt you with the truth."

"The truth? What are you calling the truth?"

Who is this angry person? I don't know him. Or maybe part of me does. Nate had a temper, I saw it with other people, but rarely with me—or her. Hell … I don't know anymore.

"Nate … I know what's in my head. And it's not a lie."

"You don't know a goddamn thing!" He clenches his fists as heat plumes up the sides of his neck. He steps toward me. What is happening?

"You don't get to say this kind of shit to me." He takes another step.

I retreat a few paces.

"I've lived with this fucking guilt for over twenty-two years. An accident that I wasn't there to prevent has eaten me up whole." His voice shakes. His entire body shakes.

I don't think he'll actually hurt me, but I also don't recognize this person.

No Morgan.

No David.

No distraction.

No one to save me.

"And now you want to dig up the past—my past—and make accusations that you can't prove. You want to rip back open my fucking heart by telling me someone *murdered* her?"

He shakes his head, stalking toward me like he's ready to rip *my* heart straight out of my chest. "No. You can get the hell out of here. I don't want to see you again."

I flinch as tears sting my eyes and anger rockets through my veins. My hand flies through the air, connecting with his face. "Fuck *you* for not understanding!"

Pure rage burns in his eyes as his nostrils flare.

I fight the urge to run. I fight the emotions knocking at my chest while stifling the raw scream burning in my throat. A light breeze could shatter me from the inside out. I'm nauseous and every muscle in my body feels weak and unsteady.

Humiliation. Pain. Resentment. *Anger.*

A lot of anger.

He grabs my arm. I rip it away so fast my feet stumble backwards until the wall catches me.

"Don't you touch me." I hug my arms to my chest.

He sucks in a sharp breath and lets it out slowly. I catch a glimpse of something besides rage.

Pain. He's in so much pain.

"Then make me understand."

He doesn't get to say that. Not now. Not after calling me a liar. Not after telling me to get the hell out of his house. I just … snap.

"Understand? UNDERSTAND?" I shove him.

He grabs my wrists with a loose grip and holds them next to his chest. I try to wriggle free. His hands tighten around my wrists.

"Let go of me! I don't fucking understand it myself. But I'm not going to protect you any longer."

His eyes narrow, jaw clamped shut.

My skin burns from my heart pounding out of control. "If she were here, she'd ask you why you didn't save her. Why you let your stupid ego drive her away. Because she didn't drown by accident." I yank my hands free and pound my fists against his chest. "I was *murdered*!"

Pound. Pound. Pound.

He doesn't stop me. While I breakdown, he stands here like a punching bag, taking everything I give him.

I was murdered.

Not *she. I.*

This is not a normal human experience. People don't recall past lives for a reason. Death is supposed to be final. The memories should die. What kind of god would allow someone to relive their death, because that's where I'm at. I'm on the precipice of reliving my death one horrific flashback at a time.

My fight loses momentum. Each jab to his chest softens more than the one before it.

Still, he doesn't move.

I stare at my hands, now idle on his chest—my labored breaths the only sound between us. Something drips onto the sleeve of my shirt, and I blink, staring at the wet spot for several long seconds before trailing my gaze up his body.

Nate's vacant, red-rimmed eyes stare off into an unknown distance behind me as new tears escape them with each blink.

JEWEL E. ANN

He didn't break me. I broke him.

"Nate," I whisper, reaching for his face.

He grabs my hand and holds it to his cheek as his face distorts into this torturous regret, and his body shakes beneath my hands.

His legs give out.

His shoulders slump.

His body drops to its knees.

I try to stop him, but I can't, so I wrap my arms around his torso and fall with him. Nate hugs me to his body tighter than I've ever been held.

"I'm so … sorry," his voice cracks.

My heart rips open, letting in all of his pain. He cups the back of my head and kisses the top of it over and over between sobs. My tears come slower. One at a time. A blanket of pain envelopes us.

I have memories of Daisy's life, but I don't have feelings from it. My emotions are those of an outsider watching a movie or reading a story. It's empathy. Heartbreaking empathy.

Silence settles around us again, and his body stills with his cheek resting on my head. "I'm sorry," he says in a defeated tone.

I peel myself from his hold, sitting back on my heels while wiping my cheeks. "Those were my words, not Daisy's. It's like I'm seeing what she saw, and when we touch…" I take one of his hands and sandwich it between mine "…I think I'm physically feeling what she felt. But I don't feel her emotions. It's not your fault that she died. And I didn't want to tell you any of this because it doesn't change the past, but I know these scattered flashes in my mind are from the moments leading up to her death. I see Doug. And this long cut on his face. I see

106

murder in his eyes. He killed Daisy, and he killed my friend Erica. And he's going to kill again if I don't stop him."

Nate shakes his head. "No. They ruled out foul play."

"They were wrong. Just like they're wrong about Erica. He knows what he's doing. He knows how to murder people and make it look like an accident. We don't know how many people he's killed."

He pulls his hand from mine and runs his fingers through his hair, shaking his head. "I-I don't know." Nate's gaze roams along my body before settling on my face—my cheeks, my mouth, my eyes. "Daisy ..."

"I can be your altar. You can confess. You can ask for forgiveness. Share your deepest, darkest secrets, but I can't give you back anything tangible, not even a whisper of hope, because she's only part of my memory. I can't give life to her in a real way."

More tears fill his eyes as his jaw clenches. "Fuck ... what did he do? Did he hurt you? Did he ..." He grimaces.

He's thinking the worst. *I'm* thinking the worst.

"I don't know," I whisper.

Is this how he looked the day his dad told him Daisy died? Is this how he looked when the doctor told him Jenna didn't make it? It has to be the same look because the only time I've seen this kind of anguish on the face of another human is when my mom found out my dad died.

He swallows hard. "If you know, you have to tell me. You *have* to tell me."

"I'm not sure. It's too fragmented."

"But do you feel her pain?" His voice escalates, and he immediately winces with regret.

"No. I don't feel her at all."

He eases to standing, a vacant look in his reddened eyes. "Go home."

The defeat in his voice strangles my heart.

"Nate …" I stand, reaching for his hand.

He pulls it out of my reach. "Just … please go home."

I nod.

Nate turns, disappearing into his office, shutting the door behind him.

I slip on my shoes and coat, pausing for a few seconds when I open the front door. How can I break him like this and just leave?

After shutting the door, I slip back off my coat. As I hang it on the hook, the most guttural roar thunders from his office followed by a tornado of *clanks, thunks,* and things shattering.

I freeze with my heart lodged in my throat. After a few seconds of silence, I creep toward his office, treading warily on the fear of what is on the other side of the door.

Easing the door open, I find Nate on the floor, his body buckled over, hands covering his face as he silently sobs amongst the remains of everything that was on his desk.

I hunch down behind him and hug his back. He jumps at first, and then more emotions rip from his chest.

"It's my fault …"

"No."

"What if he …" His words catch as his body shakes more.

"Don't do this."

"What if he did things? Un … unthinkable things."

Dropping to my knees, I crawl in front of him, grabbing his face and forcing him to look at me. I don't really know what to say. He's not thinking anything that I haven't thought. To rule out foul play, they had to do an autopsy. So nothing must have shown up. No signs of rape or anything like that. But ... the mind still goes to a million things that he could have done to her that would not have been detectable with an autopsy.

I can't go there and neither should he.

"Thinking these thoughts won't change what happened." That's it. That's all I've got.

I don't have to feel what she felt. I feel him right now, and it's the kind of pain that will never completely disappear. The ache in my chest will linger forever.

Nate snakes an arm around my waist and pulls me onto his lap, the same way he held me on his bed the first time I tried to tell him about Doug.

We hold each other like we're just trying to hold onto life, like we're holding each other together.

After long minutes, he eases his hold on me. I sit back until our faces are just a few inches apart. His hands cup my face like I'm someone very precious to him. I hold my breath. He's not going to kiss me. I'm pretty certain of it. And I wish I could define what this is between us, but I can't. Nor can I resist his touch. It's like my body craves the familiarity of it. Is it just morbid curiosity and obsession over the story of Daisy and Nate?

Epic.

Tragic.

All-consuming.

"Thank you for finding me," he whispers.

Why does he keep saying that?

My hands move to his shoulders. I just need to steady myself. I need to feel in control. "Do you really believe that? That I found you?"

His thumbs caress my cheeks and he smiles. It's sad. It's beautiful. But mostly, it's familiar. "Yes."

How can the touch of two different men reach my soul? I'm engaged to Griffin. I love him unequivocally. But when Nate's hands meet my flesh, it doesn't feel wrong, and maybe it should. It feels like he's reclaiming something that's his. It's like he's whispering an eerie "thank you for taking good care of her, but I'll take it from here."

And right now I want to melt into him.

Closing my eyes, I lean into his hold on me, ghosting my fingers along his arms. "Why did you say you loved Daisy as much as your wife? You married Jenna. You made a child with her." I open my eyes.

Nate's mouth settles into this pleasant smile, like he's looking at his daughter, not her nanny.

"It doesn't make sense, Nate. You should have loved Jenna more—so much more."

"I think we love many people for a lot of different reasons. I also think people pass in and out of our lives to give us an experience. You were—"

"Don't." I pull my head back, tripping over a few things as I get to my feet. "Don't say *you*. Say *she*."

His brows knit together as he lumbers to standing. "I don't care that your eyes are a different color. I don't care that you're fifteen years younger than me. You are my friend." His voice tightens with the last word. "Some things last forever. What if our friendship lasts forever? What if the connection we have transcends time?"

I'm certain no *what ifs* have ever been more beautiful, except this one … what if he's right?

"*You* taught me how to be a friend. You taught me how to

love. You were my first kiss and my first heartbreak. You fed my hunger. You comforted me when my family fell apart. You convinced me to dream big. You were my absolute everything." He frowns. "You didn't give me a child, but you sure as hell gave me life."

I bat away the tears before they escape. "I had this flashback. I was above you ... my hair tickling your face. You wore the biggest grin and you said, 'So, what are—'"

"So what are you going to do with me," Nate says with a grin almost as big as the memory in my head. And I know now ... he's going to be okay.

"You used to wrestle with me. I'd let you pin me to the ground, or my bed, or a patch of grass and weeds on the old abandoned property. You'd say 'ha' so triumphantly. And I'd grin because there's nothing I loved more than your hair feathering my face. I always said the same thing ... 'So, what are you going to do with me?'"

I smile. "And what did she say?"

"You licked me. It was weird. But with the most wicked intentions flashing in your eyes, you'd lick a path from my Adam's apple to the tip of my chin." He shrugs, twisting his lips to conceal his smirk. "What can I say? You were one odd chick."

I shove his chest. "Stop saying *you*. That's not who I am. She's hijacking my brain, but *I* was not the *odd chick* who licked you."

This.

We can do this. We can uncover the past together. And when one of us breaks, the other one will know how to glue all the pieces back into place.

CHAPTER FOURTEEN
Nathaniel

S HE'S HERE.
But I can't really touch her.

She's here.

But I can't really see her.

She's here.

But she's no longer mine.

"Promise me you'll stay away from Doug Mann. Promise me you won't go anywhere by yourself until we get this figured out. Always lock the door when you're here. Remember there's a panic button on the security system keypad."

Her jovial expression fades. "Don't go anywhere by myself?" She coughs a laugh. "That's a little hard to do. I don't have a bodyguard."

"You have family and friends. Find someone to go with you. Find someone to be at home with you. And if you can't, then promise you'll call me."

I hate scaring her, but this revelation has gutted me. Daisy was murdered. When she told me, it felt like my father breaking the news to me all over again.

Daisy's *body*.

Drowned.

Dead.

I didn't save her then, but I'm sure as hell not going to let history repeat itself.

Stepping over the debris, I bring her into my body and hug her. Swayze Samuels is a clash of everyone in my world. It's difficult to make sense of the feelings I have for her.

The boss in me thinks she's the perfect person to look after Morgan.

The boy in me feels elated to have his friend back.

The father in me wants to protect her like my own child.

But the man in me wants things that I shouldn't want— not from a twenty-two-year-old woman engaged to another man.

So I kiss her head like a friend or a father, even if I want to know what the skin just below her ear would feel like against my lips or what her tongue would taste like sliding against mine.

I release her, taking a cautious step backwards before my dick gets any harder. I chastise myself for letting those thoughts take form in my head. Even if Dr. Greyson would dismiss them as harmless, they don't feel harmless when I can't control an erection.

"Are we done renegotiating my contract?" She cocks her head to the side.

"You chatted with my dad?"

"Briefly."

"He liked you."

She frowns. "Daisy."

I shove my hands into my pockets. "He thought you were good for me."

With a slight headshake, she rolls her eyes. "He thought *Daisy* was good for you and that's because she fed you when money was tight."

I nod with ease, thinking about every sack of food she brought to my house, the two sandwiches she packed in her school lunches, the money she slipped in my wallet when I wasn't looking. "I didn't deserve you."

She goes to speak but clamps her jaw closed like she's giving up on correcting me. Daisy is not a separate person, she's just in a different body with a different name, but part of her is right in front of me. I'll take any part that I can get because I loved everything about her. I still do.

"I'll walk you to your car."

Swayze nods.

There's so much more I want to know. Did Dr. Albright mention hypnosis? I'd give anything for her to remember us like I remember us.

"Thank you, my big bad bodyguard."

I hold open the door to the black truck. "You're welcome."

She rubs her lips together, hugging herself as if to keep warm and as if she's waiting for something more. I'm not going to kiss her, even if that's all I want to do at the moment. There's no fucking way I'm that guy. But ... I'm not a total saint either.

"Do you have my picture in your pocket today?"

"Pfft ..." Her nose scrunches. "You're full of yourself, Professor Hunt."

I lift a single eyebrow. "Is that so?"

"Yeah, that's so." She turns to climb up into the truck.

I slide my left hand around her waist, pressing it flat to her stomach to pin her back to my chest. And fuck me if she doesn't gasp in a way that I imagine she would if my cock were sliding into her for the first time.

Knock that shit off! My mind wars with itself and my body.

The fingers of my right hand dip into her front pocket. I slide out a photo—the photo of me. She doesn't fight me. Not a word. I'm not sure she's even breathing.

"Am I still full of myself?" I hold the photo up to her face. I'd love to see her expression. "No comment? Okay." I slide the picture back into its spot. "I like riding in your front pocket."

She takes in a quick breath and turns, eyes narrowed. "Yeah, well … I bet you still have that picture of me in your wallet." Her chin tips up, shoulders back.

Happiness steals my smile. She brings me unfathomable joy. It's the reason I named my daughter after her. And I love when she says *me* and *I* instead of Daisy or her.

"Always," I say with complete sincerity.

Swayze deflates a fraction when I surrender total honesty. "The picture in your wallet makes sense." She looks down at the fraction of space between us. "The picture in my pocket doesn't make the same kind of sense."

"Then why the fascination with it?"

She shrugs. "I love the expression on your face. Your hair. Your lips. Your eyebrows. The stubble along your jaw. But mostly …" Her gaze finds mine again. "It feels like a bridge to the gap between then and now. It feels like a big piece to this puzzle that's in my head."

And since I can't stop myself, I slide my hands in her hair and kiss the top of her head one more time because I love how it feels. She rests her palms gently on my chest—I love how that feels too. Basically, I love *all* the feels—right or wrong— that I get from her.

If I were Griffin, I'd beat the ever living shit out of me for touching something that's not mine. But the problem is … when I do touch her, my head goes blank, listening only to my heart whispering *"mine."*

"Drive safely."

"Goodnight." She climbs up and gives me one last smile.

Swayze

"HEY, WHAT AN unexpected surprise." My mom hugs me when I step inside the front door.

"Griffin's working late and I wanted to talk to you."

"Did you eat?"

I follow her to the kitchen. "Not yet."

She gestures for me to sit at the table. "I'll make you a sandwich while you talk."

I'm not that hungry, but it might be easier to tell her everything when she's not staring at me the whole time like a therapist. "That would be great. Thanks."

"So what's up? Wedding stuff?" She grabs things from the fridge.

"I know why I knew more than other kids my age."

Mom laughs. "Wow. You made your father and me promise to never discuss it again. I haven't mentioned it in years. *Now* we're going to talk about it?" She shoots me an incredulous look.

Drumming my fingers on the table, I nod. "It's quite the story."

With her back to me, she opens jars and starts assembling what looks like a turkey sandwich. "I like stories. Let's hear it. Once upon a time …"

"Once upon a time, over twenty-two years ago, I was Nathaniel Hunt's best friend, Morgan Daisy Gallagher."

She stills.

I wait.

It's quite the opening line to a story.

Ever so slowly, she looks over her shoulder, lips parted.

I smile. "I know things she knew. People she knew, especially Nate. I see strangers that I recognize, but I remember them from many years ago ... as in before I was born. I just know a lot of random stuff, but now it doesn't seem so random."

The butter knife clanks against the plate, and she completely turns toward me. "Swayze ..."

I hold up my hands, palms out. "I know. Believe me. *I know*. It's crazy. Not possible. It begs for a more logical explanation. It's taken me months to even consider this could be a real possibility. But there is no other explanation. This is the reason Dr. Greyson referred me to a new psychiatrist. Dr. Albright is sort of an expert on the matter."

"Swayze ..." She moves toward me like I could attack her.

"Mom, I need you to believe me so I can tell you what this has done to me."

With unsteady legs, she plops down onto the chair next to me. "You're asking me to believe in reincarnation."

"I'm asking you to believe *me*. People pack sanctuaries every Sunday to worship God. They can't prove he exists. I have way more proof that I was Morgan Daisy Gallagher in another life than anyone has that God truly exists. Many religions believe in reincarnation. And some very brilliant historic figures also believed in it."

She chews on the inside of her cheek, forehead wrinkled. "Start from the very beginning."

And so I do. I start with the day I saw Nate in the waiting

room at Dr. Greyson's office. Nothing gets left out, not even the photo in my pocket. After an hour of trying to explain every little detail, including Doug Mann and why I went so crazy over Erica's death, my mom looks like a statue or maybe a ghost, pale and expressionless.

"What about Griffin?" She speaks her first words.

"I don't know. Sometimes I think he believes me, but whether he does or not, it doesn't matter. Either way, he hates that I have this connection with Nate. And I don't blame him, but I also don't know what to do about it. He wants me to quit my job so we can pack up and move far away from all of this, but I can't outrun what's in my head."

"He's jealous?"

"I think so. It's so hard to tell with him. He's this pillar of confidence, and he's good at hiding his emotions."

"*Should* he be jealous?"

"No."

She holds up the photo of Nate that's still on the table. "Are you sure?"

Ghosting my fingers over my bottom lip, I stare at it. After a few seconds of contemplative silence, tears burn my eyes. "I feel like I'm piecing myself together. And I don't know if Griffin will still love me the same way when he sees the whole me."

Mom sets the photo back on the table. "Tell me about these pieces."

A tiny smile fights its way to my lips. She's had so much therapy she sounds like a therapist.

"They're thrilling and utterly terrifying. When I'm with Nate and we're talking about the past, it's not weird. It feels natural. He's so familiar. It's the epitome of feeling like you've known someone your whole life. And I adore Morgan. I think I would no matter what, but when I'm there, I can't stop thinking *he named his daughter after me.* It's life-changing."

My mom makes slow nods, trying to process everything I throw at her. "Beyond the flattery of him naming his daughter after this person you believe was you, and the familiarity, how do you feel about him? What is your relationship with him? Swayze..." a bit of regret sinks into her eyes "...do you have feelings for him that go beyond just friends?"

"No. I don't have ..." I sigh. "It's complicated. It's confusing. When I'm with Griffin, I have this need for him to accept me as not only Swayze but the parts of me that are Daisy too. But when I'm with Nate, I like the separation."

"Because if you're Daisy with him, then Swayze is not cheating on her fiancé."

"Mom ..." I frown. "That's not what's happening. I'm not cheating on Griffin."

"Have you crossed the line with Nate?"

I'm not sure if I should be offended that she doesn't trust me or elated that she's protecting Griffin. Pushing out of my chair, I finish making the sandwich she started. "You'll have to explain this *line.*"

"Have you kissed him?"

"No."

He's kissed me on the head, but that doesn't count. Does it?

"Do you want to kiss him?"

I finish cutting the sandwich in half and set the knife off to the side, pausing a moment to hold back my knee-jerk reaction. This is my mom, the person who loves me unconditionally. She loves me if I meet Griffin at the altar. She loves me if he leaves me tomorrow. I don't have to hide from her.

"I love Griffin. There has not been one day since we met that I've questioned wanting to be with him—not since I met Nate, not since I've acknowledge my past, not when we've fought, not yesterday, not today, and I won't question it tomorrow."

"But?"

My gaze shifts from the knife to my mom. "But Nate has become my obsession."

We both move our attention to the photo.

"I can't shut off my brain, but the one thing that scares me more than the deluge of memories is this insatiable curiosity."

"About?" She shoots me a sidelong glance.

Biting my lips together, I search for a way to explain this without it sounding like I *want* it to happen. "I wonder what his lips would feel like pressed to my neck where he used to kiss her … or me. I wonder if it would bring forth more memories."

"Or start a fire that would burn down your whole world?" Her eyebrows lift, giving me that motherly-warning look.

"Yeah … or that."

"Do I need to give you the curiosity-killed-the-cat speech?"

I shake my head.

"Do you think that Griffin might be right? Maybe you should find another job. I know it won't change the memories you have, but it would eliminate the *temptation*."

I grab half of my sandwich and take a bite. "You make it sound like I'm going to hop in bed with him," I mumble.

"Can we talk woman to woman?"

I shrug.

"You're carrying around a shirtless picture of him in your pocket. I just worry that if he put those lips on your neck, you'd wonder what they'd feel like in other places. Where would it stop, if not in his bed?"

"It's not going there." I don't mean to sound so prickly. "We're friends, but more than that, Morgan is attached to me and I'm attached to her too. The fact is he needs me to take care of her, and I need a job. I like my job. And in a non-jumping-in-his-bed way, Nate and Morgan feel like extended family."

"I'm your family. Griffin, his parents, and his sisters are your family. We love you. This cannot end well, and you know it. *And* if what you said about Doug Mann is correct, it's not safe for you to be anywhere he can easily find you. Tomorrow you need to go back to the police and plead your case, *make* them understand. Honey, Griffin isn't trying to tear you away from Nate and Morgan, he's trying to protect you."

"The police are not going to buy my reincarnation story no matter how hard I try to sell it. And I'm not going to spend the rest of my life running. I want to figure something out so I don't have to leave my home."

"Your home or Nate?"

I bite my tongue because it's covered in defensive words that won't justify anything.

"I need to get home."

With a sad, defeated smile, Mom pulls me in for a hug. "I'm on your side no matter what. All I want is for you to be happy."

"Thank you."

CHAPTER FIFTEEN

"NICE TO SEE you again, Swayze. Please, have a seat."

"Thank you." I take my seat across from Dr. Albright. I like her. She's warm and approachable.

"Tea?"

"I'm good, but thank you."

"How have things been since we last talked?"

"Interesting I suppose is the best word. I told Nate that I think Daisy was murdered. He wasn't real receptive at first, in fact, he was quite angry, but I think we're good now. He's worried about Doug. And I think he's frustrated that the only proof we have is that of a twenty-two-year-old girl who claims to be his dead friend's reincarnated soul. The police aren't receptive to that."

She nods once before sipping her tea.

"I told my mom everything too. I think the hardest part for me is all the gaps that I haven't been able to fill in yet."

"We could try to fill some of them in with hypnosis, but you'd need to be sure it's what you really want. There are pros and cons with it. You would need to decide if the benefits outweigh the risks."

I wring my hands in my lap. "What are the pros?"

"Possible increased memory of certain events. Deeper understanding. Validation. Maybe even what it would take to put a murderer behind bars."

"Hypnosis is recognized as something reliable and valid in a court of law?"

"I'm thinking more along the lines of you remembering something that might help shed new light on the case. Something officials missed the first time."

I nod. "And the cons?"

"Well, the most obvious one is it might not work on you. Beyond that … there's the possibility that the very information that could put Doug Mann behind bars might also give you images or memories that you can't forget. The kind that give you nightmares. The kind that lead to PTSD. It's a risky tradeoff, and I don't want to downplay it at all."

"Right now I don't remember the exact details of Daisy's death. My death." I cringe. It's still so incredibly weird. "But you're saying I could. And who wants to relive their death, especially if it was tragic and traumatizing?"

"Precisely. But the chances are truly slim. The unconscious mind is there to protect you. Most of the time we can't bring forth memories that our conscious mind can't handle."

"But if Doug preys on another innocent woman, and I feel like I could have prevented it …"

"It would be hard to stomach it."

I nod. "But if I spend the rest of my life reliving my death …"

Dr. Albright relinquishes a soft sigh. "I've had personal experience with this. They were able to use hypnosis to suppress the memory I had of a tragic death. But there's no guarantee it would work. It's a really tough decision, however you look at it. That's why I want you to think long and hard before you make it. I want you to discuss it with family because it could impact them too."

"The trauma?"

Her neatly-trimmed fingernail traces the rim of her tea cup while honest eyes hold their gaze on me. "Yes, but the way you perceive yourself could change too. If you connect on a deeper level with your life as Daisy, it could change who you are as a person now."

"Because I will *feel* more like Daisy?"

"It's possible."

"I could feel closer to Nate?"

"Perhaps."

Do I want to feel closer to Nate?

"YOU'RE LATE." GRIFFIN slips on his jacket before I get the door shut.

"Late for what?" I deposit my purse on the kitchen chair.

"Bowling."

"Bowling?"

His eyes widen, disbelief rolling off every inch of his body, which happens to look hot as fuck tonight. Griffin screams filthy sex when he wears those faded worn jeans and that Doobie Brothers vintage motorcycle tee.

I press the heel of my hand to my forehead. "Bowling. That's right. That's tonight." Bowling with his work buddies.

"The look on your face says I'm going by myself."

"No. You're not going by yourself." I hustle past him to the bedroom. "I just got distracted at Dr. Albright's office. Let me change into something less homely than yoga pants and a hoodie."

"I'm already late. Don't worry about it. Where are the keys

to my truck?"

"My purse. And I'm coming. Just wait!" I hop from one foot to the other, tugging on my jeans. "Where's my red V-neck shirt?" Riffling through the shirts in the closet, I can't find it.

"I'll be home before midnight. Don't wait up."

"Son of a bitch," I mumble, seizing the first shirt I can rip off the hanger and tugging it on while I chase after him. "Just WAIT!"

My plea goes unheard. He's out the door. I snatch my purse, grab my shoes, and sprint after him. The annoyance on his face when I hop in the truck is no match for my scowl—thanks to my shoeless feet taking the brunt of his impatience.

"Hello? What the heck? I said I was coming."

Glancing in the rearview mirror, he backs out of the driveway. "Yeah, well you say a lot of things."

I bite back the what-crawled-up-your-butt-and-died comment because I don't relish the idea of being locked out of the house later. But seriously, it's an appropriate question for the circumstances.

"Is this about me being a little late? Or me being a little late because I was with Dr. Albright?" I shove my feet into my ankle boots.

His grip on the steering wheel tightens just like his jaw that's holding back his answer.

"Whatever." I glance out my window at the streetlights flickering on like a farewell wink to the last sliver of sun. Too bad I'm not good at playing the cold shoulder game. "Aren't you going to ask me about my day? No? Well, I'll tell you anyway. Morgan said 'see' but I think she meant Z because I've been trying to teach her my name. Then I ordered a sub for lunch and they forgot the pickles, and Nate doesn't have pickles at his house. Like ... who doesn't have pickles? It's a staple, no different than ketchup and mustard."

Griffin responds by turning on the radio, a nice little slap in the face.

I continue, only much louder so he hears me over the music. "Dr. Albright discussed hypnosis with me. I'm not sure I can be hypnotized, but I'm considering it."

Click.

Off goes the radio.

"What did you just say?" Griffin gives me a sidelong glance, much longer than he should since he's driving.

"Pickles. They forgot my pickles."

"Fuck the pickles." His attention returns to the road.

"Well ..." I murmur, "it's an option, but not really my thing."

My humor falls flat on my audience of one.

"Why?"

I slide my hands beneath my legs to tame the nerves. "Because Doug Mann needs to be in prison. Because I won't feel safe until he is. Because this patchy memory has left me feeling like I'm anchored to the past and losing sight of my future."

"This has gone too far. Reincarnation? Hypnosis? Murder mystery? Do you hear yourself?"

"You don't believe me."

"I don't know what to believe!" His knuckles blanch over the steering wheel.

"Then believe *me*. Trust me. Help me."

A cynical laugh cuts through the air. "Help you? How am I supposed to help you?"

"By not getting so miffed about me running late to a bowling outing because I have a job and a therapy appointment. By not freaking out every time I mention the past or Daisy or Nate."

He parks the truck and hops out. I guess this topic is on hold until we're done bowling a few rounds. This should be loads of fun.

To my surprise, he comes around and opens my door. I unfasten my seatbelt and swing my legs around, but before I can hop out, he wedges himself between my legs. The arms I love encircle my body while he rests his forehead against my chest.

"You drive me fucking crazy."

I nod several times, even though he can't see me.

"If I believe you, then I sure as hell don't want you being hypnotized to remember anything more. If I don't believe you, then it's going to piss me off if you waste time and money on something so insane."

I kiss his head, tickled by the stubbly surface of the tiniest outgrowth of hair. Uncontrolled thoughts of Nate pop into my mind. A kiss on the head isn't necessarily innocent, it can be intimate like it is when my lips press to Griffin's head. What does Nate feel when he kisses my head?

"I need to feel safe. Don't you want that for me?"

His head lifts, sincerity resolute in his expression. "I would never let anything happen to you."

"I know, but you're not with me all of the time. He was inches from me in a parking lot and you weren't there. I don't want this life, Griff."

My eyes close on a heavy blink when his hands press to my cheeks.

"You won't have this life. I promise."

I love him for making this promise, even if it's one he might not be able to keep. There's a reason I've always felt safe with Griffin. I just hope when I need his safety the most … he's close enough to hear my cry for help.

"Let's go." He takes my hand and helps me out before tucking me under his arm—my hero.

CHAPTER SIXTEEN
Griffin

S WAYZE IS A terrible bowler. She's also a skittish bird whenever one of the guys from work gives her shit about something. On the surface, she doesn't fit into my world. But in a way that lungs need oxygen and a heart needs blood, she's vital to my life.

I don't know for certain that Doug Mann killed Erica, nor do I know that he killed Morgan Daisy Gallagher. What I do know is that he got too close to the oxygen in my lungs and the blood in my heart.

"Can I say your little fiancée is sexy as fuck without you slashing my throat?"

I take a swig of my bottled water, lean back in the chair, and watch Swayze's perfect ass as she throws another ball in the gutter. "If you weren't my boss, I'd say no. But I'll let it slide because you're right, and I want to keep my job. But if you say a word to her, look at her for more than five seconds at a time, or let your hand so much as graze her hand ... fuck the job. I'll end you."

He chuckles, taking a slow pull of his beer. "Fair enough."

"Griff, I suck at this." She shoots me a pouty face with her lower lip protruding as she waits for her ball to return.

"Maybe it's all the cheap wine. Should I cut you off?"

Her head jerks back, face sour. "No. I haven't had *that*

much … uh …" Wrinkles form along her brow.

"Wine, Swayz. We're talking about wine. And the fact that you can't remember that long enough to finish a sentence just proves that you've had too much. I'm cutting you off."

A few of my friends and their significant others snicker.

She grabs the ball and swings it back. We all flinch because it would be the third time she's released it in the wrong direction. Thankfully, she holds on to it. "Then I'm cutting you off too."

I smirk. "Of water?"

She heaves it. Two seconds later, the ball clunks in the gutter. Looking over her shoulder, she scowls at me like it's my fault she's sucking ass at bowling tonight. "Sex, buddy. No wine for me, then no sex for you."

The snickers return for a second round of the Griffin and Swayze Show, but this time they're muffled behind fisted hands because they know better than to make fun of me. Payback is my favorite game.

I crook my finger at her as Breanna, Derek's date for the night, stands up to take her turn.

Keeping her drunken gaze locked to mine, Swayze wobbles toward me. "Yes, Mr. Alcohol Police?"

Holding out my hand, palm up, I wait for her to take it. After a few seconds of staring at it with apprehension, she takes it. I give her a firm jerk, and she stumbles forward onto my lap. I drag her knees up to straddle my legs.

Jett clears his throat. "There are young kids ten yards away. At least take her into the bathroom. Not that I personally have issues watching."

I ignore him. Swayze? Not so much. She turns pink clear to the tips of her ears.

"I'm not having sex in the bathroom," she tries to whisper but misses the mark by a few decibels.

"No?" I grin, lifting a single brow while sliding my hand around the back of her neck.

Her head shakes a half dozen times, eyes wide like the idea alone has sobered her up a good fifty percent.

Those wide eyes dart side to side several times before meeting my gaze again. "Uh uh."

I'm joking, even if my dick at the moment feels rather enthusiastic about the idea. Leaning closer, I whisper in her ear, "I love you. You suck at bowling, but I love the hell out of you."

"I'll give you a hundred bucks if you tell me what he said." Jett winks at Swayze.

"A hundred bucks?" Her back snaps ramrod straight. "He said, 'I love you. You suck at bowling, but I love the hell out of you.'"

Jett lifts his fisted hand to his mouth and coughs. "Bullshit."

I grin at Swayze and shrug. She frowns.

"I want my hundred bucks. Tell him, Griff."

All I can do is chuckle.

Jett lumbers to standing for his turn. "I'm firing your pansy ass if that's what you said to her."

"That's bullshit!"

Okay, she's not all that sobered up after all.

"I want my hundred bucks. I just shared ..." She points a finger at him as I hold onto her waist before she attacks my boss, who's grinning like an idiot. "Dammit," she mumbles before sinking her teething into her bottom lip. "What was I saying?"

This gets more laughter from the rest of the drunks. I'm the only completely sober one in the group.

"Yes!" Her same accusatory finger shoots up in the air. "I just shared something personal with you *only* because you offered me a hundred bucks."

Jett bowls a strike and turns, stroking his goatee. "Swayze, darling … Griff saying you suck at bowling is quite public. We've all seen you."

Aaannnd it's time to go. Swayze digs her nails into my arms, trying to pry my grip from her waist.

"We're taking off. Swayze hasn't had dinner yet."

Breanna jerks her head to the side. "There's food over there. Pizza, hot dogs, nachos—"

"Nachos? I love nachos! Griff, nachos!"

I lift her off my lap now that food has distracted her from attacking Jett. "I'll take you to a Mexican restaurant. You don't want stale chips and fake cheese." After changing my shoes, helping her with hers, and saying our goodbyes, I take Swayze's hand and pull her toward the exit.

"I think I do want stale chips and fake cheese," she murmurs as we step outside. "I'm so hungry I could eat anything."

I grin, shaking my head. "I can offer you a shot of cum on the way if you need something to tide you over."

"A shot of—wait, is that code for a blowjob?"

Everyone else in the parking lot hears the lingering echo of blowjob. Well done, Swayze.

I open her door. "It's code for get your ass in the truck."

She lifts her leg but misses the step.

"You're a fucking mess."

She giggles as I grab her waist and hoist her up. "But you love me."

I help her fasten in. "I do."

"But you were piiisssed about me being late for bowling."

I shut the door, get in on my side, and start the truck. As we pull out of the parking lot, she slips off her boots and wiggles around to get her feet tucked under her off to the side.

"Why does everyone look at you like you're meat and they're starving carnivores?" She slurs a few of her words either from the alcohol or plain old exhaustion.

"I don't know what you're talking about."

"Come on ... the women. They are so nonconspic spic not conspic ... no that's not right. Inconspic ... fuck!"

Biting my lips together, I shoot her a quick glance. "Conspicuous?"

"That's it! You're so smart, honeybuns."

Honeybuns is a new one.

"All those filthy women want you. They have no shame."

"Alcohol makes you paranoid, Swayz. What do you want to eat? Mexican?"

She leans on the console between the seats and drums her fingers together. It's a little weird. "I'm thinking a Griffin hotdog."

Scratch that. It's a lot weird.

"Never heard of that brand. So, yes to Mexican?"

Her hand cups my crotch. "I think I'm ready for that cum shot."

"I think you're too drunk, I'm too sober, and the speed limit is too high."

With a click, she unfastens her seatbelt and positions herself on her knees facing me.

"Swayz, fasten your ass in the seat."

"Tell me you don't want me sucking you off." She unfastens my jeans.

Sucking you off and *honeybuns* in the same night. Drunk Swayze has a different filter than sober Swayze.

I tighten my grip on the steering wheel while I should be tightening my grip on her hands to keep her from doing this. But as she slides her hand along my length, I stop giving a fuck about safety and all things that require optimal brain power.

"Swayz …" I make a weak attempt at stopping her.

Too late. A rush of adrenaline shoots through me, restricting the air in my lungs a bit when her warm, wet mouth first makes contact. In seconds I go from hard to really fucking hard as she shows a lot more eagerness than sober Swayze.

Focus on the road. Focus on the road.

"You taste *so* good."

Yet another phrase that's new tonight. I don't care how rich, educated, or sophisticated a man is, no guy turns this down. Except … the guy who loves a woman like I love Swayze. I can't have my future wife—mother of my children— die in a car accident before we ever get the chance to say "I do."

But it feels so fucking good.

I pull into a vacant parking lot of an office building and shove the truck into *Park*. Gathering her hair in my hands, I hold it away from her head so I can watch her in what little light filters in from the streetlights. It's a beautiful sight.

She hums.

I bite my bottom lip, letting my head fall back. My plan when we got home was to talk about this therapy of hers and the crazy idea of hypnosis. But as her fingernails dig into my thighs and she takes me deeper, I decide it can wait a day or two—the approximate amount of time it takes to get over a good blowjob, and Swayze's giving me a damn good blowjob.

"Easy, babe …" I tug her hair a bit as she gags.

I fight the urge to push into her mouth more as I get close. So close.

"Fuuuccck!" Every muscle tenses as I release.

Future wife. Mother of my children. Keeper of my cock … *gags.* Not a you-just-tickled-my-gag-reflex-but-I'm-good gag. This gag is a strong two-second warning.

One second.

Two seconds.

Blah!

Two coughs and one more upchuck.

"Oh my gosh …" she whispers, using the back of her hand to wipe her face covered in sweat, saliva, and humiliation.

A permanent cringe affixes itself to my face as I feel the warmth and wetness of wine, stomach acid, and cum covering my cock and absorbing into my jeans, clear to my ass as it runs between my legs along my leather seat.

Another first. One I could have done without tonight.

"Are you okay?" I press my hand to her cheek as she catches her breath.

"I'm so sorry. I'm so sorry. I'm so sorry."

My attention returns to the mess between my legs. I nod slowly. "It's okay, Swayz."

"It's not okay." She shimmies half of her body between the seats. "Here."

I stare at the plastic tube with the rolled up shammy I use at the carwash.

Swayze shrugs. "It's very absorbent." She pulls it out of the tube and unrolls it. "Do you want to do it or should I do it?"

I yank it out of her hand and ruin a relatively new shammy. After I get things cleaned up enough to tuck myself back into my jeans, I toss the rag out my door and start the truck again.

"That's littering." Swayze scrunches her nose.

I give her a look.

She zips her lips and fastens her seatbelt. "I uh ... have a bottle of hand sanitizer in my purse."

Shoving the truck into drive, I ignore her. It's going to take more than a bottle of hand sanitizer to fix this mess.

"Don't worry about dinner either. I'll grab something at home."

I shoot her an incredulous look.

She snorts out a laugh. "I'm sorry." She laughs some more. "It was the Zinfandel on an empty stomach. Do you want the ring back?"

There's no way I'm acknowledging her until my balls are no longer sticky with vomit.

Swayze

THE SHOWER SHUTS off. I search for a nonchalant expression, sitting on the edge of the bed waiting for Griffin to come out of the bathroom. I need a shower too, but I thought maybe he deserved to take one first. I'm nice like that.

"Your turn." He eyes me with a hard-to-read expression as he drops his towel and snags a pair of red briefs from the dresser.

It never gets old. When we're in our eighties, will I still lose all ability to speak when he drops his towel or will his body be too flaccid? Nothing more than loose skin. Will the dragon along his backside look eighty as well?

"Did you eat?"

My gaze snaps to his eyes. "Two pieces of toast."

"Go shower. We can watch a movie if you want to."

"Are you mad?"

Griffin pulls on a pair of sweatpants. "Nope."

"Really?"

He picks the towel up off the floor and flips it over his shoulder. "It was the best fucking blowjob you've ever given me … until you vomited. There's potential. We can work with that."

My eyes narrow at him. "It was the wine."

"I know. If we can figure out a way to get you that enthused about sucking my dick without first intoxicating you, then I think we'll be onto something really special."

I laugh. "Wow. That almost sounded like a speech about curing cancer or feeding the world, except the *sucking my dick* part. You should go into politics, Griff."

He replies with a naughty grin.

After I shower and brush my teeth, I grab a blanket and cuddle up on the sofa next to him.

"ESPN is not a movie."

"I was just waiting on you." He clicks off the TV.

"No movie?"

Griffin angles his body toward me. "I don't want you to be hypnotized. If you need to talk all this out with a therapist, fine. But I don't want you to be hypnotized."

"Griff, we don't even know if it will work. If you could hear Dr. Albright, I think you'd—"

"Fine." He rolls his lips between his teeth, eyes wide. "Let me hear this Dr. Albright. Let me go to your next appointment with you."

"Really? You would do that?"

"Sure. Why not?"

I leap into his lap, throwing my arms around his neck. This is exactly what I need. If Griffin sees Dr. Albright with me, he'll know I'm not crazy. He'll see why it's so important to do whatever it takes to put Doug Mann behind bars.

I'm not going to lose him after all. He will accept the part of me that's Daisy, and we will be fine.

CHAPTER SEVENTEEN

"GOOD MORNING, HUNT family." I breeze into the great room with a bakery box and a drink carrier with two high calorie over-sugared coffee drinks.

"Someone's in a good mood." Nate smirks.

"Yes, sir. I sure am." I snatch his plain coffee out of his hand and replace it with my sweet one. "Extra caffeine, extra sugar. Your students will find you to be much more fun today."

He quirks an eyebrow. "And by fun you mean passed out by mid-afternoon when I come crashing down from my sugar and caffeine high?"

"Exactly." I smile while holding open the box of donuts.

"Vanilla cake donut with chocolate frosting and sprinkles, however did you know?" He takes the donut.

He knows darn well how I knew.

"Griffin agreed to go with me to see Dr. Albright." I take a glazed donut and sit next to Morgan on the floor. She's working the army crawl like a champ. "And if it goes well, I think I'm going to try hypnosis with her. Maybe we can uncover something from my memory that will help prove that Doug Mann is a killer."

Nate sets his coffee and donut on the counter and presses his hands to the edge. "Has she explained any of the risks with you?"

"Yes. I know it could uncover memories that I don't want

JEWEL E. ANN

in my head, like how I died as Daisy. But I'd rather have those memories to deal with than another murder on my conscience if or when he kills again. And ..." I twist my lips to the side and tease Morgan with a teething toy.

"And you're afraid you could be his next victim." Concern etches into Nate's forehead.

I nod.

"I have someone looking into the case again."

"That's good."

"Are you being safe? Not going anywhere by yourself?"

I laugh. "Yes, Dad."

"No." He shakes his head several times. "Don't call me that. It's too weird."

"Everything about us is too weird. I've been reading Dr. Albright's book, the same one you have in your nightstand. There's so much that nobody really knows about reincarnation and so many different opinions. The glitch kind of theory is interesting. Like our souls are hard drives that should be wiped clean before the next life, but sometimes not everything gets wiped from it, and there's this random information that we bring forth with nothing to connect it to."

Nate shrugs. "Maybe it's not that meaningless. What if we all carry something to the next life? It's possible we just don't recognize it. Wouldn't that be the purpose of the soul? Random knowledge. Déjà vu moments. Hidden talents. Oddly familiar faces. Think about it, had you not met me, do you think these memories of yours would be anything more than the occasional weird feeling of familiarity?"

A grin slides up my face. "You believe in fate."

Nate sips his coffee and shrugs. "Why not? I don't think everything is fate. I don't want to believe you dying was fate. I

140

don't want to believe that Jenna dying was fate."

"If not fate, then what?"

"Life. Circumstance. We navigate the earth by free will. Every day we have an opportunity to choose our own destiny. But some things are more. What if young Nate and Daisy knew each other in another life? A parallel universe? What if we're destined or fated to find each other in every life?"

Morgan gets upset at her toys or maybe just too much time on the ground. I pick her up, focusing all of my attention on her because Nate's words feel like ice tickling my spine. "Sounds like a fantasy book or movie."

He squats next to me, kissing Morgan on the cheek while I take a slow, hopefully very inconspicuous, inhale of his spicy scent. "What if it's an epic love story?" Nate's gaze sweeps along my face, and I feel it everywhere because he's inches from my lips.

"You don't love me." I choke on the words as they come out like a strangled whisper.

"I do love you."

Dead. Dead. Dead.

No oxygen.

No words.

No pulse.

"Because I think I've always loved you, and I'm certain I always will." He grins, leans in, and kisses the top of my head. "Breathe, Swayze. I'm not stealing you from your fiancé." He grabs his bag and coffee. "I think a part of you will be mine to love in every life."

It's not until the door shuts behind him that I let my lungs have that sweet, refreshing oxygen.

The rest of the morning I play with a smiley, giggly baby.

When Morgan goes down for a nap, I get a text from Nate. I glance at the camera. The timing is too perfect for it to be a coincidence.

Professor: I didn't mean to scare you this morning
Me: You didn't

I lie.

Professor: I meant that I love you like family. Like someone special in my life. Nothing more.

Is *he* lying? And if not, how do I respond? *I love you too?*

Me: I get it. You remember me differently than I remember you.

I roll my eyes at my stupid comment.

Me: You have the feelings. I just have memories.
Me: Not that I don't have any feelings for you.

"No ... not that." I cringe.

Me: I think you're a nice guy.

Yeah, that's not it either. I don't look at the camera, he'll see my nervous embarrassment.

Professor: Good thing I'm not asking you out on a date. The 'nice guy' comment might sting with rejection.

Looking at his response, I hide my grin behind Morgan's head on my chest.

Me: I have a hard time believing any woman has ever rejected you.

Professor: *This girl I knew many years ago rejected me quite often. But I was persistent.*

"You're not playing fairly," I murmur while typing my reply.

Me: *I can't say for sure, since I got an F in flirting as a teenager, but from observing well-adjusted girls around me, my guess is the girl you knew was playing hard to get. IDK*

Professor: *You got an F in flirting?*

Me: *Don't you have a job to do?*

Professor: *When are you seeing Dr. Albright again?*

Me: *Tomorrow night. Why? Are you going to eavesdrop outside of her door?*

Professor: *Lol if I can get my parents to watch Morgan, I just might.*

Me: *Off topic … are Daisy's parents still alive?*

Professor: *Yes*

Me: *Do you think if I met Daisy's parents that it would trigger more memories? I mean, they're the people she saw every day for fifteen years.*

Professor: *Do you want to meet them?*

Yes. No. I'm not sure. There's a mix of fear, intrigue, and excitement swirling in my stomach. If I concentrate on Daisy and let that part of me bleed to the surface, then I absolutely want to meet her parents. I want to see her room, crawl in her bed. Riffle through her dresser drawers. Dear God, I hope they don't really still have all of her—my—stuff twenty-two years after saying a final goodbye.

Me: *I think I do.*

Professor: *I'll arrange it.*

Me: *What does that mean? You're not going to say anything about me, are you? How will you explain me—us.*

Professor: *I'll think of something. I'm incredibly smart like that.*

Me: *Gagging.*

Professor: *Work calls. Give Morgan a kiss from me.*

I tip my chin and kiss the top of her head and wink at the camera in the corner.

CHAPTER EIGHTEEN

"THANK YOU."

Griffin squeezes my hand. "Stop thanking me."

I knock on the door to Dr. Albright's office.

"Come in."

"But seriously ..." Before opening her door, I face him. "Thank you for coming with me. You could be with a million other normal women with normal names, but you're choosing me, even though marrying me is only going to change my last name. And for the rest of my life I may have to deal with freeloading spirits from past lives. Yet..." I grin "...you're still here."

"If you keep talking like that, you might convince me to turn and run. Stop while you're ahead, Swayz."

Lifting onto my toes, I press my lips to his. He kisses me back, just enough to impart his spearmint taste to the tip of my tongue. Griffin is yummy in every sense of the word.

"Hi, Dr. Albright." I slip off my jacket. "I'd like you to meet my fiancé, Griffin Calloway."

She meets us halfway and shakes his hand. "Very nice to meet you, Griffin. Please have a seat. Can I offer either one of you water or tea?"

"Tea would be lovely."

I raise an eyebrow at Griffin. He smirks.

I'm not sure I've ever heard him say the word *lovely*.

"Swayze?"

"Yes, I think I'll have some tea as well. Thank you."

"Did you both have a nice Thanksgiving?"

With a smile, I glance at Griffin. It was our first Thanksgiving together. And it was perfect. Scott and Sherri invited my mom as well as my grandparents to dinner.

No talk of Nate or past lives.

Lots of wedding talk. Good food. Laughter. And family.

Griff winks at me. He's thinking of the long weekend we spent in bed. Yeah, that was pretty spectacular too. A rewind button on life would be nice. I'd replay those four days over and over again.

"It was lovely." I borrow Griffin's word. "How about you? Did you have a nice Thanksgiving?"

"I did. It took a bit to find a few living friends, but I scrounged three and we had quite the time."

Griffin and I chuckle.

She serves us tea and takes a seat behind her desk. An easy smile settles on her face. "When Swayze emailed me, I was very happy to hear that you would be joining us, Griffin."

He answers with an easy nod just before taking a sip of his tea.

"So you're thinking about trying hypnosis?"

"Yes. I just wanted to bring Griffin in case he had any questions. I tried to explain it to him as best as I could, but I'm not the expert on it."

"Ah, then I assume Swayze discussed the possible benefits as well as the risks?"

"Can I be frank?" Griffin asks.

"Please," Dr. Albright continues to smile.

I draw in a slow breath and hold it. What does he need to

be frank about?

"I'm not one hundred percent buying into the reincarnation thing. The only reason I'm even considering it as a possibility is because I can't really give a better explanation. Do you honestly believe Swayze is this Morgan Daisy Gallagher reincarnated?"

"It's perfectly normal to question it, the same way people question God or all the beliefs about how we originated and where we go beyond this life. So all I can offer you is my *opinion*. And my opinion, both professional and personal, is that Swayze's soul and part of Daisy's soul share space in the beautiful body sitting next to you. I believe we are fabrics of many lifetimes."

Yeah, that doesn't sound crazy at all. I can't see past the stoic expression on his face to determine if he finds the "beautiful body" sitting next to him to be as much of a magical unicorn as what Dr. Albright tries to lead him to believe.

I rest my white hoof on his hand and wag my long tail, sending a rainbow of glitter in all directions.

"So let's pretend you're right."

My lips press into a firm line, and I talk my eyes out of rolling in disbelief.

This woman is highly educated, incredibly wise from years of living, and the picture of a sage. Yet, Griffin only wants to *pretend* she's right. This isn't going as smoothly as I'd hoped.

"Won't digging up old memories, like death, be pretty traumatic? She's twenty-two. Is it smart to risk that kind of psychological trauma?"

"It is a risk. That's why I want Swayze to really think this over before making a decision. She could remember things she saw, but she could also relive the feelings."

"But that's just it," I interrupt. "It's driving me crazy to have these images but no feelings or emotions attached to them."

Griffin turns to me. "So you want to remember what it felt like to die? Or worse ... to be murdered?"

"No. But I'd rather remember the feelings than let another woman actually die at his hands. And it's not just that. There were good times too. I hate seeing them in my head but not feeling them like Daisy did. This familiarity keeps clawing its way to the surface of my conscience like it *wants* to be felt. Like it *needs* to be felt."

He scoffs, shaking his head while looking away from me. "Good times? You mean *Nate*." He says his name with such contempt. "You want to remember how you felt about him?"

I glance up at Dr. Albright, but she doesn't look like she's ready to jump in the pool and save me from drowning.

"Not in the way you think, Griff."

Griffin gives Dr. Albright his attention. "Please tell me you don't condone this. We're engaged. I want to spend the rest of my life with her, but I don't want to compete with another man for her *feelings*."

She returns a concentrated nod. "Swayze, can you elaborate on the kind of feelings you want to remember. If they're not romantic feelings, then maybe you can set Griffin's mind at ease a little bit."

The muscle twitching in Griffin's jaw says I won't be easing his mind anytime soon, but I try anyway.

"We were young. And before there were any feelings of love, we were friends. Sometimes I think the reason this other life moved forward with some memories intact is because I'm here to do something for Nate." I'm not saying this right.

Griffin's expression goes from irritated to murderous.

I hold up a flat hand to keep him from losing it. "He feels responsible for Daisy's death. And her murderer is still killing. And a baby lost her mom. The timing is too coincidental. I think I have these memories to deal with Doug Mann, and take care of Morgan, and let Nate know that it wasn't his fault. His wife died. When I first saw him at Dr. Greyson's office, I could tell he was hanging by a thread."

With his thumb and middle finger, Griffin massages his temples.

"If I may make a suggestion..." Dr. Albright folds her arms on the edge of her desk "...think about you first, Swayze. What you want. What you need. What you're really willing to risk. Try to ignore any sense of debt to anyone else or the fear of guilt over Doug Mann. What is the one thing you really *need* from this?"

I don't have one need. I have a million undefinable needs. My need doesn't have a word. It's a feeling. A nagging, soul-deep feeling. And maybe I'm the only one who can understand it, but something tells me Dr. Albright does too, even if she won't say it aloud in front of Griffin.

So I go with the one thing that should make sense. "I need to feel safe."

He grunts a laugh while shaking his head more. "I told you, I'm not going to let anything happen to you."

"You can't make that promise!" I cringe.

Dr. Albright's sympathetic gaze lands on me.

I release a slow breath of regret. "You have a job. I have a job. We can't be attached at the hip for the rest of our lives."

"And no one can guarantee that hypnosis will give us the missing piece of evidence to convict a man of a possible murder that happened over twenty-two years ago. But in the meantime, you risk remembering something that could haunt you forever, or you risk …"

Releasing the end of his sentence in a quick sigh, he rubs his lips together.

"Finish," I say.

He stares off in the opposite direction.

"I need this, Griff."

"Fine." He stands and grabs his jacket from the back of the chair. "Whatever you need, Swayz."

"Griff?"

"Let him go, Swayze."

The click of the door behind him makes a tiny tear in my heart.

I hold my emotions intact, even with Dr. Albright's empathetic expression. "Please tell me you understand me."

"I do. But I also understand Griffin. He's scared of losing you to Nate."

"That's ridiculous."

"Is it? Some people would see this story as fate. Nate loses his first love, and when he loses his second love, he finds you—*again*."

"Fate?" I cough a laugh. "You think it's fate for us to be together again?"

"No. I'm not *some people*. But it's no more crazy than you believing you have memories from that life for reasons of fate. Maybe fate exists, maybe it doesn't. I love the idea of fate, but it's possible you're not recognizing your true fate yet."

"What's my true fate?"

She sips the last of her tea and sets her cup down before sharing a hint of a smile. "I have no idea. But if it's fate …

you'll find out."

"I'd better get going. I should go see if I need to call for an Uber." I stand. "If I don't try the hypnosis, I fear I may always regret it. And I don't want to marry Griffin with that kind of regret lingering."

"It's ultimately your choice, and yours alone. I'm here for you in whatever capacity you need me to be."

"Thank you."

Griffin's not outside her door, and there's no sign of him down the hallway toward the elevators. He left. The curse of Daisy has made me self-destructive.

I take the stairs to the first floor and turn left toward the entrance to the parking lot.

He's there.

I stop.

I stare.

I admire.

I dream.

And then I start to hurt.

Hands shoved in the front pockets of his jeans, and one leg bent with his foot on the wall, he pushes off and shoots me a sad smile.

I hurt more.

"You waited."

"Of course."

"But you're mad." I slow my pace the closer I get to him.

"Frustrated."

"That's code for mad."

He holds out his hand. I take it.

"It's not code for anything. Let's just go home."

I let him guide me to his truck. He even opens the door for

me. Before he steps back to shut it, I clench his jacket and pull him closer.

"Let's grab something for dinner."

He nods, eyes searching my face. Dear God, I love him something fierce.

"And then let's hide under the sheets and pause life for a few hours."

Griff kisses one side of my mouth, then the other side, ending squarely on my lips while nodding ever so slightly.

At some point we won't be able to press pause and hide from the world, but I'm going to do it for as long as I can—as long as he's willing to love me back.

CHAPTER NINETEEN

"YOU RECOGNIZE IT?" Nate asks as we pull in the driveway to the pale yellow two-story house.

There's an actual picket fence around the yard, caging ornamental grass and day lilies that need to be cut back before it snows.

"Swayze?"

I nod. I didn't know this was in my memory until now. The way I didn't know I knew Nate until I saw him. Twenty-two years isn't long enough to understand or even describe this feeling of knowing something—someone—so intimately, yet Swayze Samuels has never seen this house.

I swallow hard. "It's like ..." I shake my head. "It's like opening a new door to a new world. The second I saw you, I didn't just think *there's Nate Hunt.* A flood of memories infiltrated every inch of my brain.

"She has blond hair and blue eyes. He has slightly darker blond hair and brown eyes like Daisy. He painted the fence gray; she hated it and made him repaint it white. In the spring red tulips bloom beneath the maple tree in the backyard. There's also an old shed in the corner of the backyard. Handprints in the concrete slab just off the deck."

Unbelievable ... I shake my head and look over at Nate.

He smiles. "Your handprints."

This is the part that hurts the most. More than the missing feelings—I don't remember *me*.

"I want to *feel* this so badly. It's like I can't truly make sense of it if I can't feel it. I'm going to do the hypnosis. I have to."

Nate rests his hand on mine. He doesn't hold it or rub it. *This* is the only part I feel. How the hell do I not remember myself as Daisy, but I remember his touch?

"I don't need you to love me back … in this lifetime." He smiles.

My eyes fill with tears. How can one sentence be so beautiful and so forlorn at the same time?

I don't need you to love me back … in this lifetime.

Nate Hunt deserves to be loved back in every lifetime—especially this one.

"Maybe after today you'll see enough to be able to let go."

Narrowing my eyes, I slowly turn my hand so our palms are pressed together. Still, we're not interlacing our fingers or holding onto anything more than the familiarity of his skin touching mine.

"Let go of what?"

"Anything that doesn't serve the purpose of you finding happiness in *this* life."

My gaze leaves our two hands in search of more meaning in his eyes. "Are you letting me go again?"

He flinches. "Swayze …"

My hand slides out from under his. I pump it into a fist a few times to shake off the lingering feeling of the boy I knew before the man. "I'm getting married. I have a great job. I think happiness has found me."

If he's trying to hide his concern, he forgot to tell the line between his eyebrows.

I nod toward the house. "So you said they're excited to meet Morgan. How are you going to explain the nanny tagging along?"

"They know you're coming too. They know you're Morgan's nanny. I said you're a friend of the family and have been like a kid sister to me for years. You've heard all the stories about Daisy and you wanted to meet them."

My lips twist to the side. "I suppose it will work."

Nate opens his door. "It will work as long as you don't get too creepy about your knowledge of them or their house."

I climb out of the vehicle while he gets Morgan from the backseat. "I think calling me creepy is a bit excessive."

"It's really not." His lips wrinkle to hide his smirk as he shuts the door.

Cue the music as I enter the Twilight Zone. When she opens the door, a tidal wave of memories weakens my knees. It's like I'm seeing a ghost, but she isn't a ghost. This house isn't a ghost.

I'm the ghost.

"Nate!" Daisy's mom holds out her arms for a hug.

"Claudia. It's good to see you." He sets Morgan's car seat on the entry floor and hugs Daisy's mom.

My mom?

"Claudia, I'd like you to meet Swayze." Nate smiles at me like, *You're up. Don't be creepy.*

"Nice to meet you, Swayze. What a unique name. I like it a lot."

It's no shocker that Claudia, who gave her daughter the middle name Daisy, would like my name.

"Thank you. Nice to meet you too."

She quilts and makes scrapbooks. Cooking isn't her strong

suit, but she can follow directions with anything that's a simple add-water-and-mix. The house is neat but not obsessively clean. I don't have to run my finger along the banister or a coffee table to figure this out. I just *know* it.

"Oh, Nate ... she's adorable." Claudia presses her hand to her chest, peering down at Morgan in her seat. I think she might cry. "We felt terrible for missing the funeral, but we were in Europe and just couldn't make it back in time. We're incredibly sorry for your loss." She shakes her head. "I've wanted to come see you or call you a million times, but ..."

Nate gives her a comforting smile. "It's fine. I understand."

Of course she's emotional. Claudia lost her only two children.

"Come in, please." She shuts the door behind us and leads us to a formal living room. "Dennis should be back soon. He ran to pick up a few things from the store."

We take a seat on the sofa, and Claudia sits in the chair next to it. Nate pulls Morgan out of her car seat and hands her to Claudia.

She bounces her as Morgan springs her legs because she loves jumping. "Look at you, sweetie. So much energy. Such big smiles."

Nate shoots me a look. I feel his joy and his grief.

"What did you name this beautiful little girl?"

Oh ... fuck ...

Seriously? Daisy's parents don't know that Nate named his daughter Morgan?

"Her name is Morgan."

Claudia freezes, even with Morgan's hyper legs demanding more bouncing. Way to make Claudia cry, Nate. I bet Jenna would have sent out birth announcements so this kind of surprise would have happened via snail mail instead of special delivery.

She gasps and several seconds later she releases that breath in what sounds like a hollow *oh*.

I grab Morgan before she drops her. Claudia's fist covers her heart as tears stream down her face.

"Why don't we give you two a few minutes?" I hug Morgan to me. "We're just going to … snoop around." I say the last two words quietly. But I know all that Claudia hears is *Her name is Morgan*.

We go upstairs. There are three bedrooms and a hall bathroom. Yep. Just like I remember. "So …" I stand at the entrance to Daisy's bedroom. "This was my room, huh?"

Morgan doesn't answer me. She's too busy playing patty-cake with my cheeks. I recognize everything in this room. Holy heartbreaking hell! They haven't touched her room since she died.

I feel bad for every time I've told my mom she needs to move on from grieving my dad. He hasn't been dead all that long in comparison to the over two decades that Daisy has been dead.

Wouldn't it be something if they knew that part of their daughter resides in me? Maybe like that heartbreaking yet inspired emotion that surely accompanies knowing that a loved one's organs saved lives. That lingering physical connection.

But this is more. I carry something greater than flesh and blood. I have her memory. And on days like this, I wish I had her emotions too. I'm so numb to the familiarity around me. Sometimes empathy seeps in and disguises itself as something I think belonged to Daisy, but it's not.

"There you are."

I turn to Nate's voice and a puffy-eyed Claudia behind him. Her gaze darts to the room. I haven't left the threshold. It feels like I need permission for that.

A noise from downstairs distracts her. "That must be Dennis. Let me take Morgan." She trips on her name, blinking back more tears.

I hand her Morgan.

"Go on in." She smiles at Nate and nods toward Daisy's room. "I know it seems crazy, but I've left her room the same. All these years later, I just like to go in there and talk to her. She was and always will be my daughter. I don't want to forget her." Claudia shrugs like it's no big deal.

My twenty-two-year-old self with little true life experience would find Claudia a bit cuckoo. I think *obsessed* was the word I used with my mom. But after all summer and these first months of fall with Nate, I no longer feel qualified to judge anyone.

"We'll be downstairs. Take your time."

"Thanks," Nate says.

When Claudia is out of earshot, Nate pushes me into the room and shuts the door behind us. My eyes shoot open wide. *Holy crap! What is he doing?*

"Finally." He gives me a devilish look. I haven't seen this look from adult Nate. However, I recognize that mischief in his eyes from my memory of him beneath me, when he said *what are you going to do with me?*

Gulp!

"I was never allowed in your room."

"D-Daisy's room," I stutter as he gives me a predatory look.

He takes a step toward me. I take a step back.

"If I even looked in the direction of the stairs, your dad

would clear his throat and scowl at me."

"Her dad," I say just above a whisper because I can't breathe.

"Twenty-two years ago I would have thrown you on the bed and made out with you until you were ..." He grins while biting his lower lip and shaking his head.

I take another step back until my legs hit the bed, and I stumble, landing with my ass on the edge. My hands fist the quilt.

Until I was what? I don't want him to finish.

Shit! Yes I do.

He kneels on the floor in front of me, resting his hands on my legs. It's giving me third-degree burns.

"Do you remember this room or are we both seeing it together for the first time?"

His hands require constant supervision. I can't take my eyes off them. "Uh ..." I swallow hard. "I remember it."

"And?" He squeezes my legs a fraction.

I wish I were as numb to his touch as I am to the emotions of Daisy's life, but I'm not. It's not just that Nate is this incredibly sexy man touching me—I'm engaged to *the* sexiest man alive. It's that my body lights up to his touch like seeing an old friend for the first time in two decades. The familiarity is the drug. Like I was once a Nate Hunt addict, and after years of sobriety, I'm getting a hit again and it sends my senses spiraling into an oblivion of *need.*

"Do you remember you?"

"Not me. Daisy." I still don't let my gaze drift an inch from his hands. "And no. I have this picture in my head of her life, you, this house, her parents ... literally everything and everyone *but* her. It's as if she's been erased. And I hate not having feelings to put with the things I see."

My breath catches as his hand moves from my leg to my chin, tipping it so I look at him.

"Do you want to remember what it felt like to be Daisy?"

"Yes."

"Why?"

"To make sense of the things in my mind."

"What if it means you feel what she felt when she died?"

"I-I don't know."

"What if it makes it hard for you to ignore the two people downstairs? If your love for them comes back to life, what would that do to your relationship with your mom?"

Swallowing, I shake my head ever so slightly.

"Do you want to feel that love for them?"

It's love. Can love be a bad thing? Can we ever love too many people?

"Maybe," I say, feeling the heat from his body scorching mine.

"Do you want to feel *our* love again?" His hand slides along my neck until the pad of his thumb brushes the spot below my ear where he used to kiss me.

Yes. I want to feel it. I want to close my eyes and go back twenty-two years in my mind and let him kiss me there. I want that for him. I want that for me. Then I want to open my eyes and go on with my life like it never happened, bury the moment in the grave with my old body and never think of it again.

"I still feel you everywhere." His eyes close. The hand on my leg squeezes and his thumb on my neck presses a little harder.

Control. He's fighting for every single breath of it. If I let him kiss me, would it give him closure? The kiss goodbye that he never got. Or would it feed an insatiable hunger? Where would the kiss stop? Where would his hands stop?

More than any of that … how far would I let him go?

"Are you going to kiss me?" I whisper because I have to know before my heart explodes.

Nate opens his eyes, sharing a weightless gaze and soft smile. "No, I'm not going to kiss you." He's unhurried with his words as his hold on me relaxes. "You're not mine to kiss."

"But you think I'm yours to love."

"Part of you." His grin swells. "Yes." He stands. "I'm going to leave the physical part of loving you to your real boyfriend."

Real boyfriend …

I don't have to remember how Daisy felt emotionally to understand why she fell for Nate Hunt. Even now, at thirty-seven, that boyish grin and mischievous glimmer in his eyes disarm me with absolutely no effort.

He purses his lips, studying me for a few seconds. "Were you going to kiss me?"

"Don't be arrogant." My eyes narrow at him.

"You asked me first. Does that make you arrogant?"

"You were touching me."

"You were letting me touch you. So let me rephrase … were you going to *let* me kiss you?"

I stand, chin up while drawing in an angry breath. "I'm engaged to another man."

"It was a yes or no question."

"What do you think?" My chin inches up a little higher.

Some women go their entire life without seeing a man look at them with complete adoration. I already have two men who look at me like I'm something pretty damn special. Why? Well, who knows?

"No. You would never let me kiss you like you were mine. You would never agree to marry a man who you didn't love with every fiber of your being."

All fight drains from my body, shoulders relax, chin dips down, and my glare softens.

"And I know this because part of you once loved me like that."

I don't think. My arms fly around his neck, hugging him to me. After a few seconds, his reciprocate. "Thank you," I whisper in his ear.

CHAPTER TWENTY
Nathaniel

WHAT IF THE purpose of my life is to make sure my best friend finds happiness?

I hug her.

She would have kissed me back had I let myself kiss her, not because she doesn't love Griffin. Because ... we're testing time. Waiting for the right moment—the right life.

"Thank you," she whispers.

I hug her tighter. The curtain went down on Nate and Daisy. I mourned the end. Yet, here I am getting an encore. It won't last. Nothing lasts. But I'm not going to blink. I'm not going to breathe. With every ounce of strength I have inside of me, I'm going to stop time and live in this moment forever.

"Oh ... sorry." Dennis gives us an awkward smile as he opens the door. No throat clearing. No death glares.

Swayze steps back.

"It's emotional being in her room," I say as an excuse for what he just saw. "Dennis, this is Swayze."

"Hi." She smiles, cheeks apple red with embarrassment. A good blush always looked good on Daisy too.

"Nice to meet you." Dennis shakes her hand and gives me his attention. "I don't think Claudia is going to let Morgan go home with you."

I chuckle. "I'm glad we were able to stop by today."

We follow him downstairs.

"I'm keeping her." Claudia hugs Morgan to her, kissing her chubby cheeks.

Dennis shakes his head. "Clearly you know who to call if you need a babysitter."

"Yes." Claudia perks up. "Call me absolutely anytime you need someone to watch her."

"Thanks." I take Morgan and fasten her into the infant carrier.

"Did being in her room make you feel closer to her?"

I look up, giving Swayze a quick glance.

Her lips curl together.

"Yes. I felt really close to her."

"It's hard to believe it's been so long. I had all these things I wanted to say to her. All this advice I wanted to share with her. You'll understand as your little girl gets older. There's just never enough time."

I stand, zipping my jacket. "No. There's not."

Claudia rests her hand on my cheek, canting her head to the side. "Don't give up on love, Nate. Okay?"

I nod. "I've got more love than one man deserves right here." I glance down at Morgan. It will be hard, maybe even impossible, to love like she means after losing Daisy and Jenna.

"It was very nice to meet you, Swayze."

She smiles at Claudia and Dennis. "Can I ask what you say to her ... when you're upstairs talking to her? I lost my father. I'm just curious since it seems to help you."

Dennis gives his wife a gentle smile as he grabs her hand.

She draws in a slow breath. "Well, it's been a bit of everything. A few months after she died, I decided to just pick up from where she would have been at the time. We discussed school, driving, boys, college." She laughs. "I think I even discussed birth control with her. And Nate ..."

Claudia's focus shifts to me for a few seconds. "I told her all about you. How much you grieved her death. I told her about you not going to prom or homecoming dances and that I knew it was because you couldn't go with her."

Fuck. This kind of hurts. I didn't go. I didn't live in many ways for years ... until I met Jenna.

"I told her you decided to go to college instead of playing hockey. I had to break the news to her of your engagement." She winks. "She was jealous, but she understood."

Swayze laughs. I meet her gaze and smile.

"And more than anything, I've given her advice on navigating this world, in case she gets a second chance. Crazy right?"

"A second chance?" Swayze squints.

"Swayze, can you please grab the diaper bag?" I lift the carrier.

"What do you mean a—"

"Swayze, the diaper bag. We really should get going."

Claudia flicks her wrist. "I'm just being silly. I know there's probably no such thing as reincarnation, but it's comforting to think that her soul moved on. Our little girl had a beautiful soul."

"Funny you mention that—"

"Swayze!"

Everyone snaps their attention to me.

"Sorry. I didn't mean to raise my voice. I just remembered I have a podcast to record tonight and I'm suddenly feeling anxious that I'm not going to get it done if I don't get Morgan home and put her to bed soon."

"Of course." Claudia walks us to the door. "I can't thank you enough for bringing her by. I'm a little embarrassed we didn't make the first effort months ago."

"Nice to see you, Nate. And good to meet you, Swayze."

"Thanks, Dennis. It was nice to see you again too."

"Yes, tha—"

"Have a nice evening." I shove Swayze out the door in front of me.

"What is your deal?" She swerves to stay on the sidewalk as I nudge her forward with the infant carrier.

"I had one request—don't be creepy."

"I wasn't being creepy. Dude! She brought it up like she's open to the idea. What if she knew?"

"Shh!" I jerk my head toward her door. "Get in." I latch the infant carrier and hop into the driver's seat before Swayze decides to run back inside yelling, "It's me! Your baby girl."

"If I'm creepy, then you, Professor, are a paranoid whack job. And oh my god … good job waiting this long to mention you named your daughter Morgan. Whack. Job." She folds her arms over her chest and snaps her head into a resolute nod.

"Swayze, you can't play dead daughter reunion when you have nothing to offer them but visions. You can't love them like Daisy loved them. You have a new life, a new family. It's not okay to drop the I'm-Daisy-reincarnated bomb on them and then skip off like you didn't just blow their minds."

"I have a little more grace and tact than that, but thanks for the vote of confidence."

As we turn onto the main road a few minutes later, I shoot her a sidelong glance. "Okay. What were you going to say to them?"

Her eye twitches, jaw clenched.

"I was protecting them, not dismissing you."

She whips her head toward me. "You were totally dismissing me like a child. I know when I'm being reprimanded publicly. My parents used to do it when I'd get fed up with them treating me like a child."

I snicker. "So if they said something about you acting like a child, your answer was to act out even more like a child?"

Her nose wrinkles as she speaks with a mocking voice. "Swayze, do you need to go potty? Swayze, did you wash your hands with soap? Swayze, let me help you tie your shoe better. Swayze, you're scratching your head a lot, let me check you for lice."

"And did you have lice?"

"That's not the point. I'm just tired of people telling me what to do or what to think. That's why I want to do the hypnosis. I want my feelings and opinions about that life to be my own."

I scratch my head. "We've hugged a lot lately. That's all it takes for those pesky little parasites to jump onto someone else. Have you always been such a hugger?"

"Oh my gosh! Would you please focus? I didn't have lice." She looks out her window and mutters, "That often."

"Eww ..."

Swayze blows a stray hair away from her face. "Shut up. There were like ten identical red hats in the lost and found at school. I just picked the wrong one." On a sigh, she angles her body toward me. "But seriously, do you know how it could change their lives if they knew that Daisy did get a second chance?"

"Again, you're not listening to me. You have nothing emotionally to offer them. *If* you have some miraculous recovery of your emotions through hypnosis, and you have this dire need to run home to Claudia and Dennis Gallagher, then you have my blessing."

"Well, Dad. Good to know I have your blessing."

I remind myself that she's twenty-two, been scrutinized her whole life, and she's living with memories from a past life. She deserves a pass for the snarky, childish attitude.

"I'm sorry." She exhales pure frustration. "I'm having identity issues. Morality issues. Commitment issues. *Life* issues."

We pull in the driveway. "My head has been all over the place since we met. And I'm certain what I've felt is a tiny fraction of what you're dealing with. So no apologies. Okay?"

"Thank you for taking me to see them." She rests her hand on mine over the gearshift.

The warmth of her touch gives me something I've missed for so many months. I savor it, feeling it bone-deep. "You're welcome."

She opens the door and climbs out.

"Swayze?"

"Yeah?"

I want to deserve her. I lost her once. My wife died. Fate is this beautiful, shiny, tempting excuse to bend my own morality to fit what I want, even when she's not mine. "Don't lose yourself in search of her."

"In search of Daisy?"

I nod.

Biting her lips together, a deep line forms along her brow. "What if I *need* to find her?"

"What if you don't?"

CHAPTER TWENTY-ONE

"THERE'S MY FAVORITE grocery store guy."

Griffin glances over his shoulder, working on some metal part at his workbench. His eyes make their usual inspection.

"Still like what you see?" I grin.

"Always." He turns back to the part in his hands, inspecting it closely.

Say it. Please.

"How was your day, Swayz?"

Yes!

"I over sugared my coffee this morning. Left me a little shaky by lunch. Morgan's crawling a bit. In another week, I think she'll be everywhere."

"A fun age."

"Yes." I turn over my bucket and take a seat. This is nice. We're talking about my job like a job, not like Griffin's competition. I don't sense any agitation in his voice. Maybe I can navigate this just fine after all.

"I have three really good job options away from here," he says.

"Wait. What?"

Griffin turns, wiping his hands on a rag. "I talked to Jett about it the other day. He gave me three options, any one of them would be mine if I wanted it. We can see which location would be the better option for you finding a job. I talked to my parents about it too. They agree it's best."

"B—" My lungs burn, begging for a breath as my heart crumbles, bearing down on my stomach. "Best for who?"

"Us."

I shake my head. "What are you talking about? Why are you doing this?"

"I love you."

Adrenaline dumps into my legs, shooting me off the bucket. "This isn't love!"

"I want you safe."

"You want me away from Nate."

Griffin nods, eerily calm like he's holding a royal flush.

"Nate's not a danger to me. You can't take me away from them. You can't ask me to leave my mom. You can't ask me to leave Dr. Albright just when we're getting ready to have this breakthrough."

"I love you. I want to spend my life with you. Protecting you is my number one priority."

I start to respond, but the words vanish, leaving me choking on a breath of nothingness. It feels like my world is crashing down around me while Griffin shows no signs of stress, anger, or regret.

"Protect me from who? Nate?"

"Yourself."

I fight back the tears that sting my eyes. "This isn't love. This is your jealousy. This is you not trusting me. You not believing me. You think hauling me off to some place far from here is going to make the memories I have disappear. But they're not going anywhere, and unless I find a way to bring them to life, I'll never be able to let them go."

"We'll leave after the holidays, whether you find a job or not." He turns his back to me.

"Is this an ultimatum?"

"It's an intervention."

I cough sarcastically. "An intervention? I think that requires more than one person."

He shrugs. "Fine. I'll call my parents and your mom."

"My mom? Really? Because the last time I talked with her, she was on my side."

"Swayz, we're all on your side."

As he turns, leaning against the workbench with his hands on the edge, I bat away the tears that sneak their way out.

"Forcing me to do something I don't want to do is not being on my side. I am not a child. I am *so* sick and tired of everyone thinking they know what's best for me." The lump in my throat swells, making my words break apart. "I was Morgan Daisy Gallagher whether you choose to accept it or not."

Griffin rubs his hand over his head. "Swayz, I believe you. I accept it."

"Then why?"

"Because I don't want to risk someone fucking with your brain on the slim chance that you might remember something that will make a difference in the fate of Doug Mann. I don't want to risk watching you lose your mind to some awful death. And …" His Adam's apple bobs as his forehead wrinkles.

I hug myself as if I can physically hold everything together. "Finish it. You've come this far. Just … finish."

"I don't want you *feeling* things toward him. I'm begging you to leave all the emotions buried in the fucking ground with her body."

My jaw slides side to side. "And you've shared all of this—

Daisy, Nate, the reincarnation—with your family?"

"Yes."

I grunt, shaking my head. "And they believe it?"

"They don't know what to believe. But given the fact that you have a psychiatrist who believes you, it's hard to make a case for anything else. However, they agree that leaving Madison—leaving Wisconsin—is the only way we stand a chance."

"Oh my god ..." I run my hands through my hair, nudging the edge of hysteria and delirium. "It *is* an ultimatum. I agree to go and we stand a chance. But what if I refuse to go?" I hold my hands out to my sides, palms up. "Then what?"

For the first time tonight, I sense genuine pain coming from Griffin. "Swayze ..."

Great. I'm Swayze now. This isn't happening. Someone please wake me the fuck up from this nightmare.

"I'm leaving no matter what."

Pressing my mouth into a firm line, I nod slowly, focusing on the floor between us. "So this isn't really about what's best for me. You just want to move."

"Jesus ..." He sighs, finally showing an edge of agitation, pacing several steps in each direction, head bowed, hands shoved into the back pockets of his jeans. "It's *all* about you! Don't you get that?"

"Then why would you still move if I say no?"

He stops in front of me, grabbing my face with a firm grip. "Because I'm not going to watch you self-destruct. I'm not going to watch you fall in love with another man. I'm not going to watch you be a mom to a child that's not mine. You want the perfect proposal and the perfect wedding. But I just want *you*. Since the day we met, it's been that simple for me. And I'll take you with the souls of a million lives woven into yours. I'll listen when you need me to listen, I'll protect you when you're scared, I'll be whatever or whomever you need me to be ... but I won't be *him*."

"I don't want him," I whisper.

"No?" He cocks his head to the side.

"No."

"Then move with me."

"Please don't ask me to do that."

"Ask you to do what? Marry me? Have a family with me? Move away with me?" His words gain a sharper edge as his hold on my face tightens. "Be faithful to me?"

I swallow around the jagged boulder in my throat. Griffin's nostrils flare as he lets go of me with one hand and reaches around to his back pocket.

"Carry a picture of *me* in your pocket?" He holds up the photo of Nate.

I don't have to ask where he got it. I'm wearing leggings today. Griffin does our laundry, and I just got sloppy and forgot the photo was in the pocket of the jeans I left on the floor of our closet.

How could I be so careless to leave it there? How could I be so stupid to have it in the first place?

He wads up the photo and releases it to the ground while his other hand palms the back of my neck, pressing our foreheads together.

"Swayz ..." My name bleeds from his chest as heavy breaths fall between us.

I blink and the dam releases all the heartache that I can no longer ignore.

He draws in a shaky breath. "You're. Breaking. My. Fucking. Heart."

I try to speak, but painful sobs smother my words.

His lips press to my cheek. Even now, when he has every right to be angry, all I feel is his love—his pain. I've hurt my grocery store guy. And I don't know how to make it right.

"If you don't walk away from this…" he ghosts his mouth over my face, erasing my tears with his lips "…I won't be able to hold on."

My fingers curl into his shirt.

Don't let go.

"Griff …" I bury my face into his chest. "I love *you.*"

His hands fall limp to his sides, leaving a chilling ghost of his touch along my face. After I make a wrinkled wet mess of his shirt, he takes a step back, tearing us apart.

No… I'm the one who's tearing us apart because I'm so messed up in the head. It's a morbid thought, but at this moment I wonder if a brain tumor would be less painful for both of us.

"I know you love me." Griffin saying that to me, while his gaze remains affixed to the photo of Nate on the ground, is a self-inflicted dagger to my heart.

This is so much worse than Apple sitting on my bucket. This is Griffin taking a trip to California with her. No … this is worse. There's no way a night locked in our bedroom, under the sheets, will fix this.

When his red-rimmed eyes find me again, I don't look away no matter how much it hurts. And dear God does the anguish and disappointment ever hurt. So I confess, hoping there's something to "the truth will set you free." I don't think it will, but Griffin deserves honesty from me.

"This other life wants to consume me, and I don't know if I can stop it. I want to let it go, but it's stronger than any drug.

It's bigger than me. It's larger than life. So I can fight it for the rest of my life, or I can submit to it."

"*It* or *him?*"

Of course he thinks this is about Nate, there's a photo on the ground that flashes Nate's name in neon lights. But it's not about him.

"Her. It's about Morgan Daisy Gallagher. I can't let this go until I know who I'm letting go of."

Griffin turns, grinding the wadded photo under his boot. "Me," he murmurs, walking away. "You're letting go of me." He raises the garage door, slips on his jacket and helmet, and rides off without another glance in my direction.

CHAPTER TWENTY-TWO

Griffin

I FOUND THE photo when I ran home over the lunch hour. Maybe there's a reason I wasn't looking for love the day I met Swayze. Love like this is a fucking miserable emotion.

The photo of Professor Hunt isn't from their childhood. It's a photo of a shirtless, virile *Nate* in his twenties, close to my age, I'd guess.

Did he give it to her? Or did she take it?

I don't know. It doesn't matter. I'm losing her and there's nothing I can do about it.

Love like this is a fucking miserable emotion.

"Hey." My mom looks up from wiping the kitchen counter. She gives me a sad smile.

I shrug off my jacket and return the same solemn expression. "Hey."

"You're back. Does this mean it didn't go well?"

After I found the photo, I debated tracking down Professor Hunt and beating him until his last breath. Instead, I came here. My parents have a way of diffusing my anger.

"Something like that."

"Where's Swayze?" Mom asks just as my dad comes down the stairs.

He gives me the same look, easing into the kitchen chair next to me.

I glance back at my mom as she tosses the rag in the sink and leans her back against the counter. "I assume she's at home. After I confronted her, I just left. I didn't know what else to say."

"I called Krista after you left earlier. Come to find out, she and Swayze had a heart-to-heart about this. Krista knows about the photo too. I could tell her heart's really breaking for Swayze."

I blow a quick breath out my nose, shaking my head. "Jesus! My heart's breaking for her too. But I can't save her if she doesn't want to be saved. I can't make her want a future with me if she doesn't even know who she is. There's no way I can compete with this. She said it herself. This is bigger than all of us. But I wasn't part of that life. *He* was. I don't have answers for her. *He* does."

Resting my elbow on the table, I close my eyes and massage the tension from my brow.

Mom hugs me from behind. "She loves you. Krista said it. I'm saying it. We all see it."

I grunt a laugh. "I know she loves me. If I didn't believe it, I'd just leave. But I'm not. I'm making my case, but I *can't* leave things how they are and wait for them to get worse. If she does this hypnosis and things get worse, it's not going to be *my* shoulder that she wants to cry on. The emotions will be Daisy's. And we know I'm not the love of Daisy's life."

With a kiss to my ear, my mom releases me and sits opposite of my dad. "We love Swayze like a daughter. But you are our son. You come first. Don't give more than you have to give. If she's going to fall, and you can't save her, then get out of the way before she takes you down with her."

"I hate this," I whisper, keeping my eyes closed to keep the emotions in check.

IT'S COLD AS fuck as I ride around for another hour on my bike. I welcome the numbness—if it would only hurry up and wrap around that miserable blood-pumping organ in my chest. Swayze hasn't tried to call or text me. Maybe I should be thankful that she's giving me space, but part of me wonders if she's too far gone to save what we have left.

The back door and wood floor both creak to announce my arrival. Everything in this house creaks when the temperatures fall.

"Hey." Swayze whips her ponytail around and tugs out her earbuds, eyeing me over her shoulder from her hands and knees on the kitchen floor. "Slip your boots off on the rug. I'm just about done scrubbing the floor."

She doesn't scrub floors.

I bend over and untie the laces to my boots while she goes to town on the last corner of the floor by the lazy Susan.

"Why are you scrubbing the floor?" It's as though I'm watching a video of her in fast forward.

She stands, wipes the sweat from her brow, and sighs. "It gets dirty quickly this time of year."

"Yes. But why are *you* scrubbing the floor?" I slip off my boots.

Tossing her phone and headphones onto the counter, she washes the sponge. "I'm just trying to stay busy."

"It's nearly ten o'clock."

She grabs a wad of paper towels and dries her hands, lifting her shoulders. "My mind won't shut off yet, so I find listening to music I hate mixed with chores I hate to be both physically and mentally taxing. Do you need to use the bathroom? I'm cleaning it next. Maybe that will be the tipping point for my exhaustion."

"When did you start having trouble sleeping?"

"Since I decided to do whatever it takes to keep my fiancé from leaving me."

I rub the back of my neck. "Swayz, I don't want to leave you. I want to *take* you."

"This makes no sense!" She balls her fists. "We're planning a wedding and you want to up and move? How's that going to work? Are we sneaking back in town to tie the knot? Is our family going to come to us instead? Are-are-are—"

"Stop!"

She winces.

With my hands planted on my hips, I lean forward. "I found a picture of a half-naked guy in the pocket of your jeans."

She bites her lips together. Even from this distance, I know it's to keep her emotions in check. It doesn't hide the slight quiver of her chin. "That's just it. I forgot your birthday and you locked me out of your house. You found a photo of Nate in my pocket … but I'm still here. I don't understand."

"I overreacted with my birthday."

"Why?"

Rubbing my forehead, I chuckle. "Because I was excited about asking you to move in with me. Because you caught me completely off guard. Because I was having a moment." I hold my hands out. "I don't know, Swayz, because I'm fucking human. You put me on this pedestal, and I'm never going to live up to what's in your head. Sometimes I'm going to be short-tempered and unreasonable. But I'm not going to carry around some fucking picture of another girl!"

She flinches.

Again, I'm showing her my imperfections. I'm showing her my love disguised as jealousy and my pain disguised as anger.

She rubs her lips together, focusing on the floor between us. "I'm sorry."

I know she is. But it's not what I need to hear.

"Do you want to know the places Jett can find me a new job?"

Her head shakes, but she doesn't look at me. Grabbing the bucket of cleaning supplies, she keeps her gaze on her feet all the way to the bathroom.

The door clicks.

"Fuck you, Morgan Daisy Gallagher," I whisper.

CHAPTER TWENTY-THREE

"YOU'RE STILL HERE." I rub my eyes and yawn as I pour a cup of coffee that my non-coffee drinker fiancé made for me.

I don't deserve him. But I want him.

"It's snowing pretty good out today. I'll drive you to work and pick you up." He rinses out his smoothie glass in the sink.

I don't deserve him. But I want him.

"Thank you." I take a sip of coffee, eyeing him over the steam. I missed those arms around me last night. As much as we want to believe that beneath the sheets our physical connection can right all wrongs in the world, it can't.

My heart waited half the night in my throat, desperate for his touch. It didn't have to be sex. A kiss. A brush of his hand against mine. *Anything* to give me the tiniest bit of reassurance that we would be okay.

Nothing.

Griffin turns, catching me gazing at him longingly. I take one more sip of coffee and set it on the counter. "I'll grab my socks so we can go. I don't want you to be late to work."

His lips pull into a smile. A barely-detectable one. It's the kind of smile a stranger on the street might give me if we happened to make brief eye contact.

Is that what we are now? Strangers?

Does Griffin look at me and wonder who I am? The girl he

met in the grocery store would follow him absolutely anywhere. That girl would never carry a photo of some other guy in her pocket.

I don't deserve him. But I want him.

He glances at his watch.

I take the hint and hustle to grab my socks. Griff looks like all kinds of sexy waiting for me at the door with his jacket on and a black beanie on his head.

"Okay." I sling my bag over my shoulder.

He takes my hand and it nearly stops my heart. "I shoveled the drive, but it's still slick."

We step outside and I squeeze his hand, not because it's slick. I squeeze it because I don't want to let go. Because I'm dying inside. Because it's how my heart feels.

Suffocated.

Strangled.

Desperate.

There's nothing I can do to make this pain go away—to make *her* go away. So I watch the snow fall as cars creep along the white streets and listen to the radio, filling the awkward space between us. He pulls into Nate's driveway that's been cleared as well.

I unfasten my seatbelt. "Thanks for the ride."

He doesn't say anything. Instead, he gets out, comes around, and opens my door. And I fall in love with him even more than I thought was possible. Griffin doesn't send me a dozen roses on my birthday. He hands me a single petal every day. Sometimes it's a look. Sometimes it's a whisper. And sometimes it's opening my door, helping me out, and holding my hand all the way to the top of the steps.

"Five?" Griffin releases my hand and slips his hands in the

pockets of his coat.

"Five." I lift my shoulders to my ears to block the wind.

He nods, turns, and walks down the steps.

"Griff?"

He turns.

I drop my bag by the front door, make my way down the four steps, and throw my arms around his neck. "You're my favorite person in the whole world. My love ... my friend ... my grocery store guy." I bury my face into the warmth of his neck. "Know that. *Always* know that."

He doesn't hug me back. And that's okay. He's dropping me off on the doorstep of the man whose picture he found in my pocket. This is on me. All of it. He's mine to love or mine to lose.

Without meeting his gaze—because I know it would break me—I pull away and run up the stairs, grabbing my bag before disappearing behind the front door. Leaning my back against it, I try to calm my breath, holding back the tears.

"I'm glad to see you got a ride," Nate calls from the kitchen.

I slip off my coat and boots.

"Good morning. How were the roads?" he asks.

I smile at little Miss Morgan working the sloth crawl. "Typical early winter snow. Slick. And riddled with drivers sliding into each other. It's Wisconsin, not Texas. How do people forget their winter driving skills so easily?"

Nate hands me a cup of coffee. "Eight more inches expected later today. It's going to make for a fun commute home."

"Thanks." I take a sip. "Good thing I have a driver today."

"Good man."

I chuckle, shaking my head. "I don't think you'd say that if you knew what the last twelve hours have been like for me."

"Oh?"

"Yeah." Setting the mug on the counter, I turn my attention to Morgan. She grins when I get down on the floor with her, tempting her with a toy. When I start to speak, my voice cracks. It's raw. Very raw. Clearing my throat, I start again like I'm reporting the news instead of sharing my anguish. "Griffin wants me to quit and move away with him."

After a few seconds of silence, I look over my shoulder. Maybe Nate didn't hear me. His brows are drawn so tightly they look like one instead of two.

He heard me.

"Really?"

"Yes. Really."

Nate nods once. "So are you giving me your notice?"

I turn back to Morgan, pivoting her the other way so she doesn't get frustrated with her head hitting the sofa since her crawl doesn't involve a reverse mode yet. "I don't know. I don't want to move. But …"

"Is it his job?"

"He doesn't want me to pursue anymore with Dr. Albright. The hypnosis."

"So don't. But why does that mean you have to move?"

"Don't? I have this person inside of me, and I don't know her. She's the key to putting a murderer behind bars." I stand, picking up Morgan and bouncing her as she starts to fuss. "This isn't like returning something to the store. Moving isn't going to erase Daisy from my head."

"Is that truly what he thinks?"

Glancing out the window, I blow out a slow breath. "He

found the picture of you in the pocket of my jeans." When I return my gaze to Nate, his eyebrows shoot up his forehead.

"Swayze ..."

"I shouldn't have taken it. I shouldn't have carried it around in my pocket. A million different I shouldn't haves, but I can't change what's happened. It's just not fair of him to ask me to quit my job and leave my family because he doesn't ..." I bite back my words, with a wrinkle of pain on my face.

"He doesn't want you near me." Nate rubs his lips together, nodding slowly.

"I know. It's ridiculous. And—"

"It's not." Sadness crinkles the corners of his eyes as they narrow a bit.

"What do you mean?"

He scoffs. "Swayze, you had a picture of another man in your pocket. Not a ninety-nine cent baseball card of your favorite player. How did you expect him to react?"

"So you think this ultimatum he's giving me is justified?"

"Ultimatum?" He hands me Morgan's bottle as she starts to fuss some more.

I sit in the chair and give it to her. "Yes. He didn't suggest I quit and we move. He told me he's leaving with or without me the first of the year."

"Then go."

My jaw unhinges. "W-what are you talking about? What about Morgan? What about Doug Mann? Daisy? My mom? His family?"

"What about you?" He hikes his bag onto his shoulder. "Do you love him? Is he the one?"

Tears prick my eyes. I blink them away. "You're defending him."

Nate frowns, walking toward the chair. He kisses Morgan on the head. And then he kisses me on the head. I hate that I want him to do it. I hate that it feels so natural and expected. "Maybe I am." He stands straight.

"Why?"

With a soft chuckle, he scratches the stubble on his chin and jaw. "If I were Griffin's age … never mind his age. Hell, at my age, if I had a fiancée and I found a photo of another guy in her pocket, I'd hunt him down and knock his head straight off his body."

"You would not."

He quirks a brow. "Now that's the young naive Swayze talking. The one who doesn't really know me. Give it a second. Once you start thinking like Daisy, you'll know I'm one hundred percent truthful." He shrugs. "Proud? No. I'm old enough to know that violence doesn't solve anything, but I'm not too old to remember what it feels like to want the girl beyond all reason."

I search for the right response, but there isn't one, so I blink at him over and over.

"I have to get to work. Stay warm."

More blinks.

"Nate?" I say just as he opens the door. "So you want me to leave?"

"Hell no. I'm still the boy who wants the girl beyond all reason."

The door clicks shut.

Thirty minutes later, I get a text.

Professor: *Stop holding your breath. I want my 'friend.' That's all.*

CHAPTER TWENTY-FOUR

"LAST WEEK GRIFFIN gave me an ultimatum. Move away or lose him. We've been coexisting in near silence since then. I have less than a month decide to stay or go."

Dr. Albright offers a sympathetic smile, but I don't sense an ounce of surprise.

"I want him, but I don't want to leave. I mean ... he said he believes me. He believes that I was Daisy and he can accept that."

She listens, giving me a slow nod.

"But he's worried about Nate. Daisy's feelings for him. My feelings for his daughter. And ...."

Dr. Albright continues to offer a receptive smile. I love her patience with me. It's not tick-tock time's almost up. She looks at me like she gets me.

Of course she does.

"Go on. Take your time."

Yeah. This is the grueling part. I know how much it hurts me, and I can only imagine it's multiplied by a million for Griffin. "He found the picture of Nate. It was in the pocket of my jeans."

"That must have been hard. Painful."

I nod, blinking back the tears. "The need to know, to *feel* this other life has made me reckless. I'm making bad decisions, but they don't feel like mine. And just saying that aloud makes me feel certifiably insane. No one gets acquitted for murder because the voice in their head was from another life. At best they end up in a mental hospital until they slit their wrists with a sharpened chicken bone."

I laugh. It's not funny, but I need to save myself. "I bet they only serve boneless cuts of meat in psychiatric hospitals. Huh?"

Dr. Albright smiles. It's big. Not the contained humor of Dr. Greyson. "I don't have all the answers. And I won't pretend that I do. I wrote those books as a means of therapy. I wrote them, too, so maybe other lost souls wouldn't feel so alone. Sometimes the memories make you feel empowered. Sometimes they feel like your demise."

She sips her tea and holds up a finger. "Remember … this is a new journey for you. A journey full of choices. Acknowledging your past life is a choice. I know it doesn't feel like it right now, but it is. Not everyone gets the opportunity to make that choice. If you need to know, then you need to know. Don't feel guilty for that."

"But what about Doug Mann? What if the reason I remember this other life is because Daisy's soul wasn't finished? Is that possible?"

"Absolutely. There are many possibilities. But your job isn't to figure out what Daisy wants, it's to figure out what Swayze Samuels wants. And it's okay if it's the same thing, but it's also okay if it's not. You are Swayze. This is your life. You cannot go back and live her life."

"You're saying I should follow Griffin." She's probably right. After all, he's downstairs waiting for me, protecting me even when I'm where he doesn't want me to be. Either he's biding his time to say he did all he could or he loves me *that* much.

"I'm saying you should follow Swayze. She's got a lot of roads to take. And maybe some wrong turns along the way. That's all part of living life. Don't steal anything from the past or borrow anything from the future. Pay your dues today. That's living life."

Fuck.

Yeah, I'm twenty-two, but I feel twelve because I don't know what that means. But I have this feeling in my gut that it's the most important piece of advice anyone will ever give me. I should tattoo it on my forearm and stare at it every day until the meaning sinks into my soul.

"How was your day?" I break the silence on the way home.

"That's my line," Griffin says, eyes on the road.

"Well, you don't have the copyright on it, and you haven't said it in a while, so I'm trying it on for size."

"My day was good. I did some training this morning, and then I was interviewed for a magazine article." That's the most he's said to me in a week.

"That's cool. I can't wait to see the article. Is it just online or an actual paper publication?"

"Both."

"So a good day."

"Yeah, she took me to lunch for the interview. Nice place. Picked up the tab."

She.

No big deal. No need for my mind to wander into jealousy land. Nope. Not me. It's not like she sat on my bucket or shared a single bottle of beer or invited him to California.

Dammit.

I'm burning up with a fever of jealousy. He doesn't have a half-naked picture of her in his pocket. *He* would never do that.

"What are we doing?" I ask as he pulls into a strip mall parking lot.

"In case it's escaped your mind, Christmas is around the corner. I need to get some gifts. Do you need to get home right away?"

"No. Good call. We should shop." I'm still on my firsts with him. It's our first holiday season together. Griffin has a Christmas list. I like that. He could click a few buttons on the computer, but he's not. He's shopping. I like this a lot.

We hold hands. Another thing I like. A little something I took for granted.

"Coffee?" I glance up at him as he holds open the door to a coffee shop. "Now we're talking."

"Not for you. My mom likes a very particular coffee, but my dad gives her crap about spending money on it because it's not cheap."

"Sorry ... all I heard is 'not for you.' Now I feel like I *need* this coffee."

He gives me a frown before shooting the lady at the counter a killer smile while releasing my hand.

My emotions are on crack. I'm up and down, jealous and paranoid. Reading into every little look he gives me or *doesn't* give me.

The lady gets Griffin two bags of the coffee and one really obvious flirty bite of her lip while batting her eyelashes. That look used to not faze me. I was the girl he took home. The girl he undressed. The body he worshipped. Now I feel on the verge of being his biggest disappointment. His biggest mistake.

"Can I get you anything else?"

"No—"

"Actually…" I give her a smile just as sugary "…I'd like a small cup of that to go. Please."

Griffin frowns at me again. WTF. Why the frown?

I scowl back at him. He looks away.

"Ring mine up separately."

She puts a lid on the cup and sets it on the counter.

"It's all together," Griffin says with a bit of exasperation.

Flirty Face's eyes ping-pong between us as she totals it up.

Griffin pays cash and grabs the bag. "Thank you." He shoots her *another* awesome smile.

Dammit! I want that smile.

She bites that stupid lip of hers again and nods, releasing her lip and falling sober when she catches my raised eyebrow.

"Swayz," Griffin says, holding open the door.

I take a few more seconds to stare her down like she's the villain in my nightmare. But she's not. That girl resides in the mirror.

Pivoting, I give Griffin the same stare-down look.

"What is your deal?" he asks when the door shuts behind us.

"What is *your* deal?" I lengthen my strides to stay a few steps in front of him like I know where we're going next. But I don't. "No coffee for you, Swayze. No smiles for you, Swayze." My head bobs animatedly side to side.

I'm hitching a ride on the looney train. The clock is ticking, we're just not counting down aloud. The toxic mix of anger, fear, resentment, jealousy, and bone-deep love is stripping every last piece of my sanity.

Every day I think he's going to cave and say we don't have to leave. We'll work things out right here. Instead, every day he inches away from me a little more—not as many glances, hardly any words, rarely a touch.

Maybe he's protecting his heart.

I wish I could protect mine, but I can't. It's going to break no matter what. There's no way for this to end without me giving up a piece of myself, without me saying goodbye to part of my shattered heart.

"Are you done?"

I glance over my shoulder. Before I spew any more venom, I bite my tongue and nod. He's hurting. *I'm* hurting him. This is on me. I don't deserve good coffee or great smiles.

"In here." He jerks his head toward the bookstore.

I backtrack several steps and follow him inside. "Who's getting books for Christmas? Your dad?"

"Yep." He takes the lead this time like he knows exactly where he's going.

"I love that your dad reads so much. He's always got his nose in a book."

Griffin weaves through the maze of books as I sip my coffee.

"History?"

He nods, thumbing the pages of a book on World War II.

"I'm going to look through the kids' section."

For Morgan. But I don't say that to him. He nods without looking at me. I meander around the kids' book aisles, politely declining help every time an employee asks if I'm looking for anything specific.

"Don't spill your coffee. You're terribly accident prone."

Fear seizes my heart, making it impossible to breathe. I back away from the voice while turning, bumping into a display. Several books fall to the floor.

Doug Mann grins that fucking psycho grin as he shakes his head. "As I was saying …"

I make a quick scan for Griffin, but he's nowhere to be found. "Get away from me."

Doug holds up his hands. "I'm not doing anything. Just saying hi."

I hug my coffee cup to my chest, but I should throw it in his ugly, scarred face.

Oh. My. God.

I … *she* cut his face. My eyes close briefly. Behind them I see a jagged piece of rusted metal clutched in a young girl's shaky hand.

Her hand. My hand.

"You don't have the balls, little girl," he taunted her.

"I want to go home. Let me go and I won't hurt you," her voice trembles just like her hand.

Still, I don't see her. I only see him. I see what she saw. But I don't *feel* what she felt. The only thing I feel right now is my own fear.

"Griffin!" I slap my hand over my mouth as my own cry for help startles me. I don't remember thinking I should yell for him, it just happened.

The already quiet bookstore becomes eerily silent.

Doug takes one step back, two steps back. A few people gather around with concern etched into their faces. My wide eyes shift from Doug to the brooding man stalking up behind him.

"Hey!" Doug holds up his hands in surrender as Griffin

grabs the front of Doug's jacket and backs him out of the store.

"Are you okay?" one of the employees asks me.

I nod.

I shake my head.

I nod again.

Without answering her with actual words, I take cautious steps toward the store's entrance. Just as I grab for the door handle, it opens.

"Let's go." Griffin grabs my hand.

My coffee falls to the sidewalk, splattering everywhere. When I look down, I see a hunched-over Doug Mann struggling to his knees, buckled in half, grabbing his stomach. Griffin practically drags me to the truck, opens the door, lifts me inside like I can't do it on my own, and stalks around to get in the driver's side.

He starts the truck. "Are you okay?"

I fold my hands so tightly I can barely feel them.

Griffin pulls out of the parking lot. "Swayze, are you all right?" His voice raises a notch.

I nod. Why I nod when I don't mean yes is a mystery. But I seem to do it a lot. My gaze darts around the truck until his reddened knuckle on his right hand snags my full attention.

He beat a man up for me. A murderer. What if Doug comes after Griffin?

"Swayze?" Griffin's impatience snaps me out of my thoughts.

"Yes."

"Yes, you're fine?" He rests his hand on my leg.

I blink and tears surrender.

"Did he hurt you?"

No. Doug didn't hurt me. I hurt him. I cut him. *She* cut him and I didn't know it until tonight. These memories demand a voice. A second chance. "No," I whisper.

"You're crying. Don't lie to me. Did he hurt you? Threaten you?"

Another headshake.

Griffin sighs, but it's the heavy kind that's from frustration, not relief.

I can't help it. My tears are because he's touching me, and I fear my days of feeling him touch me are numbered. Daisy's life isn't fading, it's intensifying. She's ruining my life, and I don't know how to stop it.

When we pull in the driveway, I hop out before Griffin pulls to a complete stop.

"Swayz?"

I run into the house, making it to the toilet just in time to vomit. As I finish brushing the yuck from my mouth and rinsing with mouthwash, Griffin appears in the doorway.

"I'm sorry he got that close to you."

I shake my head, wiping my mouth with the towel. "You can't live by my side."

"It won't happen again."

It will. It will happen again and again until Doug seizes the opportunity to get me alone or until I find a way to prove that he's a murderer without having to die—again—in the process.

I step closer. He shifts to the side to let me past him. I don't want past him. I just want *him*.

"Touch me," I whisper, stepping closer until the hallway wall prevents him from retreating another step.

"I can't." Pain settles along his brow, seeping into the depths of his eyes.

"Why?" I rest my hands on his chest, making him flinch.

"Because I'm leaving soon, and I don't think you're coming with me. My parents are buying the house to rent out. They'll rent it to you if you want to stay in it."

Sometimes emotions hit with so much force it doesn't even take a blink for the tears to pour out in relentless streams. "Don't go." I choke on two little words.

"Come with me."

I curl my hands, grabbing his shirt. "Choose me ... please."

The pain on his face sinks deeper into his forehead. "You were never a choice. It's always been you. But I asked you to marry me, so now it's your turn ... choose *us.*"

I drop my head to his chest, next to my clenched fists. Emotion racks my body, but he still doesn't touch me. I see that jagged piece of metal. The shaky hand jerks out of control, slashing Doug's face, erasing his sadistically taunting grin, replacing it with blood and rage.

I died. *I* died.

The bloodied dagger drops to the floor. She runs.

I run.

Out the door. Down the rotted steps. Weaving through the brush and trees.

"He killed me!" I cry.

"Her. Not you." Griffin says with such control.

"H-he's going ... t-to do it a-again."

"You're safe."

Finally ... he wraps his arms around me.

Slowly.

Tentatively.

It doesn't matter. I'm in his embrace. And maybe it's torturing him to let this happen, but I don't care. I just need him. It's desperate. It's selfish.

It's an illusion.

Griffin has to know this too. He has to know deep down that he can't protect me from a killer.

CHAPTER TWENTY-FIVE

B ENEATH THE SHEETS, Griffin gives me his embrace. I want to pretend that we can get lost in the physical, numbing the emotional. It won't solve anything.

He knows it.

I know it.

But as I wake in the early hours of the morning, I *need* more. I need him to ease the pain and hide the memories under a veil of physical pleasure.

Anything.

Minutes. Seconds.

I'll take absolutely *anything* right now. Anything to make the visions in my head disappear long enough to catch my breath.

My hand covers his hand resting on my abdomen, just below the bunched-up hem of my tee. He doesn't flinch, just even breaths ghosting the back of my head. My hand guides his down beneath the front of my panties.

His body twitches, stilling again behind me. I hear him swallow hard as my lips part to let out tiny breaths, trying to keep up with the flutter of my pulse.

My middle finger presses down on his middle finger, like playing a piano key. The calloused pad of it brushes my clit. Closing my eyes, I inch apart my legs, welcoming his touch deeper between them.

He stiffens. I try not to let his apprehension seep into my conscience, my heart. With everything I have, every last thought, every last prayer, I silently beg him to roll me toward him. Cover my body with his. Bury himself inside of me. And just … *be.*

He doesn't.

But he moves his hand without me guiding him anymore. Fingers spread like he's claiming something that should already be his; he slides two fingers inside of me.

The slow build of my panting breaths is the only sound in the room. With the heel of his hand he rubs my clit.

It's slow, but hard and so desperately demanding. He's giving me pleasure. I'm giving him pain. I feel it with every stab of his fingers. The pleasure builds, blinding the visions in my head.

His erection presses against my back. I need him to make me whole. Tears burn my eyes. I try to turn, desperate for his mouth on mine, but he jerks my back firm to his chest as his hand rubs hard circles over my clit, fingers as deep as they can reach. I'm a prisoner to his touch, fighting to arch my back. My hands reach behind me to grab his head. He buries his face into my neck.

As I come, his teeth sink into my shoulder until I cry.

Until I fall apart.

Until I die in this moment.

"Fuck you, Daisy," he whispers with a hauntingly raw voice.

Still reeling from the blinding sensation, I can't register what he's doing until I'm alone in bed. The toilet flushes. The water turns on. The bathroom door opens.

I wait.

Nothing.

In a blink, the pain returns. The visions come back to life. And I'm alone.

Because he's right.

Fuck you, Daisy.

I WAKE JUST as lonely as I fell asleep. There's no hazelnut coffee aroma. No Griffin.

On the sofa there's a pillow atop a neatly folded blanket. I don't stare at it or the pictures of us on the fireplace mantel or his running shoes by the door.

In fact, I can't get out of the house fast enough.

"Hello?" I call, removing my coat and boots inside Nate's entry.

"Shh ..." Nate's hushing sounds from his office.

I peek inside the door. "Lazy morning for little Miss Morgan?"

"Yes." Nate keeps his focus on his computer screen, fingers pecking at the keyboard with the grace of a bull racing down the streets of Pamplona. "A nice gift this morning since I had a few things to finish up."

"I won't distract you, then. I'll just grab some coffee and keep an ear out for her."

He shakes his head. "You're fine." Slapping down the lid to his computer, he grins and unfolds his tall body from the desk chair. "I'm done." After slipping it into his messenger bag, he struts toward me. "Good morning. How are you?"

I can't deny him a small smile, even if it doesn't fit my mood today. "I'm good."

With his thumb and middle finger, he pinches my cheeks together like a duck's. "You need to work on selling it better. What's up?" He continues toward the kitchen.

Everything is up. Or upside down. Or just plain old fucked-up.

"I'm considering giving you my two weeks' notice."

He stops, back to me. I wrinkle my nose, waiting for a response.

And I wait some more …

"Okay." He resumes his steps without giving me a backwards glance. "But I'm going to need something more concrete than you're *considering* it. I can't *maybe* look for a new nanny."

"That's it? Okay? Not, why? Not, please reconsider? You paid me five thousand dollars to be here when school started. But now it's no big deal?"

"Don't do this." He turns. It's the same pathetic pained look Griffin gave me. I'm the injured animal on the side of the road while everyone passes by waiting for someone or something to come along and put me out of my misery.

Nate sighs, leaning back against the fridge. "I asked for a week. This is bigger. This is your future. I'm not going to ask you to stay. If you don't want to go, then—"

"What? I want to be with Griffin. I just can't get rid of the past. Every day I feel like I remember more. And Doug …" I grab the back of my neck with both hands and shake my head, the fear still raw and nauseating. "He cornered me in the book store last night."

"What?" Nate pushes off the fridge.

"I saw it. Her … me. She was holding a jagged piece of metal. The scar on his face … she cut him and then she ran. Every time I see him, more comes back to me."

"*What* did he say to you? Why were you alone last night?"

I continue to shake my head. "No … Griffin was there, just a few aisles over. And he didn't say much. It's the way he taunts me. He knows I know about Daisy and Erica. I'm next, Nate." My voice trembles along with every muscle in my body.

He wraps me in his arms. "I won't let that happen."

Something inside of me snaps. I push him away. "You can't say that. Griffin can't say that. Nobody can say that unless you're going to be by my side twenty-four hours a day. Griffin was literally ten yards away, yet Doug got to me. Was it a coincidence? Did he just happen to be there? Or was he following me? Is he trying to prove that he can get to me no matter who's supposedly watching over me? Is he toying with me?" I run my hands through my hair, tugging it with frustration.

"I'll see if there's something I can do."

I laugh. "Great idea. In the meantime, I'll just be … dead." My laugh grows into something borderline hysterical. "I'm going to die twice at the hands of the same man. But that's okay. Maybe I'll figure it out the next time around." My body buckles over in laughter. I'd give absolutely anything to be the average "normal" woman I was six months ago. My poor soul really sucks at this thing called life.

Nate grabs my shoulders and shoves me upright and straight into the wall. My laughter stops like a bullet to my temple.

"Stop." He grits his teeth. "You don't get to do this. *You* going to the lake by yourself when I told you to stay the fuck away, was not okay. You walking away from me because I had a moment with my stupid ego was not okay."

Angry tears fill his eyes. "You *dying* on me was not okay."

I can't breathe. Or blink. Or move any part of my body.

"You coming back to life when I need you more than any-thing, only to tell me you're in love with another man is *not* okay. You stealing my daughter's heart is not okay. Your fucking two weeks' notice is not okay. And you laughing about this man who killed you is NOT..." he rams his flat hand into the wall right next to my head "...OKAY!" Another *bang* on the wall.

Morgan cries.

He doesn't let any tears escape, but I feel every single one in my soul.

Morgan cries more.

The ridged muscles of his arms start to relax. He has me caged against the wall. He's let twenty-two years of emotions slash into my heart, but now he has to let me go soothe his crying daughter.

I start to peel my back off the wall, and he grabs my head and kisses me.

Oh. My. Fucking. Hell.

My brain and my heart explode at the same time. This isn't a chaste kiss on the head. This is the kiss that reiterates every single gut-wrenching word he just said to me. This is an explosion of two lifetimes. This is the ruination of my life as Swayze Samuels. This is the kiss that sends souls to Hell.

I don't know when my hands made it to his hair, but they're there. And it's familiar.

I don't know when my lips began to move, but they're moving against his. And it's familiar.

I don't know when my tongue decided to taste his, but they're dueling like they can't get enough. And it's familiar.

Every inch of his body pressed to mine, every touch, every

moan … it's all too fucking familiar.

And then … it's over.

He disappears down the hall to Morgan's room. With one hand, I trace my bruised lips and with the other hand I ghost my fingers along my neck, just below my ear. *That's* where I needed his lips. One kiss.

Gentle.

Reverent.

The way he first kissed me.

Nate wasn't supposed to obliterate my world. He wasn't supposed to break the fragile thread holding me to Griffin.

But he did.

I lock my knees to keep from falling over as he carries Morgan to me, wiping the tears from her eyes. She grins the moment she sees me.

This little girl loves me, even if she can't define love yet. I love her too. And if I'm honest with myself, I love her daddy too. Much like her, I don't know how to define my love for Nate.

When our eyes meet, I fight to hold back the toxic emotions. Regret falls off every inch of his body in relentless waves. He doesn't have to say anything.

"I …" He shakes his head with this look like he just ran over the family dog. "I'm …"

"It's …" My head shakes, mirroring his. It's what? Fine? No. It's the opposite of fine. It's the definition of insanity. It's the worst thing I have ever done. Yes. He kissed me. But I kissed him back. And I didn't stop him. I'm not sure how long I would have let him kiss me had he not stopped when he did. My mom's words echo in my conscience. *Where does it stop?*

"You kissed—"

"Daisy."

"Yeah," I whisper.

He kissed her because he remembers everything. But that doesn't explain why I kissed him. A million excuses plead their case in my head. Valid, reasonable, believable excuses.

"I should not have kissed you," he says.

"Can you see if your parents can watch her today? I need to …" I swallow the pain, the thick, suffocating guilt. "I need to do something."

He nods. "I'll see if they can be here within the hour."

"K." I take her from him. "Let's get you changed and fed." Brushing past him, I take her back to the nursery.

A few seconds later, the back door shuts, and I break down, hugging Morgan to my body because … I lost my grocery store guy.

CHAPTER TWENTY-SIX

"TO WHAT DO we owe this honor?" Jett winks at me as I stomp the snow off my boots inside the front door of the dealership.

"I was hoping to catch Griffin on a break."

"Griff never breaks, but I can probably see if he'll make an exception for you."

I force a smile. It hurts like hell. "Thank you."

He nods his head toward the service department. "Follow me."

Griffin's at a computer. He looks up.

"Your woman wants you to take a break. The bathroom door has a lock." Jett smirks.

Griffin doesn't acknowledge him. Neither do I. It's like he can see through me, like he knows what I'm going to say. I'm the girl who forgot his birthday. I'm the girl who kissed another guy. And Griffin is just the boy who fell for the wrong girl.

My chest hurts so badly it's crushing me. I have to tell him what happened. And even though I know without a single doubt that it meant nothing to me, it's going to mean everything to Griffin. And that's fair, because the world's kindest grocery store guy deserves a girl who would never let another man kiss her.

I look around, but there's no one else in sight. Griffin shifts his weight on the stool, propping one boot up on the metal rung, hands crossed over his chest.

"You've never looked more miserable," he says.

I laugh a little, fighting back the tears.

"If you're not coming with me, then you don't have to say anything."

I bite my quivering lips together and blink. As soon as he sees my tears, he looks away. I close my eyes.

"Tell me about your day, Swayz." Griffin shot me this killer grin on our third date.

We were eating dinner at his house for the first time. He baked salmon and steamed asparagus. I brought a bottle of wine and cookies that I tried to pass off as homemade, but I was pretty sure he knew they were store-bought.

It was the first time he called me Swayz. No one had ever given me a nickname before. In that moment, for the first time in my life, I didn't hate my name.

"It was good." I shrugged, still struggling to keep eye contact with him for more than five seconds without blushing like a schoolgirl.

"Good is a terrible description. I need details." He took another bite of salmon and pinned me with the sexiest look.

"Details, huh? Well, nothing too exciting. I got fitted for my cap and gown—"

"No." He shook his head. "Start from the beginning. Breakfast. What did you have for breakfast?"

"Really? You want all the details? I'm not that exciting."

"I'll be the judge of that."

My face hurt from smiling so much. "Toast and butter. Coffee with sugar. I like a lot of sugar in my coffee. So much so I'm not sure if my jolt is from the caffeine or the sugar. Barre class. Show-

er—"

"*Tell me more about this shower.*"

I giggled with a full-on blush. "*It was wet.*" My hands covered my face. "*Gah! I can't do this.*"

"*Swayze Samuels naked and wet. I can work with that. Do you wash your hair or soap your body first?*"

Shaking my head, I continued to laugh. "*I can't do this. It's like phone sex without the phone.*"

"*Fine. We'll save phone sex without the phone for after-dinner conversation. So how much sugar are we talking about? Like would you say you have coffee with sugar, or sugar with coffee?*"

"*Probably the latter.*"

"*Barre class. Are you a dancer? Please say yes.*"

I giggled more. I never knew giggling was my thing until I met Grocery Store Guy.

"*No. My coordination is quite challenged, but I like the burn and it's supposed to lift my butt. I think the jury is still out on that.*"

His chin jerks up. "*Stand up. Let me see. I'll happily be the judge of that.*"

"*You're a total flirt.*"

"*Just with you.*"

"*Ha! I doubt that.*"

Griffin gave me this look, the kind of look that came with an exaggerated pause like he needed to process something. Something new. Something unexpected.

I liked that look because unlike the casual flirting, it felt like something he hadn't given to anyone else.

We sat at his two-person kitchen table for almost two hours, flirting, laughing, and sharing special looks.

"*Can I talk you into sitting on my sofa?*" He stood, holding out his hand.

I rubbed the rim of the wine glass over my bottom lip. "Is there something special about your sofa?"

"It's more comfortable than these old wooden chairs."

"Are you inviting me to get comfortable?" I grinned, trying to be flirty, but ... man oh man I was so nervous. Third date and no kiss. In all fairness, it was our first evening date. The other two had been quick meals over his lunch break.

Three dates in three weeks, but we texted every day. Lots of texts about the most random stuff.

Griffin: Strawberries are on sale. Do you like strawberries?

Me: I cut my sandwiches diagonally. Do you cut your sandwiches in half?

Griffin: Going to the speedway with some friends. Do you bat your eyelashes to get out of speeding tickets?

Me: Never do a vinegar rinse after shaving your legs.

Griffin: Getting another tattoo.

Me: Sparrow. The name of the new girl in my barre class. Parents are stupid.

"Yes. I'm inviting you to get more comfortable."

I placed my hand in his hand. It fit. It felt right. No, it felt perfect.

"So how many tattoos do you have?"

"Quite a few."

We sat on the sofa. A small grin tugged at his lips when I left a full cushion between us. My nerves were firing on all cylinders. There was a hundred percent chance of me whimpering if our bodies got too close.

"You don't keep count?"

"Nope."

"Do you have a favorite one?"

"The dragon."

My gaze inspected the tattoos on his arms.

"I'm wearing too many clothes for you to see it."

Heat crawled up my neck and in lower places as well.

"Do you have any ink?"

I shook my head. "Just a birthmark."

His gaze made a quick inspection of me.

I grinned. "I'm wearing too many clothes for you to see it."

"Cute." He leaned back in the opposite corner, crossing his inked arms over his chest. "I know what you're doing. And it's not going to work. I'm not that easy."

"What am I doing?" I chuckled.

"You're pretending you have a birthmark so I'll agree to show you my dragon if you show me your birthmark. And only after I'm standing in front of you, completely naked, will you reveal that it's not really a birthmark, just an odd-shaped mole. No ..." He shook his head. "I'm not falling for that. If you want me naked, you're going to have to show me the birthmark first."

Amusement.

Shock.

Embarrassment.

And need.

They all hit me at once. Griffin wasn't just a flirt. He was good ... really really good.

I swallowed hard. All that my brain made sense of in that moment was a simple exchange. Me lifting my shirt a few inches in exchange for him getting naked. I needed to see the dragon. After all, it was his favorite tattoo, and who doesn't like dragons?

"It's not an odd-shaped mole." I leaned back in my corner of the sofa and slid up my T-shirt.

Griffin's tongue made a lazy swipe along his bottom lip. I rubbed my lips together, hoping, praying that said lips would get to press to his mouth soon. We were on date three, but all the random texts made me feel like I knew him more like an eighth date. My body just wanted to catch up to my mind.

"That's quite the birthmark. I can't see the whole thing." His gaze flit to mine, eyes gleaming with this sexy challenge.

My shirt was tucked up just to the bottom edge of my bra, but the birthmark extended a half inch to the underside of my left breast.

"I'd have to remove my bra." I faked confidence. Like no big deal.

He glanced at the nonexistent watch on his wrist. "I don't have any plans for a while. I've got time. Do you?"

"We haven't kissed, but you want me to take off my bra for you?"

He smirked. "Swayz, you make it sound like a strip tease. I just want to see all of your birthmark before I show you my dragon."

I scraped my teeth along my lower lip, eyeing his tight sexy graphic tee and muscular legs clad in worn denim. Sinewy, inked arms. Shaven head. At least two days' worth of stubble along his jaw.

Sitting up, I inched my shirt off, the rush of adrenaline obvious in the exaggerated rise and fall of my chest.

Griffin's Adam's apple bobbed just before his lips parted.

"Here." I slid the bottom of my bra up just enough to show him where my birthmark ended.

"That's a sexy birthmark."

I slid my bra back down. "It's no dragon."

His grin grew so big I felt it along every inch of my skin, but nowhere did I feel it stronger than the heavy pulse between my legs.

In one full motion, he stood and shrugged off his shirt. I swallowed back my whimper and squeezed my legs together.

He turned, showing me his back and the dragon that started

midway and off to one side. I tried to speak, but he unfastened his jeans, leaving me fumbling for a single coherent thought.

Gulp.

Granted his back was to me, but … but … butt!

Sigh. Drool. Whimper.

He let his jeans slide to his knees and shoved his briefs down on the side where the dragon's tail snaked over his holy-fucking-perfect ass and halfway down his leg.

I told myself to close my mouth and stop panting, but my body didn't respond.

Griffin glanced back over his shoulder. My gaze shot to his, and I snapped my mouth shut, but I'm pretty sure he saw the trail of saliva running down my chin.

"Female dragon. I'm thinking of naming her Swayze."

I barked out a laugh. He grinned while sliding his briefs back over his ass and pulling up his jeans. He faced me again, but his jeans weren't fastened. I told myself not to stare at his erection straining his briefs, but it wasn't my fault God gave me twenty-twenty vision and a naturally curious mind.

Seconds or maybe a decade later, Griffin's voice broke my trance. And his words started what became Griffin and Swayze— sex on demand. Every. Single. Day. "Tell me to fasten my jeans and put on my shirt."

Like a shameless hussy, I let my hungry gaze take its leisurely time meeting his eyes. "Why the hell would I do that?"

He kneeled in front of me and peeled off my jeans. My legs shivered. Teeth chattered. I had never been so scared to want something so much.

"Are you going to kiss me anytime soon?"

I didn't usually—okay, ever—get naked with a man before the first kiss.

Griffin gripped my hips, jerking me to the edge of the sofa. I *sucked in a sharp breath, grabbing his biceps to steady myself. His erection pressed between my legs, shielded by two thin layers of cotton.*

Our lips lingered a breath from touching. His hands slid up my back, deft fingers unhooking my bra.

I leaned in to kiss him before my heart exploded. He pulled back just enough to deny me. I tried again. And again he denied me, wearing the devil's grin.

"Griff ..." I whispered. "Kiss me."

Keeping his sable eyes locked to my gaze, he eased my bra off my arms. My eyes fought to stay open when his hand cupped my breast.

He just looked at me with what could only be described as wonder. After years of scrutiny, someone was looking at me like they didn't need to figure me out.

"Please ..."

He nodded slowly, his gaze sweeping over every inch of my face. "I think I will." Pearly whites flashed a second before he kissed me.

For a girl who didn't believe in fate or anything written in the stars, I knew with one kiss that I would never want to kiss another man again.

But I did. I kissed Nate. And it didn't feel entirely wrong, but it should have. So I have to let my grocery store guy go be someone else's perfect man. No one will ever love him more than I love him, but maybe they'll love him better.

I don't try to stop the tears or even wipe them from my face. Everything is too numb. Everything except my heart. It feels like it's gone ten rounds in the ring. Would someone please just knock me out already?

Griffin finally looks at me. He grimaces, pumping his fisted hands several times. "Who are you?"

I swallow, trying to keep the pain from suffocating me. "I don't know."

Sliding off the stool, he pulls in a slow breath that expands his chest, pushing back his shoulders. He's always had this confidence I can't imagine finding in a million lifetimes.

He steps toward me. I step toward him. His knuckles brush my tear-stained cheek. "Remember when you were mine?"

I choke on more sobs, making it impossible for him to catch all of my tears. Nothing good can come from telling Griffin that Nate kissed me. It feels cruel if I'm not leaving with him—if we're over. But that's not us. I tell him about my day, and he tells me about his. We share the highs and lows.

I should have shown him that picture. I should have told him how confused and curious it made me feel.

Griffin *was* my person. And if we carry pieces of other people with us, woven into our souls, then I will take part of him with me to my next life. And if I touched him the same way, I don't want us to end on a lie, hidden beneath a secret.

"Nate kissed me, Daisy. His friend."

His jaw steels, face distorts into anger. But nothing but pain shows in his eyes. "Did you kiss him back?"

"Yes." My mind screams at me. *Tell him it wasn't you who kissed Nate back, tell him it was Daisy.*

I don't say any more. There's no way to make this okay for him. No excuse. No begging for forgiveness or mercy. I want to always remember Griffin as the most honest, purest part of myself.

"I'm sorry."

"For what?" he says with a tight voice.

For my insecurities. For being a bad housekeeper. For

shrinking your wool shirt. For putting ginger in the Alfredo sauce. For forgetting your birthday. For vomiting on you. For taking the wrong job. For kissing Nate.

"I'm sorry you got in the wrong line at the grocery store."

"Jesus ..." he whispers as pain fills his eyes.

I slip off my engagement ring. "You are unequivocally the greatest moment of my life." Sliding the ring into his hand and closing his fingers around it, I lift onto my toes and press my lips to the angle of his jaw. "I love you, Grocery Store Guy." Releasing his hand, I step back and smile through my tears. "Always."

Leaving my heart at his feet, I turn and leave.

Okay, Daisy, finish this.

CHAPTER TWENTY-SEVEN
Griffin

I LOST HER.

It's a special kind of Hell. But I can't compete with something that took place before I took my first breath.

I'm not sure what will ease the pain. Something tells me this isn't the answer, but for lack of a better idea, this is all I've got.

"Griffin ..." Professor Took Something That Was Mine doesn't even pretend to be surprised to see me waiting at the door to his office. "I have a class in fifteen minutes."

I glance around at the hallway congested with students. "This won't take long."

He nods at me. It's slow, like he knows exactly why I'm here. "I'm sure it won't," he mutters, opening his office door. He takes three steps inside. I shut the door behind us. The second he turns, I land one fist into his gut. As soon as he buckles over, I land another fist into his face. Stumbling back a few steps, he presses his fingers to his bloodied lip.

Not an ounce of shock on his face.

Not a bit of rage in his posture.

Not a single balled fist.

Not the breath of a word.

"You want her to be someone she's not." I shake out my fist and ball it again because I'm not sure if I'm done bloodying his face. "So you can kiss her. You can fuck her. You can pretend she's your baby's mama. But it won't bring her back. She's dead. You're chasing a ghost. One day *Swayze* is going to wake up and realize she settled for a borrowed life. And that's the best case scenario." I shake my head, clenching my jaw. "If you let that shrink try to bring back memories … it will destroy her. And that's on you."

Thunk!

I land a final hook into his jaw. He bounces back like he's taken more than a few jabs to the face. "Fuck you for taking my whole goddamn world."

I turn and grab the door handle.

"She doesn't love me," he says.

Gripping the handle tighter while pinching my eyes shut, I let his words die behind me. "I know."

Swayze

"HEY, SWEETIE. WHAT a surprise—"

The second my mom opens the door, I fall into her arms. I let every single emotion go. "I-I lost h-him."

"Oh, Swayze …" She hugs me, stroking the back of my hair.

"Why …"

She pulls back, cupping my face that's contorted into an ugly cry. All of my heartbreak reflects on her face. "Why what?"

"Why can't I be normal?" I choke on another sob. "M-my whole l-life … I just wanted … to be normal."

Kissing my forehead, she hugs me again. I used to think she

could make everything better with a magical hug.

I used to think the same thing about Griffin's embrace. But the demons inside of me are untouchable. They demand my attention. I'm a slave to their intentions.

"Sit. Let's figure this out."

If only …

I sit in the leather recliner, and she kneels in front of me, handing me several tissues before resting her hand on mine. When she squeezes it, it wrings out more tears.

"Sherri told me about Griffin finding the picture."

I nod. God, I love her for not giving me the I-told-you-so look.

"He's moving." I sniffle, blotting my eyes.

"Sherri said he wants you to go with him."

Another nod. "But I can't."

"Swayze … you can. I don't want you to move, but after talking with Sherri, I think Griffin's right. If it's going to work, you need a fresh start. You need to choose a life."

"I can't. Doug Mann murdered me. And he's going to do it again if I don't do something."

She cringes. I know talking about myself as Daisy in first person must sound crazy. But I can no longer separate the two.

"I have to let Dr. Albright try hypnosis on me. If I can remember all the details, then they can arrest him." I shake my head. "I can't live my life looking over my shoulder. I can't run."

She lets out a slow breath. "We're not talking about catching a thief, Swayze. If the pieces of what you remember are true, he's a serial killer." Squeezing my hand again, she leans into me. "If he murdered Daisy and her soul resides in you, then you're asking Dr. Albright to bring back memories of someone *murdering* you. My dear child, do you get that? People commit suicide because they have memories of abuse, rape, war, and torture stuck in their heads."

"Then she hypnotizes me and takes away the memories after Doug is in prison."

Mom frowns. "Griffin said Dr. Albright can't guarantee that will work."

"It worked for her."

She sighs. "Please. I'm begging you. Let Griffin take you away from all of this. Let him keep you safe."

I pull my hand from hers and lean back in the chair, hugging my arms to my body. "This isn't a switch that can be flipped. This isn't a bad experience in school. This isn't a missed opportunity. This isn't anything you, or Sherri, or Griffin, or anyone can even begin to understand!"

Her forehead wrinkles. "Swayze, calm down. I wasn't—"

"I can't calm down! Don't you see? I am a grade-A fucking mess."

"Swayze ..."

"I can't run. I can't just decide to let go of something that is gnawing at my very existence. I can't shut it off. And I can't go with Griffin."

"Please ... you're going to lose every—"

"I'VE ALREADY LOST HIM!" I drop my head in my hands, shaking with grief.

Mom rests her hands on my legs.

"Nate ... kissed me." My voice shatters into small sobs.

"Oh, honey ..."

"And ..." The shame. It's a heavy weight bearing down on my chest. A knife digging into my gut. A cancer in my brain. "I kissed him back." I lift my head. "It felt like I'd done it a million times. It was wrong, but in the moment it didn't *feel* wrong."

Tears fill my mom's eyes. "It's going to crush Griffin."

I blink big crocodile tears.

"Swayze ..." She shakes her head slowly as her gaze inches to my chest. I let her pull my arm away from my body. Her fingers ghost over my naked left ring finger. "What did you do?" she whispers.

I swallow back a thick lump in my throat, blinking my swollen eyes. "I need answers. And it doesn't feel like a choice. It's like I'm telling my lungs to stop breathing. No matter how hard I try, I can't stop whatever this is. And ..." I draw in a shaky breath. "I had to tell him *because* I love him."

"He's going to leave. With or without you. That's what Sherri said. You're going to lose him for—"

"Ever," I whisper.

Her head eases to the side. The pity on her face compounds my self-loathing. "It's not a break. He's not taking a vacation. This is forever. Tell me you *really* comprehend this. Tell me you know that some girl is going to pick up all the pieces to his heart and mend them."

"I know." I don't feel anything right now. Everything is numb.

If I could change the cards in my hand, I would. But I can't. So I'm going to play them and pray that I live to tell about it.

CHAPTER TWENTY-EIGHT

G RIFFIN'S WORKING IN the garage when I get home.
Home.

I'm not sure where my home is anymore. It used to be simple—Griffin was my home. When my soul can't decide on a life, how am I supposed to find a home, a husband, or any sort of normal existence?

This doesn't even feel like a breakup. It feels like a tragedy. A brain tumor. Terminal cancer. A soldier going into battle. Cupid with a busted arrow and a tear in his eye.

At twenty-two my dreams have been stripped of hope. Unicorns, Santa Claus, the Easter Bunny, and happily ever afters don't exist.

I stop halfway to the back door and turn. Eyeing the door to the garage, my feet take me there. He's leaving. I know.

We're dying. I know.

But he's not gone yet. And my heart still gallops in his proximity, so ... we're not dead.

He could hate me. But what if he doesn't?

Doug Mann could run my vehicle off the road tomorrow and Griffin leaving me wouldn't matter. My mom never planned on living alone in her forties.

I ease open the door.

Fuck. My heart ...

Griffin doesn't acknowledge me. He's boxing up his tools.

He's leaving me. Oh … my … heart …

I close the door behind me. It's warm in here. The heater in the corner kicks on.

I drop my bag by the door and look around the garage. My bucket isn't in its usual spot. Did he hide it? Throw it away? Pack it?

The workbench is clear, so I hop up on it, fold my hands in my lap, and watch Griffin. I wonder if twenty years from now I'll remember how much I loved just watching him. I hope so. I hope, if he finds love again, she knows how amazing it is just to *be* with him.

I hope she has exciting days to share with him. And I hope she knows how incredibly rare it is to find a man who genuinely gives a shit about her day.

Maybe I shouldn't be out here. Maybe it's a slap in his face. Maybe it's salt on the wound. My brain—my conscience—knows this. But my heart doesn't understand.

I wonder if my heart will ever understand.

Does he wonder why I won't leave, like I wonder why he won't stay? Or do we both know the answers. But … yeah … the heart doesn't think. That's not its job.

My head knows I should be inside packing up my stuff, at least an overnight bag to take to my mom's house. But my heart keeps my ass planted to this workbench, my eyes tracking his every move.

Seconds give way to minutes. I spend them thinking of every memory we've marked in time. Memories eat up almost two hours—two hours that I don't feel Daisy.

Two hours of the girl who met the guy in the grocery store. I like her. I like them.

I glance up from somewhere in the past when the lights go

off. Griffin stands at the door, holding it open. My lips turn upward. A tiny smile he can't see.

Our gazes meet for the first time tonight when I brush past him, stepping out into the chilly night. After several steps, I turn, remembering my bag on the floor.

But it's not in the garage. Griffin has it clutched in his hand.

Our gazes meet again. It's not like earlier today. It's … peaceful. Maybe it's acceptance. So I turn and let him carry my purse. I let him follow me into the house.

Yeah, I'll flashback to Griffin Calloway for the rest of my life.

He sets my bag on the kitchen table and washes his hands. I make my way to the bedroom, grab a bag from the closet, set it on the bed, and start to put some clothes into it. I told my mom I'd be back to stay with her. She's probably worried about me.

I walk back into the kitchen to grab my phone from my bag. Griffin has two plates on the counter, and he's making sandwiches.

My lips find that tiny smile again as I tip my chin toward my phone, shooting off a text to my mom.

Me: *Sorry, I'm running a little late. Packing my bag now and grabbing a sandwich. Be there soon.*

Mom: *OK. Text me when you leave so I can keep an eye out for you.*

Me: *Will do.*

Griffin sets the two plates on the table, but he doesn't look at me. He sits down and starts eating. I miss him already. Taking a seat next to him, we eat in silence. It's sad, but comforting. And with no spoken words, we say so many things. *I'm sorry. Life's not fair. This hurts. I'll never forget you.*

And when we're both done, he finally looks at me. And it's clear that the only words left are the ones that change nothing, but mean everything.

I love you.

When he takes our plates to the sink, I go back to the bedroom and finish stuffing a few things into my bag. I zip the bag and draw in a long breath, releasing it a little at a time along with the weight of the world while glancing around the room.

If I stayed, if I rented the house from Sherri and Scott, I'd have these memories. Some days they'd give me comfort, other days they'd suffocate me with grief. I guess that's life, a steady pendulum. Balance is nothing more than a breath in the middle. Maybe at night, I could pretend that he's next to me in bed; maybe then I could find balance and take a breath.

I think I can do this—I can survive on one good breath a day.

Griffin startles me when he sneaks up behind me, reaching around to grab my bag. His chest brushing my back. Of course he's going to be the gentleman, the protector, and walk me to the car.

Thunk.

He drops my bag on the floor.

I turn. Our eyes meet. He grabs my face and kisses me. It's hard and demanding. It's impossible to breathe. That's okay … I only need one good breath. I'll catch it later.

He erases every trace that another man held me—kissed me. It's not right and it's not wrong. It simply *is.*

It's Griffin and Swayze.

And maybe this is futile, a team down by twenty points

with ten seconds left in the game. But who doesn't love watching the losing team play hard until the clock runs out?

Griffin pulls back, breathless and beautifully haunted as he gazes upon me. Is he making sure all he sees is his Swayz?

He shrugs off his shirt. I shrug off mine. And we kiss again, leaving it all on the field. His hands fist my hair as my fingernails dig into his back.

It's not a race. We're slow to make a pile of clothes on the floor. There are too many kisses to be had to rush anything. The future holds no promises, so we take our time making another memory.

It's a good one.

He eases my naked body onto the bed beneath his.

"I know every curve of your body ... I know what each curve feels like under my hands."

I love his hands. In my favorite dreams, they were made to touch me. Only me. Always me.

He takes his leisurely time making sure his lips touch every inch of my flesh. I writhe beneath him, committing this feeling to the deepest parts of my soul. If I take something with me when I die, this time it's going to be how incredibly revered I feel by this man.

Griffin

I'M LETTING HER go and it fucking hurts. Finders keepers doesn't apply to humans. But she's here now and so I'm taking now, and I'll take every minute of later that she gives to me— only me. Then I will walk away. I'll let her find what's missing, but I just can't be here when she realizes it's not me.

For now, I'm leaving my touch *everywhere*. When *he* touches her, I want her to remember my lips were here first.

I roll her onto her stomach. She arches her back, stretching her neck up. "Griff..." she murmurs as I drop kisses down the length of her spine. Her arms stretch over her head, hands clawing at the sheets. She's never looked more beautiful, bowed beneath my touch.

If this were our life, I could keep her for eternity. She loves me. *Swayze* loves me.

But this isn't our life. This is just a small reward for surviving the hard stuff.

As I tease the curve of her ass with my teeth. She lifts onto her elbows, glancing at me over her shoulder.

I kiss the teeth marks, looking up at her with a grin. She smiles in spite of the glassy emotions held hostage in her eyes.

"Are you marking me?"

"Yes." I bite a little lower.

Another bite. And another ...

She giggles, squirming until she's escaped to the top of the bed, back pressed to the headboard.

I'm not sure what hurts more, the grenade exploding in my own chest or knowing that beneath that smile of hers, she's wrecked and lost. And there's nothing I can do to make it better. Stretching out my legs toward her, I crook a finger.

She bites her lower lip and shakes her head, hugging her knees to her chest. I nod.

She shakes.

My brows lift slightly. She releases a silent sigh and crawls toward me, straddling both of my outstretched legs.

Palming her ass, I guide her down onto me. Her eyes flutter as she grabs my biceps.

"Baby …" I whisper over her lips.

She brushes her mouth over mine, slowly rocking her pelvis against mine. I resist the burning urge to flip her onto her back and fuck her into some grand apology—until she begs for my forgiveness—until every memory of Daisy and Nate vanish forever. Until … she chooses a life with me.

"I didn't get in the wrong line at the grocery store."

She stills, moving her hands to my cheeks, so much pain on her face. "I can't go with you." More emotions pool in her eyes.

"And I can't stay." I cover her hands with mine. "But, Swayz … I didn't get in the wrong line at the grocery store."

She blinks out another round of tears. "Fuck you, Daisy." It's something between a sob and a laugh.

I smile and nod once. "Fuck you, Daisy."

We kiss and it's all *us*.

I can't change what's on the outside. I can't save her from another life. So I devour her like I may never eat again, or take another breath. And after a few more seconds of this slow build up, I flip her onto her back and try to fuck some sense into her.

I'm not a hero. I'm human. But still … I want the impossible.

CHAPTER TWENTY-NINE

"**N**O," GRIFFIN GRUMBLES in a sleepy voice, tightening his hold on me as I try to slide out from underneath his arm hooked around my waist.

"I have to pee and text my mom. She thinks I'm coming over." I already know I have a gazillion missed messages from her. I'm surprised she hasn't driven over here. The fact that I let her track my phone location is probably the only thing keeping her home.

"I'm leaving you. You're not leaving me."

I don't know whether to laugh or cry. It's a little too soon and a lot too raw for those words.

He releases me. "Go. I'm kidding. But come back. I'm not done ruining you."

For another man—Nate.

I'm fine with being Griffin's ruination. At least I know he can put me back together. The thing is … he's leaving.

I slip on Griffin's discarded tee, grab my phone, and go into the bathroom. Yep. Six missed messages and two missed calls.

Me: *SO sorry.*

Me: *Got distracted.*

Me: *Staying here.*

Me: *Talk to you in the morning.*

Mom: *Oh? That's good. Yes?*

Me: *It's still heartbreaking. But, I want it.*

Like a drug, the withdrawal is going to suck. I hope to God I survive.

Mom: *Love you.*

After I'm done in the bathroom, I tiptoe to the kitchen to get a drink of water. It's starting to snow again. I watch it for a few minutes.

The floor behind me creaks.

"More snow," I say.

Griffin towers behind me. He takes my glass and drinks the rest of my water before setting the glass off to the side on the kitchen table in front of me.

"I like you in my shirt. I always have." His hand slides around me, under the front hem of the shirt.

My jaw relaxes, releasing tiny erratic breaths between my parted lips. His fingers tease me while his other hand finds my breast, pinching my nipple. I jerk back against him until his cock nudges my back.

"Bend forward." His words rasp along my ear. "I'm going to fuck you on *our* table. Because I can."

Yeah. He's ruined me because—*Lie on your back, I'm going to gently make love to you*—will never do it for me. It will never feed my hunger to be physically and emotionally owned by a man like Griffin.

I bend forward and rest my cheek on the cold wood, gripping the opposite side of the table. A cool shiver shoots along my spine when he slides up the shirt, exposing my ass. His fingers tease me, fucking me, until I pulse my pelvis against his hand. The head of his cock replaces that hand, and he drives into me on one hard thrust. Followed by another. And another ...

The table scrapes along the floor a fraction every time his hips slam against my backside.

It's him.

It's me.

It's us.

Swayze and Griffin—sex on demand.

"I WANT TO cry. But I think my tear ducts are broken." I frown at Griffin when he hands me a cup of coffee.

He returns a sad smile before tipping my chin up with his finger and pressing his lips to mine for an easy kiss. "Good morning."

"Morning." Good? I can't say that.

He's going to work. He has to know I'm going to work too—at Nate's house. Yet, he's showing a shit ton more confidence than I could muster on my best day.

"How do you do that?"

He fills a water bottle at the sink. "Do what?"

"Last night. This morning. The picture. The kiss. The forgotten birthday. Daisy. The returned engagement ring. We're unraveling and you keep clipping the thread like it's no big deal. But what's going to happen when it's the last piece of the thread?"

"Then I leave." He slips on his jacket.

I might find a way to squeeze out a few more tears if he keeps saying stuff like that. Shrugging, I shake my head. "So ... like no big deal."

He pulls a beanie onto his head, eyes narrowed a fraction.

"It's a whole fucking big deal. But at this point, I can't control you, your thoughts, or our fate. You've made up your mind. You want to pursue a life that's not mine. And I've made up my mind. I don't want to watch you walk off a cliff knowing I will never be able to catch you. I can't put you back together if I don't know where the pieces fit."

"This hurts," I murmur.

He nods several times, opening the back door. "It sure as hell does." The door closes behind him.

CHAPTER THIRTY

"HEY," I SAY, void of all confidence.

"Hey," Nate says with his back to me as he washes a few bottles.

"She still asleep?"

"Yeah."

I ease up onto the barstool. When he turns, I'm going to feel all sorts of pain and regret. But I can't hide forever.

"Things go okay with your parents watching her yesterday?"

"Yeah."

I nod. One *hey* and two *yeahs* ... good thing things aren't awkward.

"I see Dr. Albright next week. We're going to try hypnosis."

Nate dries his hands and turns.

"Jesus ..." I stand, making my way to him. "What happened to your face?" When I reach to brush my thumb across the cut on his fat lip, he pulls back and sidesteps me, grabbing his coffee container.

"I kissed my best friend."

"What are you talking—" It hits me. "Griffin? He came here? Yesterday?"

Nate screws the lid on to his container, shooting me a sidelong glance with a crooked smile tugging at his swollen lip.

"No. I give him credit for making his point in my office, instead of my house with my parents and Morgan."

"Nate, I'm so sorry—"

"Sorry?" He chuckles, shaking his head. "That's Swayze talking. I took a lot of hits for Daisy. And she never felt bad. I'm pretty sure that fell under what a real boyfriend was supposed to do. And I sure as hell wanted to be her real boyfriend. But it makes me feel bad for you, *Swayze,* that a guy stood up for you, for what the two of you have together, and you're *sorry.*"

He leans back against the counter, one hand holding his coffee and his other hand slipped into the front pocket of his dark jeans. "When Jenna and I were on our honeymoon, this guy sitting on the other side of her at an outdoor bar decided to hit on her. Right there in front of me. The shiny wedding ring clearly in plain sight. She politely told him her husband happened to be sitting on the other side of her. The dick had the balls to rest his hand on her leg. I broke his nose. Blood everywhere.

"Jenna grabbed my hand and dragged me into the hotel and straight up to our room. It was the most passionate sex we ever had. All because it turned her on seeing two guys get into it over her."

"Not the same thing. I kissed you back."

"Daisy kissed me back."

"That's just it. I don't feel her like you do. You remember all of her. I don't. So what if it wasn't Daisy who kissed you back?"

His lips twist, forehead drawn inward. "It doesn't matter. *I* kissed Daisy. I would never have kissed you had you not been her in my head at that moment."

I shake my head. "How can you say that for sure?"

"Because you're engaged to another man." His voice escalates to the edge of control. "That's not me. I don't touch what's not mine. I have morals. I'm a professor. A father. I'm not a thief."

I rub the empty spot where my engagement ring used to reside. Nate's gaze follows my movement.

"Swayze ..." He grimaces.

Fisting my left hand, I cover it with my right hand. "It wasn't you. It was me. I gave it back. He didn't ask for it. But I can't pretend that I wasn't her. I can't pretend that Doug Mann isn't a murderer. And I can't ask him to love me—to marry me—if I can't tell him who I am."

"Go apologize. Salvage it. Beg. Grovel. Whatever it takes." Nate snatches his coat from the back of the sofa and puts it on.

"What? Did you not hear me?"

Zipping his coat, he glances up at me. "Perfectly."

"He beat you up!" My sanity wanes.

Nate chuckles. "I stood in front of him and willingly took three solid punches. Not gonna lie, my face hurts more than it used to. Could be my age. But I can promise you ... I didn't get beaten up."

Slipping his bag over his shoulder, he stops in front of me. "Had I found out you told him about the kiss and he didn't pay me a visit, I would have been sorely disappointed in him."

"He's leaving. I'm staying."

"Don't be stupid. Let *her* go."

I laugh. "That's rich coming from the guy who named his daughter after *her*. The guy who visits her grave."

He stares at me, unblinking, for a few seconds. "Make sure the front door is locked. Have a good day."

I HAVE A good day. Then I have another good day. And this good day streak continues into the following week. Nate masters treating me like a nanny. Griffin masters fucking me like it's a sport. Even Scott and Sherri stop by a few times to chat like nothing is going on.

My mom is the only one besides me who sees the devastation just around the corner. She stops trying to talk "sense" into me. Instead, she vows to be the one to catch me if I jump off that cliff.

And today I'm getting ready to nudge closer to that cliff.

Dr. Albright smiles. "I'm going to start slow, just to see if and how you respond. If this works, we'll start with easy stuff. Happy memories. Let's not risk ruining your holidays with bringing forth a possible murder memory."

I nod, releasing a long breath. "You're the only one who doesn't think my need to know is crazy. Thank you."

A sad smile curls her mouth. "You're welcome. But I'm sorry that you're losing Griffin over this. I see both sides. They can't really see your side. As someone old enough to be your grandmother, I empathize with the feeling that you're young and this has the potential to change you—and maybe not in a good way. I believed our unconscious minds never bring forth more than we can handle. But after I had nightmares about a death, I realized the worst case scenario, albeit a slight chance, can happen. I was lucky to be able to have those same memories repressed."

"But not knowing and feeling so much anguish is its own kind of torture."

She nods several times.

I relax on her sofa. Since I'm an unofficial patient, she suggested we do this at her house. I worry about not remembering. I worry about remembering. I worry about everything until my mind starts to relax and all I hear is Dr. Albright's voice.

TWO HOURS LATER, I walk through the back door after my mom drops me off. She agreed to be my chauffeur per Dr. Albright's suggestion.

It takes me a few seconds to find Griffin perched on the sofa, watching ESPN. There are boxes everywhere, some empty, some taped and labeled, and some half-packed.

"Hi." He shuts off the TV.

"Hi." I close the door behind me and shrug off my coat. "You've been busy."

"Yeah." He sits up, resting his elbows on his knees. "It's about done. The rest of the stuff I'm leaving for you."

Yeah. This is happening.

I nod. "Thanks. But don't leave anything that you want or need. Really, I can replace whatever."

Except him. I can't replace him.

"Do I want to know if it worked?" He clasps his hands together.

"It worked. We didn't go too far. Happy memories. They weren't all clear, but I *felt* them. Like my mom and dad—Daisy's mom and dad. It was more than a disconnected vision or memory. It was deeper." I want to tell him every tiny detail. That's what we do. We share everything. But when I see the anguish on his face that he can't quite hide, I realize that's not us anymore. We're on the verge of not being *us*. And I know deep down, Griffin was hoping hypnosis wouldn't work on me.

I can't blame him for wanting something so badly. For wanting *me* so badly.

"We're waiting until after Christmas to go any further."

He stands. "The moving truck is coming the Monday after Christmas."

"Oh … I thought you weren't leaving until after New Years."

"I want a chance to acclimate for a few days before I start my job. Get settled."

We've discussed a lot. We've avoided a lot. We've skirted many topics in favor of just being in the moment with each other. I've never asked him this one question, and he's never offered it to me either.

"Where are you moving to?"

He grabs the tape from the coffee table and seals a box. "I think it's best for you to not know that."

"You what?" I try to keep my jaw from actually touching the ground.

"It has to be a clean break. I don't want you thinking about me and where I'm at. I don't want you second-guessing your decision and showing up on my doorstep because you need me to put you back together, only for us both to realize you still don't know who you are—but you had a weak moment and we're back at square one again."

Ouch.

He tosses the tape on the sofa and gives me an apologetic look. "I'm sorry."

My head inches side to side. "No. I deserve—"

Griffin wraps his arms around me. "Everything. And I wasn't trying to be mean. I just need everything or nothing.

And I want every last minute of everything we have left. But I can't live my life wondering if we're really over. If you're going to change your mind. It will drive me fucking crazy."

"Griff..."

"Maybe it just wasn't our time." He kisses the top of my head.

I pull back, looking at him. *Really* looking at him. Yes, I've always thought he has an old soul. And most of the time he has this militant control over his emotions where I have none. He's showed me silent anger, pent-up anger, a clenched jaw, and the kind of anger that just walks away.

Silence seeps in. I see the conflict in his eyes. His jaw clenches. And he crashes his lips against mine, almost knocking me off my feet. It's hard. It's *painful* to depths beyond any physical sensation.

My hands push on his chest. He resists me. I push harder. He lets me go, both of us breathless.

"Say it."

That sharply-angled jaw of his clenches again. "Say what?"

"Everything."

Tipping his chin down, he scratches the back of his neck. "What are you talking about?" His voice is thick.

"I can take it. I'm stronger than you think I am."

He turns back to the boxes, shaking his head. "I'm going to carry these boxes out to the garage. Will you hold open the door?"

"Say it."

He ignores me, stacking two boxes on top of each other and picking them up. I back up to the door, pressing my back against it.

"Open the door."

"Say it."

"Swayze, open the damn door."

"Say. It."

"You don't know what you're—"

"Say it!"

"I HATE THAT YOU'RE STAYING!"

Clunk.

The boxes hit the floor.

"I hate that this life isn't good enough for you. I hate that you're choosing a life you know nothing about over a life with me. I hate that this small part of me actually believes that you were her. I hate the way you look at him. I hate that you had that stupid picture of him. I hate that you let him lay one fucking finger on you. And I ..." He blinks and a tear slides down his cheek. "I want so desperately to hate *you*, but I don't. I love you..." he swallows hard, nostrils flaring as he tries to control his emotions "...and loving you right now is incredibly fucking miserable."

Maybe ... just maybe dying and trying on a new life wouldn't be such a bad idea. Maybe I would get a life without Doug Mann. A life without memories of the one before. Maybe I'd get a normal life. A normal childhood. A normal name. And I would find normal love. Maybe a boring job and a doting husband. Two kids and a dog. Simple and average would feel extraordinary.

I would have stellar self-esteem. No pity parties. No drama. Just ... beautifully boring.

I'm sorry won't cut it. I'm not even sure where the apology would start. Lord knows there would never be an end to it. I think the "excuse me for living" catchall is no longer accepted.

"I'll leave," I say with total defeat.

Griffin steps over the boxes and presses his hands to the door above my head, caging me with his body but not touching me. His angry breath brushes my forehead. "No. I will tear myself away. I'll *let you go*." His raspy words take several layers off my already raw heart. "But not yet."

My gaze meets his and *now* I let him kiss me like he hates loving me. I let him strip me like he hates my clothes. I let him possess my body even if I feel his hatred for wanting it so badly.

And then my mind goes numb. I react to the physical and let go of all the hatred and all the things in this moment that don't serve any purpose.

CHAPTER THIRTY-ONE

W E FINISH OUR shopping.

We celebrate Christmas with family like our relationship isn't dead.

Griffin gives me a tutorial on all the important things I need to know about the house, like where the breaker box is located.

Then …

It's moving day.

I wake up to the aroma of hazelnut and an empty spot next to me in bed. After a long goodbye last night, I thought he'd at least let me wake up one last time in his arms. Instead, I settle for one last walk down the hallway to his good morning smile and outstretched hand with my mug of coffee.

It's always the little things.

"Add waking up to hazelnut to the list of things I'm going to miss." I stop in the kitchen, looking around. There's a pot of coffee with the warmer turned on and an empty mug next to it. "Griff?" I peek back down the hallway. The bathroom door is open, light off.

I stand in the middle of the living room and look around. His coat is not on the hook by the door. None of his shoes or boots are by the door.

My heart slows.

No.

I try to swallow the lump forming in my throat.

No.

My feet take cautious steps back to the bedroom. His pillow is gone, pillowcase folded in its absence. The two suitcases that were at the end of the bed last night are gone.

No ...

I. Can't. Breathe.

Running to the back door, I rip my coat off the hook and shove my feet into my boots while threading my arms into the sleeves, only having it halfway on as I run out the door into the frigid air.

"Griffin!" My cries form evaporating clouds of desperation. His truck is gone. The side door to the garage is locked, I look through the window. For the first time ever, my car is parked in the garage. Everything else is gone.

The motorcycle.

The boxes.

The few pieces of furniture he decided to claim as his to take.

All gone.

My grocery store guy is gone.

There are some things you can never prepare for, like loss. It's this debilitating emotion that life serves up without an instructional manual.

We didn't talk about this day, not how we'd handle that final goodbye. I knew there would be tears, but I didn't know I'd cry them alone.

How can something so unfinished be so final?

I collapse to my knees on the snow-covered sidewalk and I cry.

IT TAKES ME three days to shower. My mom respects my need to be alone. She needed time to grieve my dad. And now I need time to grieve Griffin. Nate knows nothing yet because he's on holiday break, which means I'm on holiday break.

By day five, the intervention starts. I wonder if Griffin left my mom and his family a guide to Swayze.

Give her five days then please step in and offer her a hand and a hug.

"Hey, sweetie. Happy New Year." My mom smiles, walking in the back door with Sherri behind her.

They're just now coming in the house, but I've seen my mom's car and the Calloway's vehicles pulling in and out of the driveway for days. I'm pretty sure they peek in the windows at night just to make sure I haven't slit my wrists. That chance at a new life, albeit appealing, isn't what I want quite yet. I'm hell-bent on finishing one good life.

Unfortunately, *the good part* left me five days ago with no real goodbye, but I forgive him.

I blink several times. Today I make it to the sofa, but all I can do is stare at the wall where the TV used to be. He offered to leave it, but I don't watch it, so it would have been a silly thing to leave behind.

"I have soup. Today you should eat."

I nod once, my head still heavy from days of grieving, pulse palpable in my swollen eyes.

"Coffee, the good kind." Sherri hands me a cup of coffee and sits next to me.

It's not hazelnut. Doesn't matter. I'm thinking about giving up coffee and all other parts of my life that remind me of

Griffin. Agreeing to stay in this house was a stupid idea. The memories only serve as painful reminders.

"He wanted me to tell you he made it safely to his destination." Sherri rests her hand on my knee as I continue to watch the blank wall.

His destination. The place I'm not allowed to know about. A clean break. There's nothing clean about this break. It's so fucking messy I can't see past the cluttered images in my head. It's a maze with a hundred marbles crashing into each other and no way out.

"Tell him I'm good," I say in a monotone voice.

Mom hands me the soup and a spoon. Sherri takes the coffee from me.

"Are you?" Sherri asks.

I nod several times, stirring the wild rice soup. "I will be."

I don't know that at all. There's a lot on my docket: forgetting Griffin, resurrecting the dead, and catching a killer. No big deal. At least Scott's been shoveling the driveway. If he could arrest Doug, that would be awesome too. Something tells me that's not what a CPA does.

A shame.

"I'm going to grab groceries later. I'll pick some staples up for you too," my mom says from the kitchen.

I'm guessing she's inspecting the fridge. It's pretty pathetic. Yesterday I decided to give my stomach something to digest besides itself and a shitload of grief, but the best I could find was that crappy sprouted grain bread. I doused it in butter. It worked.

"I'll go to the store."

She peeks her head around the corner. "You will?"

I don't know why she looks so surprised. Well, maybe I do.

The death-warmed-over look might lead outsiders to believe that I'm struggling a bit.

It hurts to look at Sherri without feeling shame. What must she really think of me? Even if she wants to believe that I am Daisy reincarnated, she can't know for sure. At least part of her has to think "maybe she's just crazy."

A tiny part of me thought that too, until Dr. Albright hypnotized me. And now I know without a shadow of doubt, I was Daisy.

"It wasn't fair to go with him … and it wasn't fair to ask him to stay." After a pregnant pause, I look at Sherri.

She gets a little teary-eyed. "I know. But at least he left with things good between the two of you. No hard feelings."

My lips attempt a small smile. By the time Griffin left, I'm certain the only feelings between us were hard, raw, and painful. It simply hurt more to be apart than it did to be together.

"So …" Sherri slaps her hands on her legs. "The girls are on break for two more days. Let's all go get manicures and pedicures. My treat."

I love her. I love all of Griffin's family. I love the way they've not only welcomed me, but they've formed a special bond with my mom. Do I have to break up with them too? What will happen when Griffin comes home to visit them? Will I be given notice to stay away?

I set my soup on the coffee table. "I'll be right back." Without actually running, I retreat to the bedroom and shut the door, leaning back against it. My heart feels so laid bare. Vulnerable to every thought, every memory. Eventually, it won't feel this hard to breathe when I think of *never* seeing Griffin again. But I'm not there yet. Not even close.

Fisting both hands to my heart, I dig deep to find that elusive next breath. Then I dive back down and find another one.

One breath.

One second.

One day at a time.

"Swayze?" My mom knocks at the door.

I open the door and she slips in, shutting it behind her.

She tucks my hair behind my ear and rests her hand on my cheek.

"It gets easier, right?" I choke on the pain.

"Yeah." She offers a sympathetic smile.

"I was Daisy, Mom. I wish you could have seen the memories I saw. It was a good life, even if a short one ... it was good. For the first time, I *feel* her."

"I ..." She shakes her head. "I don't know what to say. It's hard to think of you as anyone but my child."

"It's weird." I step back and run my hands through my hair. "What if I piece it all together and it's still not enough because ..." My voice starts to stumble and crack from all the *feelings*. "Because I don't have my grocery store guy?"

"Maybe you weren't meant to be with Griffin. What if some people are meant to pass through our lives instead of walking along beside us?"

I gaze out the window like I'm waiting for a black truck to pull in the driveway. "Was Dad meant to pass through your life?"

"I didn't think so because we seemed to walk beside each other so well. But I was wrong."

"Dad's dead. Griffin is alive. You don't have to imagine someone else living life with your greatest love."

She hugs me from behind, resting her chin on my shoulder.

"You're twenty-two, my dear girl. There's a great big world out there. I think you will find another great love. And the timing will be perfect. You'll know who you are. You'll be ready to give of yourself completely."

If I live that long.

I laugh through the threatening tears. "How will I know?"

Her arms squeeze me tighter. "Oh, you'll know."

CHAPTER THIRTY-TWO
Nate

"THANK YOU FOR seeing me."

Professor Albright motions to her love seat. "Of course. You said it couldn't wait until after winter break. Naturally, I'm intrigued. Can I get you something to drink?"

"I'm good. But thank you."

"Where's Morgan?"

"My parents are watching her."

"Ah. I bet they love that."

"Yeah." I rub my forehead.

"Nathaniel, you look positively tortured. What's going on?"

"I need a favor."

"Of course."

I grunt a laugh. "Don't agree before I tell you what the favor is."

"Oh dear ..."

Oh dear is right. I hate that I'm here asking for this favor. But I have no choice.

"I need you to do something unethical."

Her eyebrows slide up her forehead as she drums her fingers on the arm of the chair.

"I know you hypnotized Swayze. I know it worked."

"And by unethical you're asking me to disclose what happened in my session with Swayze?"

"No."

"No? Well, now I'm confused."

Leaning forward, I rest my arms on my knees and fold my hands. "If a memory is too painful, too dangerous, the unconscious mind won't let it pass into consciousness. Correct?"

"Usually. But there are exceptions. I was one."

I nod. "I need you to make sure Swayze doesn't remember all the details of Daisy's death."

"It's unlikely that she will anyway if she's not ready."

"I get that. But ..."

"But?"

Biting my lips together, I draw in a slow breath. "I need you to make sure there is a *zero* percent chance of her remembering it. Ever."

"You want me to talk her out of it?"

"No. She's not heeding any sound advice at the moment. I want you to hypnotize her. I want you to not go there. The death. Doug Mann. I don't know ..."

I shake my head. "Try to repress every single memory of that life that you can repress, especially Doug Mann."

"If she's right about Doug Mann, there's a murderer on the loose. That's a big part of her motivation. She has a valid moral obligation to make sure he doesn't kill again. And every day we wait is another day that he has to stalk his next victim. What if that's Swayze?"

"It's not."

"How do you know?"

"I just do."

"Nathaniel. You can't ask me to do something unethical and not give me *all* the reasons why I should risk my career, my license."

We have a stare down.

I lose.

I risk it all to save *her*.

AFTER CALLING MY parents to check on Morgan, I drive to Swayze's house. It reminds me of the house I lived in on Gable Street, only hers is in better shape.

After ringing the doorbell several times and knocking, I assume she's not home. I stop just before getting back in my vehicle. There's music. It sounds like it's coming from the single-car garage, so I follow it.

I ease open the door. Swayze looks up from her spot near a workbench. She's sitting on an overturned five-gallon bucket. The most depressing alternative music plays on her phone that's clenched in her hand.

"Hi," I say.

She fails at her attempted smile.

"Did you get locked out of your house?"

"No."

I step inside. It's not a happy place.

"Want to talk about it?"

Swayze stares at her phone. "No."

"Do you want me to suggest songs for a better playlist?" That makes her smile a little more believable.

She turns off the music and stands. "Where's Morgan? If you left her in the car, I'm going to have to report you." Brushing past me, she walks outside, scuffing her boots like a lazy child.

I follow her. "My parents are watching her while I run a

few errands."

"I'm an errand?" Banging the snow off her boots, she opens the back door to the house.

"Yes. You're my last errand." I slip off my shoes after stepping inside and shutting the door.

"You want to know about the hypnosis. Am I right?" Plopping on the sofa, she snatches the blanket off the back of it and wraps it around herself.

"No. I'm just checking on you. That's all."

"Oh, well, here's the update: I'm still relatively stable. You don't have to worry about my mental state. Morgan will be safe with me."

"I trust you implicitly with Morgan. I'm only here as your friend. Even mentally stable people need friends sometimes."

Her lips twist, eyes narrowed a fraction. "Fine. I like the kind of friends who braid each other's hair. Do you know how to braid hair, Professor Hunt?"

"I can't tie a tie. Do you really think a French braid is in my repertoire?" I sit next to her on the sofa.

"You have a daughter. You need to learn how to braid. I won't be around forever to do things for you."

"No? Where are you going? I hope somewhere warm."

She nudges my leg with her foot. "Are you trying to get rid of me?"

"Never."

Her smile keeps slipping. I want to catch it and glue it in place. She has the brightest smile. It's crushing to see her without it.

"The hypnosis. Mostly my parents and my eleventh birthday party." Her gaze finds mine.

I just listen.

"I got a new bike. And my mom—Daisy's mom—was my friend. I'm friends with my mom now, but when I was younger, she was more concerned about my potential than things like helping me find the right dress for homecoming or braiding my hair." She grins a little more. "Daisy's mom braided her hair. See how girls remember that? You need to learn how to braid hair, Nate."

"You know, that life is gone. Is it worth giving up everything just to remember it?"

"You mean Griffin?"

I nod.

"Limbo is a miserable place. I'm a miserable person feeling stuck in the middle. I need to know everything or nothing. It's like walking barefoot on the beach is no big deal, but having a few specks of sand in your shoe is unnerving. Griffin deserves to be with someone who isn't stuck in the middle. And Doug Mann needs to be in prison. It's that simple."

"Swayze, you deserve happiness. It's *that* simple."

She shrugs. "I'll find happiness when the time is right. Our timing just wasn't right." Looking away, she swallows hard, negating everything she just said.

"If Doug Mann weren't part of the equation, would you still feel this burning need to know more? Would you have let Griffin leave without you?"

An unvoiced snort-laugh escapes her nose. "It's a moot point. But after what happened between us …" She turns back to me.

I want to shrivel up and die like the asshole I am for kissing her.

"I had to let him go."

"It was just a kiss."

Her face contorts into a painful scowl. "It wasn't *just* a kiss. And you downplaying it only pains me more."

"If not just a kiss, then what was it?"

"Stop." Tossing the blanket aside, she paces the room. "In college I had sex that was less stimulating than that kiss."

I bite back my chuckle. "Maybe you just had low standards."

"Fuck you." Her eyes narrow at me.

"Yeah, fuck me." I stand.

"Why?" Her voice loses all fight. "I get the kiss. There's this part of me that's wondered what it would feel like. This deep-seated curiosity grew more with every story you shared about you and Daisy. The more I felt like I *had* to be her, the more I wanted to *feel* what she felt. And…" she shakes her head, arms hugged to her chest "…the one thing I wanted to feel more than anything else was you."

"Swayze …"

Continuing to shake her head, she steps back as I step toward her.

Her hand presses to her neck just below her ear. "I thought you'd kiss me here, like you kissed her. Like her dad kissed her mom."

After a few seconds of staring at the floor between us, or years into the past, her eyes find mine. "I wanted red and orange popsicles and stolen chocolates. I wanted to feel that young love. The butterflies. The anticipation. I thought it would flip this switch for me, and I'd remember what it was like to be that girl who fell in love with you. I thought one kiss could make that life real in my head."

Popsicles and chocolates. I'm an asshole.

"But you didn't kiss me like a fifteen-year-old boy would

kiss a fifteen-year-old girl. You kissed me like an animal emerging from hibernation. Like a man coming undone from the inside out. Like if you didn't kiss me, you would cease to exist."

Like I was looking for that piece of myself that you took with you when you died.

Glancing away for a brief second, she draws in a shaky breath. "And I kissed you back like I just … needed to know."

"Needed to know what?"

Her gaze meets mine again, and I feel her pain bone-deep. I don't know if what's happened is fate or irresponsible. Can fate be this reckless? I just don't know. I love her—even if I'm not sure on any given day who she is or how to define this love.

"I needed to know if another man could make me feel the way Griffin made me feel. In my heart, I knew that was impossible. But you've been in my head, in my dreams, a picture in my pocket … and I needed to know if my heart would betray me."

Don't ask. Don't ask. It doesn't matter. She's not yours.

"The heart can be quite fickle and a foolish slave to desire."

"So I shouldn't trust my heart?"

I shrug. This isn't the conversation I want to have with her. I'm no expert on love. All of my experiences have ended in tragedy. That's why I need to protect her.

"I'm just saying there should be a good checks and balances between your mind and your heart. Neither one should have total say in big decisions."

"Kissing you wasn't really *my* decision."

Because I'm an asshole.

"It wasn't really a decision for me either. It was total impulse. My mind didn't catch up until I was in my vehicle, pulling out of the garage. I'm sorry."

"Then why did you kiss me?"

I turn and pace the same path she paced just minutes earlier, head down, hands on hips. "I don't know. Do we have to discuss this? It was wrong. I can't take it back. It won't happen again. I'm truly sorry. I don't know what else to say."

"Did you stop by to discuss the kiss?"

I stop my motion. "What? No. Of course not. You brought it up."

"Then what did you want to discuss?"

"I just wanted to make sure you're doing okay. I know Griffin left town, and ... I don't know. I assumed you might be having a rough time."

"Who told you he left town? We haven't talked since before Christmas."

Fuck.

"He contacted me. Asked me to keep an eye on you. To check in after a few days."

"Bullshit." She shakes her head. "There's no way."

"Not bullshit."

"He beat you up. He doesn't ask the guy who kissed his fiancée to look after her. I'm young and sometimes a little naive, but believing that would make me stupid. What's your angle? Why are you saying this? Who told you he left? Dr. Albright?"

"Dr. Albright would never discuss you with me."

I'm going to Hell. Or in *my* next life I will return as a cockroach.

"Then who."

"Griffin."

"You're pissing me off."

"What do you want me to say? Call and ask him."

She deflates. I grimace. It's over. She really ended it with him. All for a past—a lifetime ago.

"It doesn't matter. I see Dr. Albright tomorrow. I'm going to remember what Doug did to Daisy—to me. And I'm going to make sure he pays for what he's done. I'm tired of looking over my shoulder, walking to my car with my heart in my throat, jolting from my sleep every time I hear a noise. I've been sleeping with a steak knife under my pillow since Griffin left. I want to stay with my mom, but I don't want to worry her, so I play it off like I'm not scared. But ... I'm scared shitless."

I still the forward motion of my hand. I want to hug her, touch her, comfort her so she knows there's no need to be scared. Instead, I shove both hands into my pockets to keep them from caving to such urges.

"You're in good hands. I know Dr. Albright will give you the help you need." That's it. That's all I have to give her.

Pathetic.

CHAPTER THIRTY-THREE

"I DON'T UNDERSTAND."

Dr. Albright has this pained expression on her face. I'm used to the empathetic one, but not this one. "Swayze, the mind has a natural instinct to preserve your wellbeing."

"But it worked last time."

She returns a slow nod. "I'm sorry. We can try again later. You've been under a tremendous amount of stress lately. We need to listen to what your body and your mind are trying to tell us. It's just not ready."

"Fine. I'll get some good sleep. I haven't been sleeping well lately. Maybe you could prescribe something for me, and we can try again tomorrow."

"I think we should give this more than a day. Perhaps I can show you some relaxation techniques instead. Chamomile tea. A good book. Maybe you could get a massage."

"A massage? A good book? Chamomile tea? Are you serious? I could be dead by tomorrow. That murderer could be hiding in my backseat at this very moment. And tomorrow you could find out that I drove off a bridge. They'll call it suicide—after all, I've been awfully troubled lately. All because he's mastered how to get away with murder, and I can't remember a damn thing to stop him!"

"A little Xanax as needed might be a good fit after all." She holds up a finger. "Prescription pad is in my office, give me a quick sec."

Fisting my hand at my mouth, I nod. That wasn't a finer moment for me.

Dr. Albright sends me home with a "chin up" and a prescription that I'm only supposed to take if absolutely necessary.

After checking the backseat, I pick up my prescription and drive home. What if I never remember? I didn't really think that hard about it being a possibility. I don't have a plan B. There was only plan A.

I call my mom as soon as I walk in the door and deadbolt it behind me. What if he's in here? Hiding in the closet. Behind the shower curtain? The hypnosis not working today has messed with my mind. It's skyrocketed my paranoia.

My mom doesn't answer. I open the little white bag and pull out the bottle of pills. Maybe I just need sleep. But who will protect me if I fall into a deep sleep and don't wake up when he breaks into my house?

For safe measure, I grab another knife out of the drawer and slip it into my back pocket. Maybe I should call Sherri and Scott. No … what if they tell Griffin. I don't want him to know how fucked-up I am right now. He'll feel bad and rush back to save me. One of the reasons he left was to avoid watching me self-destruct.

Fuck! That's what's happening.

I have a bottle of Xanax in my hand and a knife in my pocket.

A bottle of Xanax and a knife.

Setting my phone on the kitchen table so my mom thinks I'm here, I open the door and go back to my car with nothing more than my purse, a knife, and a bottle of Xanax.

It's a little past two in the afternoon. Most of the world is still working, with the exception of some college students relishing the last day of winter break. Dougly Fucking Creepy Mann is a night owl. It's possible he's not even out of bed. Erica used to roll her eyes at his odd hours, which coincided quite well with her manic hours at the hospital.

I park on a side street two blocks away from the apartment building. Pulling up my hood and slipping on sunglasses, I trek to the building. Without a key, I can't get through the main door. And I don't want to announce my arrival to the man I'm going to visit. So I hang out by the door for a few minutes and, sure enough, someone walks out of the building.

"Oh thank God," I murmur just loud enough for her to hear me, keeping my chin tucked to my chest while riffling through my purse. "Stupid key always gets lost at the bottom and it's cold as the arctic out here. Thank you."

"No problem," the lady says while holding open the door for me.

In spite of the arctic temperatures, a few beads of sweat trickle down my back as I climb the stairs. Each step robs a little more oxygen from my lungs, the weight of what I'm about to do bearing down on my chest. My pulse pounds out of control, making it impossible to hear anything but the whisper of fear.

I stop for a moment and stare at my old apartment door. After a few breaths, I turn the corner and ascend the final set of stairs. My eyes stay focused on *his* door. If I glance right, at Erica's door, I will lose it.

When my shaky fist raps on his door, my heart attempts to break out of my chest. He killed Erica.

I knock again.

He killed Daisy.

I knock a little harder.

He's been taunting me.

Knock! Knock! Knock!

I think I could tear down this door. My plans to drug him before stabbing a knife through his heart could get derailed by the revenge running through my veins. When he opens the door, I'm going to have a hard time not skipping the drugging part. All I want to do is *kill him.*

"Miss? I think you might have the wrong apartment."

I jump at the unfamiliar voice wafting down the stairs from the floor above.

"No," I say curtly, turning my back to the middle-aged gentleman taking his final step to the landing behind me.

Bang! Bang! Bang!

"Miss, I hate to be the one to break the news to you, but Mr. Mann committed suicide several days ago."

My fisted hand stills on the door, leaving my adrenaline-fed panting as the only sound in the stairwell.

"What?" I inch my head round, eyeing him over my shoulder.

The messy blond-haired gentleman zips his coat, nodding. "Hung himself. Landlord found him when he went in there to fix a plumbing issue that Mr. Mann had reported the week before." He slips on his gloves. "My condolences if you knew him, miss."

My feet remain rooted in their spot as the man makes his way to the lower level.

Doug's dead.

AFTER A NUMBING drive home and a Xanax, I sleep for ten hours. The drug doesn't last that long, but peace of mind worked synergistically with it. I wake with a residual numbness. It's like someone knocked my puzzle on the floor and I may never get all the pieces back in their right spot, but maybe it doesn't matter.

I sit on the edge of the bed, missing the body that used to lie bedside me. After staring at my phone screen for a few minutes, I message Griffin.

Me: *Doug is dead.*

The message says *undelivered.*
I resend.
Undelivered again.

I shouldn't call him. His voice would render me a sobbing mess. If he's not getting the message, maybe if I called it would just go to his voicemail anyway. I hope.

My pulse begins to surge like it did yesterday at Doug's door. What if Griffin answers? After a few minutes of playing chicken with myself, I press call.

It rings once.
Shit! He's answering it.
I can't breathe.

It's not him. It's a recording saying the number is no longer in service. I don't understand. I call him again, dialing the number with the area code.

Again, the same recording.
Next I call Sherri.
"Hey, Swayze."
"Hi, Sherri."
"How are you doing? The girls sure had fun getting mani-

cures and pedicures with you and your mom."

"Yeah, um … me too. Hey, I was just seeing if you knew anything about Griffin's phone. I tried texting him and calling him, and it says the number is no longer in service."

My legs bounce off the side of the bed, filled with out-of-control nerves. She doesn't respond.

"Sherri?"

"Yeah, Swayze. Listen, sweetie …"

Nothing good ever comes after the words "listen sweetie." My legs still so all my body's focus goes to listening.

"He has a new number."

"So it has his new area code instead of this one?"

Another awkward silence.

"Sherri, what's going on?"

"Do you need to get a message to him? I could relay it."

"I'll do it if you give me his new number."

"I'm sorry. He asked me not to do that. I'm really really sorry, sweetie."

Wow …

I feel like the loner sitting at the lunchroom table all by myself, catching the occasional "sorry sweetie" glances and hand-fisted-over-the-mouth snickers.

So this is a clean break?

Wow …

"Tell him …" I shake my head. If he were truly worried about me and my safety, he wouldn't have cut all ties. Not with me living by myself, knowing Doug has been taunting me since Erica died—since he murdered her. "Never mind. There's no message."

"Swayze—"

"I have to get ready for work. I'll see you later." I end the call.

No tears. I'm done being sad. I'm pissed off. Hurt. But seriously *pissed off,* whether I really have any right to be or not.

We didn't end badly. We ended with a long night tangled in each other's bodies.

And then ... nothing.

He left. I let him. But I didn't think he would do this.

This doesn't feel like love or even self-preservation. This just feels cruel.

CHAPTER THIRTY-FOUR

I STOP. I just ... stop.

For the next month I function in robotic mode.

No psychiatrists.

No mention of Griffin to my mom or anyone else.

No prolonged contact with the Calloways.

When Scott comes over to clear the drive, I give him a polite wave and set a cup of coffee on the workbench in the garage for him. When Sherri calls to see if I want to come to dinner or have lunch on the weekends, I always find an excuse.

Nate doesn't ask me about anything.

Not Doug.

Not Dr. Albright.

Not the hypnosis.

Nothing.

In fact, he doesn't say much at all. He's become the employer I needed him to be months ago.

Polite.

Grateful.

Friendly.

Professional.

A month without mentioning Daisy.

It's not that I've forgotten her or the parts to that life that reside in my mind. Something happened to me that day. And I'm not sure if it was Doug's death or the total loss of connection to Griffin.

I guess I'm still trying to figure out how I got to this place in my life. Or maybe I'm trying to figure out exactly what place this is.

My mom is the only person who knows about Doug. She needed to know that her daughter was safe. Then I needed her to promise to never mention his name to me or anyone again.

"Look at you go, pumpkin." Nate grins as he walks in the house and sees Morgan standing up to the sofa, hips gyrating to keep her balance. Her grin is the brightest light I have ever seen.

Hands down she is the best thing in my life at the moment. I want her to be smart, but not too smart. Popular but kind. And I want her to meet a boy just like her daddy used to be, but I don't want some sick bastard killing her before she can truly live life.

Just random thoughts. Wishes upon stars. Prayers to an unknown god.

When Nate comes over to pick her up, she lunges for me. ME. I shouldn't gloat, but I need this. I need something.

"Who does Morgan love?" I hug her, smirking at Nate. "Swayze. That's who."

He takes her from me, shooting me an evil glare that doesn't totally hide his smile. "You're fired."

I laugh. "I have her five days. You have her two and maybe one to two waking hours in the evenings. What do you expect? Of course she thinks I'm awesome."

"She got wobbly and fell in your direction, and you read *awesome* out of that?"

"Don't be petty about it. You think I'm awesome too."

"Whoa … your hungry ego has a voracious appetite today."

"I'll bet you three hundred dollars I can get you to say I'm awesome."

He lifts an eyebrow. "Now we're betting on your awesomeness or lack thereof? And not the typical hundred-dollar bet, but the interesting amount of three hundred dollars?"

I shrug. "My dishwasher went out. Three hundred dollars for a new one."

He studies me. "I'm not going to take pity on you. A dishwasher is not a necessity."

Of course he would say that. Growing up, he didn't have one.

"I don't expect pity. I will earn the *Swayze, You Are Awesome* award fair and square."

"He nuzzles Morgan's neck and she giggles."

"Ready?" I grin.

Nate smiles. It's big. It's familiar. It's the boy who loved me in that other life. "Do your worst."

I take Morgan back from him, holding her so she's against my chest, facing him. My mouth nuzzles her ear as I whisper so only she can hear me.

"Da da ..." she says with a grin.

Nate looks like he's in shock. I'm not sure if he's going to pass out, cry, or swallow his tongue.

It's just conditioning. She doesn't really connect that word to him yet, but she can say it—thanks to *me*. And it's her first official word.

That incredible smile eases up his face as his gaze moves from her to me. I smile back. Not a gloating smile, just genuine happiness. It's the Jenna-died-but-Morgan-will-adore-you-forever smile. I can't really articulate how much I want him to have something special in his life last forever.

"You're awesome," he says in a choked whisper. And he'd never admit it, but those are the beginning of unshed tears in his eyes.

This feels like butterflies in my tummy and orange and red popsicles on hot days. Like my life makes sense again. Maybe I'm here to make Nate smile. Maybe I'm simply here *for* Nate, and he knew it, even Griffin might have known it, before I was ready to admit it.

"You're welcome."

After a few more seconds of total bliss, he slides his wallet out of his pocket and thumbs through a wad of bills, depositing three hundreds on the counter.

"Who just happens to have three hundred dollars in their wallet on a whim?"

"People who pay cash for everything." He takes Morgan back with a goofy grin permanently pinned to his face.

My lips twist to the side. "I can't take your money. The look on your face was enough. Besides, you're right, a dishwasher isn't a necessity. And I don't cook much on my own."

"Thought you were renting. Shouldn't that be something your landlord replaces?"

"Probably. I don't want to ask."

"Why not?" He sets Morgan back down, and she crawls straight to the sofa to stand up again.

"My landlords are my ex-fiancé's parents." I still don't say Griffin's name aloud.

"So? If you're paying rent, they should fix or replace it."

I nod, not really agreeing to anything, just acknowledging that I heard what he said. "Whatcha doing for dinner? Wanna order pineapple and jalapeño pizza?"

"Excuse me?" He chuckles. "You're a cheese girl."

"Maybe. I've never actually tried pineapple and jalapeño. It just sounds disgusting. But maybe it could be my jam. You once knew a girl who liked it. I might like it too."

He does a crappy job of hiding his apprehension, but I keep my chin up and what I hope is an irresistible smile on my face.

"Order it. But you're buying with your three hundred dollars."

Grinning, I grab my phone from the counter. "I think there's an online coupon I can use. You know … since I'm buying."

And so it begins. My friendship with Nate Hunt. It doesn't start on a school bus this time. It starts over a large pizza, a smiley baby girl, and lounging on the sofa watching hockey together after he puts Morgan to bed.

I make stupid comments like I don't understand the sport—just to get a rise out of him—and he playfully nudges my leg, giving me a narrow-eyed look. Just before eleven, he walks me to my car after it's been warmed up because … yeah … he started it for me fifteen minutes ago.

"Thanks for the pizza," he says.

I laugh. "Anytime. I had fun watching those guys hit that disc thingie with those paddle thingies around the ice."

"You are no good. Zip. Zero. One hundred percent trouble."

"But you love me, right?"

Oh shit …

I said that. But I meant it in a playful banter kind of way. My gaze drops to my feet as I scuff my boots against the driveway dotted with a few patches of caked-on snow.

"Yes. I do."

My head snaps up, jaw dropped.

Nate slips his hands into his pockets, shoulders lifting to his ears in an innocent shrug. "Always have. Always will."

"Nate …" I say because all other words fail me.

Keeping his hands in his pockets, like they're there to keep him out of trouble, he bends forward and kisses the top of my head. Staying there, he murmurs, "It's not an expectant love. It's not a romantic love. It's not an inappropriate kiss. It's not even my daughter saying my name."

Turning his head, he rests his cheek on my head. I press my hands to his chest.

"It's just what's always been in my heart. You died, but I lived and so has my love for you."

He straightens.

"Nate …" Yeah. That's all I've got.

He smiles. "It's an innocent love. It's a beautiful love. I think it's even an eternal love. But … I don't know yet. Maybe in another lifetime we'll see. We'll find out if our souls share something that transcends time or if they are nothing more than epoch."

"Epic?"

"E-p-o-c-h. It's a memorable event or period in time."

"Epoch …" I grin. "I definitely think this is epoch. But I also think it could be transcendent … and that would be e-p-i-c."

He reaches behind me and opens my door. "Drive safely."

"Safe." I start to get in my car and stop. "It's weird."

"What's that?"

"It's been over a month since my fiancé left, since I told you that I was sleeping with a knife under my pillow. A month since you knew I was going to have hypnosis to remember what happened. But you just …" I shrug, face contorted in confusion. "You never asked. Like you just stopped caring. I feel like everyone stopped caring. It's like the moment my parents gave up on me being anything extraordinary."

Nate has this unexplainable look on his face. It's odd. Cautious? Contemplative? "How's all of that going?"

I cough a laugh. "Are you serious? *How's all of that going?* I'm not dead, that's how it's going, but gee … thanks for asking a fucking month later."

He flinches.

"Seriously! What has to happen for the people who supposedly love me to give more than two shits?"

"Swayze …"

"You have video cameras in your house, yet my safety doesn't warrant so much as a 'Hey, are you locking your doors?' or 'Has that psychopath tried to get near you again?'"

"Has he?"

"No!" I throw my hands up in the air. "Because he's dead!"

Nate nods.

He. Fucking. Nods!

"Then you've been safe."

My head whips back like a close encounter with a bus on a busy street. "He's. Dead."

Nate nods again. A slow nod with that look. That cautious, contemplative look. "That's a relief."

"What's going on, Nate?" My breaths turn shallow, and I feel weak in the knees.

"What do you mean?"

"I mean you're not reacting in a normal way. I say Doug Mann is dead, and you have no questions. None. Not 'Are you serious?' Or 'When? Where? *How?*' How, Nate. The normal reaction is to wonder how he died. Heart attack, cancer, car accident, or a knife to his heart. *My* knife, Nate. I took a knife and a bottle of Xanax to his apartment."

His eyes narrow, wrinkling the skin around his eyes.

"I was going to *kill* him because the hypnosis didn't work. I was going to *kill* him because that's the only way I could live. That's the only way I could feel safe. That's the only way I could ease my conscience that no one else would die at his hands."

"I'm sorry."

He's sorry. That's all wrong. What is going on?

When I start to speak, he brings me into his arms, stifling my attempt to speak. I don't want a hug. I want answers. I want to know how the two men who have claimed to love me the most just abandoned me when I needed them the most.

I pull back. "Nate—"

"Shh …" He drops his head, hovering over my lips, one hand sliding into my hair, palming the side of my head while he rubs the knuckles of his other hand over my cheek, rendering me speechless and breathless.

The pad of his thumb slides over my bottom lip, jumbling my thoughts. His thumb trails downward, his lips follow in its wake.

When his thumb rubs my neck, just below my ear, my eyelids surrender, finding solace in memories of a lifetime ago. I grab his arms to steady myself when his lips press to my neck.

This is what it feels like.

To be cherished.

To be adored.

To be loved beyond words.

To be young.

To be alive.

"Swayze," Nate murmurs against my ear, "you're safe because those who claim to love you actually *do* love you." He kisses my neck.

I die.

He kisses my cheek and lets go of me, turning and not giving a glance back as he makes his way up the drive. "Goodnight."

CHAPTER THIRTY-FIVE

I THINK IT'S time to revisit Dr. Albright. Then I change my mind. She's called me once a week since my failed hypnosis session, just to see how I'm doing. There's no pressure to go visit her. There's no pressure to share anything at all with her. Sometimes the only thing I share is a new recipe gone wrong and why wasted food is the reason I eat out so much.

She's being a friend, someone who knows my journey so well. A true friend's hand is always outstretched. Knowing I can take that hand whenever I need it is a comfort all of its own.

This Monday morning, I might need that hand. My knees wobble with each step I take toward Nate's front door. The kiss on the neck Friday night left me dazed and confused. Nervous and giddy. That kiss on the neck gave me sound sleep. I didn't wake up once reaching for Griffin. I didn't shed a single tear over his absence, and I didn't hate him in the morning.

Loving Griffin hurts too much. Hating him might be extreme, but when I think of him abandoning me and cutting all ties, all means of communication, the hate is just easier. But for two nights, I felt like myself again. Not the girl who lost the guy.

"You're late," Nate calls from the nursery.

I peek around the corner. "Two minutes." And it's only because it took me so long to get the nerve to open his front door.

Nate snaps Morgan's outfit and picks her up, depositing a big smooch on her chipmunk cheek before handing her to me. "Now *I'm* two minutes late." He kisses me ... on the head. I don't know what to think of these head kisses.

"So fire me, Professor."

"I'm thinking about it, Miss Samuels." He grabs his coat and bag while Morgan and I shadow him. "Have a good day, ladies."

I step as close as I can to him when he gives Morgan one last kiss.

"Where's mine." I grin.

He lifts an eyebrow for a second before kissing me again, on the head.

"I have lips that work well for that too, ya know. Maybe you should give them a try *again*."

It's crazy to deny it any longer. Nate is my destiny, even if my heart isn't entirely convinced. Griffin made quite the mark on it, so it could take a while to get it completely on board. But my mind makes total sense of it. We fell in love in another life. I came back into his life when he needed me. Morgan needs me. We fit.

"I think I've said this before, and if I haven't actually said it, I've thought it a lot."

"What's that?"

A sad smile forms on his face. "You're not mine to kiss. Not like that."

I laugh. "Uh ... okay. Then whose am I?"

"You know that answer." He continues to the back door.

"No. Actually, I don't. Last I checked, I was a single woman making my own decisions."

After opening the door, he turns. "He left, but he loves you."

"*Loved.* He loved me. And you're right, he left me. But what he didn't leave was any way for me to contact him—ever. I don't know where he lives. He got a different phone number *and* he told his family to not give me any of that information. It wasn't a goodbye, it was…" I glance at Morgan then back to Nate, mouthing "…a fuck off."

Nate has these looks. Some of them make me feel like a child. Some make me feel like I'm a guilty pleasure. Some of them—specifically this one—makes me feel like I break his heart.

"Can you do me a favor? Since you didn't listen to me when I told you to stay away from the abandoned property …"

This. When he sees me as Daisy, he gives me the heart-breaking look.

"What's the favor?"

"Chase happiness. Never settle. Fight for what you want, not what you think you deserve. Dream big … enough for two lifetimes."

I love him. I know Daisy loves him. But I'm certain Swayze fell for him along the way as well.

"What if you and Morgan are my dream?"

Another heartbreaking look. "I'll see you two later."

When later comes, I talk him into ordering Thai. We both prefer ordering in. I add it to the list of things we have in common. We play with Morgan. I stand outside of the nursery room door, listening to him read her a book. I watch TV while he grades papers on the sofa. He walks me to my car and kisses me on the head.

This happens day after day. I feel his eyes on me all the

time. I know he's trying to figure out what we're doing. I tell myself I'm chasing happiness, still fighting with my reluctant heart.

Damn you, Griffin Calloway!

I'm not sure what Nate's doing, but I've got all the time in the world to wait for him to open his eyes to the second chance right in front of him.

Nathaniel

BY SPRING BREAK, after months of avoiding Swayze's advances toward me and months of trying to forget how my heart hammered in my chest with *need* and *desire* the day I kissed her against the wall, she starts to get a little edgy about everything.

The chaste kisses on her head.

The way I playfully warn her to keep her distance when she tries to snuggle up to me on the sofa. The way she longingly stares at me when I give her the I-could-bite-you line, like she *wants* me to bite her.

I want her like a friend wants his sidekick. But I also want her like a man dying to lose himself in a woman—but not in Daisy. She's inside of Swayze. My desire is *all* for the physical woman that is right in front of me, the parts of her I've touched, the parts of her I've seen, and the parts of her I've fantasized about too many damn times.

Somewhere along the way, the man inside of me developed a strong physical attraction to this young woman.

The inappropriate thoughts.

The heated looks.

The innocent touches that make me instantly hard.

It's all *killing* me because she isn't mine.

"What should we do next week?" Swayze asks as I pull off my tie for the start of my week off. I've officially learned to tie a Half Windsor knot—in Swayze's words—*like a big boy*. She's so proud of me and of herself for teaching me.

"Actually, I talked with Brad, Jenna's brother. Rachael is flying out to D.C. to spend the next week with him. Brad asked if I'd bring Morgan and hang out with them too. So I managed to get us a flight out on Sunday afternoon."

"Three tickets?" she asks.

"Two."

"You suck."

"I'll give you the week paid." I toss my tie over the back of the chair and smile at Morgan as I unbutton the top two buttons of my shirt.

"You're going to miss me. You're going to wish you had Morgan's unicorn nanny with you."

She has no fucking idea how much I'm going to miss her.

"She needs a Swayze detox. Maybe by the end of spring break she'll smile at me like she smiles at you."

Like I smile at you.

"You suck." She frowns.

Yeah, I'm going to miss this woman every day for the rest of this life.

"You said that. Get some new material."

"You *really* suck. Where's my winter bonus. I've never been to D.C. Would it kill you to bring the world's best nanny with you?"

"How am I going to explain why I need the nanny with me to go visit Morgan's aunt and uncle?"

She crosses her arms over her chest as I sit on the sofa, playing with Morgan, who's cruising around the furniture like a champ.

"We could drop the nanny label. I could be your friend. You know, we used to be friends."

If only …

Yeah, I want to be her friend. I want to be her everything. But it's not our time.

"My dead friend, Daisy, or my twenty-two-year-old friend, Swayze? To their ears, both scenarios will be equally cringeworthy."

"So you're never going to tell your family or Jenna's family about us?"

"Us?" I give her a questioning brow raise. "Again, are we talking about my dead friend?"

"No. We're talking about me, Swayze. You know, the girl you kissed. The girl you imagined giving you head after I sent you the wrong text."

"I didn't imagine—"

"Bull! Don't even try that with me. Griffin told me there's no way you *weren't* thinking inappropriate thoughts. And that's fine. Because I had inappropriate dreams about us. I looked at the picture and wondered what it would feel like to kiss those lips, run my hands through those wavy locks. And now I know because *you kissed me*. And I want you to do it again. But not on my head like you'd kiss the family dog. I want you to kiss me like you did against that wall over there. But this time I don't want you to stop kissing me."

Fuck me …

I want to just say screw it, put Morgan to bed, and take everything Swayze's offering me. She makes me want to be selfish and indulgent. But I can't …

"You're not mine to kiss."

"Stop saying that!"

I shoot her a disapproving glare as Morgan startles from the outburst like she might cry. But as soon as she sees Swayze's small, apologetic smile, she matches it and continues on with her cruising.

"Griffin doesn't deserve my kisses. He doesn't want my kisses. He left me alone in the same city as the man who wanted to kill me. Why do you defend him? To ease your own guilt of not watching out for me?"

"Nothing happened to you."

"But it could have! Stop taking credit for luck, as if you somehow knew—" Her face turns ashen, like the blood in her veins just turned to ice. A whoosh of air sweeps past her lips, and her brow tenses as if she can't find her next breath.

I know the feeling because I know where this is going. The reality feels like my own lungs are nothing more than two sandbags bearing down on my chest.

I avert my gaze to Morgan. I can't even look at Swayze. Not when she's putting it all together.

"Oh my god … How could I be so blind? All the unanswered questions. That night when I grilled you about Doug's death, when I really pushed you … you kissed my neck, the one place you knew would render me speechless. The ultimate distraction. It wasn't your physical desire for me. It was all mental. You manipulated me."

"Swayze …" I glance up at her.

"No …" She shakes her head, eyes narrowed at me. "Doug Mann, the master at staging murders to look like accidents or suicides, committed suicide himself. It never sat well with me, but I let the relief distract me. But that's not what happened, is it?"

"Doug was murdered. Someone did to him exactly what he did to Daisy, and Erica, and who knows how many other women."

Her hand covers her mouth. "Oh my god ... you killed him."

I shake my head, returning my attention to Morgan. Yes, I know I look as guilty as a man caught on camera pulling the trigger, but I don't know what to do. My job is to watch her and protect her. How do I protect her from the truth?

"That's how you knew I was safe. That's why you didn't ask about my progress with Dr. Albright. That's why you didn't act surprised when I said he was dead. You didn't even blink. That's why you said what you did. *You're safe because those who claim to love you actually do love you.*"

She runs her hands through her hair. "Of course ... who better to know how to kill someone and make it look like suicide than an anatomy professor?"

Her hand clenches at her chest as she kneels on the floor beside my feet, demanding my attention. "Why would you do that? You have a child. Why risk everything for me?"

After a few seconds of nothing but Morgan's little squeals and giggles, I turn my gaze to hers. "I should have saved you over two decades ago. I didn't. Someone had to save you this time. Someone had to ensure your safety. Someone had to give you a chance at a long life filled with happiness."

Her mouth falls open, and she shakes her head slowly. "Nate ..." She presses her hand to my cheek.

No ...

"You killed for me. You risked everything for me. Your love for me knows no boundaries. You're my *someone*."

No ...

Swayze kisses me. I jerk back so fast it startles her. The pain and embarrassment on her face slashes my heart. God ... I want to kiss her. I want to be her hero, her everything, but ...

"I'm not your someone."

She flinches like I just slapped her in the face. "Why are you being this way? Why kill a man for me and then reject me? Don't you want me? Is there something wrong with me?" Tears fill her eyes. "Am I not enough like her? Am I not pretty enough? Smart enough? Tell me, because right now I feel like I'm losing my mind. Like that kiss meant nothing."

I scrub my hands over my face, shaking my head. "That's not it."

"Then what?"

I stand, blowing out a frustrated breath while resting my hands on my hips. Morgan drops back down to her bottom and chews on a toy. It must be nice to be disconnected from the heartbreak of the world.

"Swayze, you're *everything*. The stars and the earth. The sun of a million lifetimes. You're the girl I fell in love with. You're the woman I want to love. You're Morgan's every smile. You're my peace of mind. My salvation. You're beautiful beyond words. Smart. Sexy. Just ... *everything*. Except ... mine."

She eases to standing, hands fisted, jaw clenched. "Stop talking about *him*." Anger laces her words.

"Swayze." I go to cup her face with my hand.

She jerks away. "Don't Swayze me. And don't touch me unless you're going to touch *all* of me. Unless you're going to kiss me like you did before. Unless you're going to help me forget *him*."

She laughs, but it's a crazy kind of painful laugh. "You killed a man for me. You *have* to be my someone. If that's not fate, then what is? I just ... I just ..." Tears fill her eyes as she hugs herself. "Love me—" Her words crack or maybe she cracks.

I grab her face and kiss her cheeks, her nose, her jaw ... I kiss her everywhere, teetering on the edge of control, but I don't kiss her mouth. And it's *killing* me.

Her hands cover mine, clawing at my skin as her lips chase mine, desperate for what I won't—what I can't—give her.

"Love me ..." she says in an anguished, strangled sob.

"I do." My grip on her tightens while my heart slams into my chest, pushing all the raw emotions into the pit of my stomach where they will stay.

"Kiss me ... *please.*"

My forehead presses to hers, rocking back and forth as I pinch my eyes shut. "No."

"Yes." She moves her hands to my face, trying to hold me still so her mouth can find mine.

"No!" I grab her hands, stilling them.

"W-why?" she cries, crumbling into a fit of sobs. Her body collapses into mine.

I hug her to me. "Because I'm not. Your. Someone. Do you get that?" I refrain from kissing the top of her head. It's so instinctual by this point. "But I would have been. I would have risked it all for you. For over two decades, I've felt this gnawing guilt that I didn't save you."

I hold her at arm's length. She hiccups on her emotions.

"I didn't kill Doug Mann. But ..."

Her face contorts into something even more painful or confused. "*But* what?"

This wasn't supposed to happen. She wasn't supposed to know—ever.

"Tell me!"

"But *someone* killed him to save you—to protect you."

She blinks out more tears as her lips part, eyes unfocused. "Don't," she whispers, frozen in place as if my words shot into her like a tranquilizer. Her head inches side to side. "I need to hate him. Don't ... don't do this."

As long as Griffin Calloway is alive, she will never be mine. I knew it the first time I met him—the way he looked at her. It was the way I looked at Daisy. It's how I look at Morgan now—like they're your whole world.

Griffin didn't have to tell me he killed Doug, but he did. He walked to the edge of the world and jumped off the fucking cliff just to make sure no one would ever hurt her.

She's not mine. And she never will be.

He asked me to keep an eye on her, to make sure that she finds happiness, because that's what people do when they love someone to the depths of their soul.

She's not mine. And she never will be—not in this life.

So I did my part. I asked Dr. Albright to betray Swayze's trust, to trick her. I risked my future as well as Griffin's future by confessing the murder. But deep down, I knew Dr. Albright would understand. And she did. The only way to save Swayze from self-destruction was to betray her. Both Dr. Albright and I will take that secret to our graves, knowing that a young woman has a chance at happiness because of that lie.

But ... I am not her chance at happiness because she is not mine.

Morgan works her way to my feet and tries to climb up my legs. I pick her up.

"I lost him," Swayze whispers.

I take Morgan's hand and rub it over one of Swayze's cheeks to dry her tears. Swayze forces a heartbreaking smile.

"Possibly." I bop Morgan's pointer finger on Swayze's nose. Griffin didn't kill Doug to get Swayze back. He did it to protect her, and he did it to let her go.

"But you'll find a man who loves Swayze Samuels. And you won't have to feel bad that he risked everything for you. And he won't have to feel bad that he didn't. Because he never has to know that at one point in your past, you needed someone to take the life of another human to save yours.

"Bury the past. Find a teaching job. And let happiness just … happen."

Swayze is right. Some things just flat-out *suck*. And this is one. She needs to let Daisy go. *I* need to let Daisy go. The only way to really do this is to let each other go.

"Nate, why are you doing this?"

She's breaking me, one tear at a time. But I don't tell her that.

"Because I'm your *friend*."

She shakes her head. "You could try to be a real boyfriend."

I grin. "I could, but we both know that's never been my gift."

"This hurts. You're hurting me."

"No …" I press my palm to her cheek, tilting my head to the side. I adore this young woman. *All* of her. "I'm giving you an out."

She sniffles. "An out for what?"

"To be Swayze."

"Are you firing me?"

Yes. No. I bite my lips together. And then I do the right

thing. "Yes. When school is out, I will let you go. Set you free."

Her gaze wanders to the window. She blinks several times and swallows hard while giving me a slight nod. "I need to …" Her jaw shifts side to side. "I need to go."

I nod as she returns her attention to me. She gives Morgan a half smile and hugs her before pressing her lips to my cheek, letting them linger for a few long seconds.

My eyes close.

Bye, Daisy.

"Safe travels," she whispers over my cheek. Stepping back, she wipes her eyes and finds a bigger smile. "It still sucks that you're not taking me with you."

I chuckle. "And you still haven't found a better word than sucks."

She shrugs. "Bye."

CHAPTER THIRTY-SIX

Two months later

"TOMORROW IS YOUR last day?" Dr. Albright asks.

It's been forever since I've seen her in person. Once I stopped feeling like a failure for giving up on remembering the past, I decided it was time for one last face-to-face conversation, not as doctor and patient but as friends.

"Yeah. It's bittersweet. Right now it feels more bitter than sweet. Nate and Morgan are family. I love them deeply. Like ... I wonder if I'll love my own child as much as I love her." I chuckle. "That's stupid, right? Of course I would. It's just hard to imagine right now because she's my—everything."

"I'm sure you'll still get to see her."

I smile past the desolation. "Actually, I'm leaving."

"Oh? By any chance ..." She gives me a hopeful smile.

"No. I moved out of the house last month. I've been staying with my mom. I haven't talked to his family for quite some time. My mom still has lunch with Sherri, but we don't talk about it. To my knowledge, my mom still doesn't know where he's living. Sherri and Scott have been very respectful of his wishes. I think they know telling my mom would be like telling me. And over the past five and a half months, there have been many times I've wanted to get in my car and just ... go to him."

"And now?"

I rub my hand over my chest, not aware that I'm doing it until Dr. Albright's gaze shifts to my hand. It's possible I always do it when thinking about Griffin. My heart refuses to let him go. For the rest of my life, I could possibly have to massage this ache.

"I hope he's happy. I really do."

I rub my chest a little more. What we had was explosive and a whirlwind of mad love. Of course a part of him will always feel like a piece of shrapnel lodged into my heart.

"You've grown, Swayze. So much in such a short amount of time. You've reconciled your past. You've accepted the things you can't change. And you've done it with grace."

"Ha! I don't know about that." She doesn't know that I went to Doug Mann's apartment with a bottle of sedatives she prescribed me and a knife. She doesn't know about the fit of jealousy I had over Apple sitting on my bucket. "But thank you. It means a lot coming from you. I admire you immensely."

"Thank you, dear. So … where are you off to?"

"I don't know." I laugh. "I'll know when I get there. Crazy?"

Her Cheshire cat grin makes me feel an odd sense of empowerment. "I think crazy is exactly what you need. Send me a postcard."

I stand and we hug. "I will."

Morgan Daisy Gallagher
Beloved Daughter and Friend

I SIT CROSS-LEGGED on the ground over the grave, picking at

the green grass. "This is it. This is where I leave you … for now. In case he forgets to tell you, Nate kinda dibbed the next time around. So pencil him in for a century from now as your real boyfriend. I think he'll be a good one."

Drawing in a long breath, I hold it for a few seconds and let it out slowly along with a rebel tear or two. "You really did a number on my life this past year. I'm not mad. I get it … Doug needed to die and Nate needed closure. Wish I would have figured that out from the beginning. Maybe I could have saved what I had with a certain guy from the grocery store. Maybe not." I shrug.

"I thought I wanted completely in your head and heart. But I'm glad it didn't work out that way. I think it would have made it harder to find myself. Not that I've really managed to do that yet. Wandering seems like the best thing for now since I'm not sure what exactly it is I'm looking for. A new place. A new job. New everything. Hell, I might even get a new name. Shh … don't tell my mom."

I reach into my pocket and pull out the wrinkled picture of Nate that I salvaged from the garage floor after Griffin rode off. "Here. He's all yours." I wedge the bottom of the photo between the ground and the headstone.

"You burying me?"

I jump as my hand flies to my chest. "Nate?"

He hunches down next to me and pulls the photo of Daisy from his wallet. "Maybe you're right. It's time to let them go." He slides the photo of her next to the one of him.

"Why are you here?"

"Yesterday was your last day. You said you'd come by to say goodbye before leaving town, but the hugs you gave to me and Morgan felt like *the* goodbye." He shrugs. "I get it. Nobody likes to say goodbye."

I nod slowly. It was goodbye. My heart couldn't take making it official.

"I thought you might stop by here. Of course I didn't know for sure. I didn't know when. But ... here we are, unknowingly bending to fate."

I stare at the letters on the headstone. "Fate ..."

"But here's the thing ... I need a real goodbye. One that's by choice."

"Griffin just left. He didn't say goodbye." I continue to keep my gaze straight ahead.

"And every day you feel cheated."

I nod.

"Then don't cheat me."

Inching my head toward him, I surrender a smile. He stands, holding out his hand. I take it and let him pull me up. My arms immediately go around him.

"I love you." I let my emotions out. It's true. I love him.

Not like a lover.

Not like a best friend—I don't remember *us* that way.

Not like a father.

It's hard to describe. I simply love him like Nate. And maybe the best way to describe it is to say that I love him like a piece of myself.

"I love you too. So much." He hugs me tightly, his voice thick with emotion. "Thank you for finding me. Thank you for giving me back what I'd been missing for so long."

"Daisy?"

"Me." He presses his lips to my neck, just below my ear. It's soft, so soft. Like twenty-two years ago kind of soft.

I slide my fingers through his hair, fisting it to hold him to my neck as silent sobs rack my body.

Yeah, goodbyes suck.

I let Griffin go and regret tore me apart. Now I'm letting Nate go, and my heart hates me. It doesn't understand. It's not its job. So I just let it *feel*.

The pain.

The grief.

The *love*.

"Let me know you're alive. Okay?"

I nod, sucking back the uncontrolled emotions.

"Send me pictures of Morgan."

He nods.

I wipe my eyes as he releases me.

"Find a real boyfriend. Okay?"

A laugh escapes past my labored breaths, still fighting to deal with all the emotions. "I'll try."

Nate smiles. It's beautiful. I wish I had *this* picture of him. "I'll see ya around." He takes a step backwards and then another, looking handsome and too dang flirty for his own good.

"Ya think?" I grin, trapping my lower lip between my teeth.

He shrugs, taking another backwards step. "I do. We're timeless."

More tears blur my vision before I blink them away, my smile growing with each step he takes. Then he turns and continues toward his vehicle, every few seconds glancing back at me. Our eyes meet again when he gets in the driver's seat. He pulls out, waving like a goofball.

It's the perfect goodbye.

CHAPTER THIRTY-SEVEN

"SPARE BATTERY TO charge your phone?"

"Yes, Mom." I load the final few boxes into my trunk.

"And you promise to pull over for the night as soon as you're even a little tired?"

"Yes, Mom." I shut the trunk.

"And you have no idea where you're headed?"

"Nope."

With her arms crossed over her chest, she bites her thumbnail. "I'm envious of you doing this. And I'm scared to death too. I'm proud of you. But yes ... I'm scared to death too."

I laugh, giving her a big hug. "You could come with me."

"No." She releases me. "This is your journey. Make it magical. Be daring ... but safe."

I chuckle. "Daring but safe. Got it."

"Sunblock and bug spray?"

"Yep." I open the driver's door.

"Condoms and lube?" She smirks.

"I'll pick some up along the way. I think for now, my vibrator will do just fine."

"Oh. Do you have bat—"

"Yes, Mom. I have batteries for my vibrator." I slide into the seat and fasten my seatbelt.

She laughs. "Okay. But in all seriousness, take lots of pictures along the way."

I hold my hand out. She takes it and gives mine one last squeeze.

"I love you, Mom."

"I love you too, Swayze."

I start to shut the door.

"Swayze?"

"Yeah?"

Tears fill her eyes. "You've exceeded my expectations." She bats the tears away and swallows hard. "I'm so proud of you. And if your father were still alive, he'd say the same thing too."

Well shit. I thought I was going to squeak by without actual goodbye tears. I guess not.

"Thank you."

I PULL OUT onto the street and think about all the goodbyes. They still suck. Every time. But that doesn't deter me from making one last stop before I leave town.

"Swayze!" Sherri lights up with surprise.

"Hi." I step inside.

She hugs me. "How have you been? We've missed you."

"I've missed you too. I'm actually just on my way out of town. I wanted to say goodbye."

"Your mom said you were leaving. She didn't tell me where you're going." Sherri frowns. "But that's fair."

Griffin. She's talking about him and his secrecy.

"There's nothing to tell." I shrug. "I'm just following the road until I find a place to land. I don't have a job lined up yet. No house. Nothing. Just me and the road ... and endless possibilities."

"Oh … well, you be careful."

"I will."

"Hey, look who's here." Scott comes down the stairs and pulls me in for a hug.

"Girls, Swayze is here. Come say hello," Sherri yells out back.

The girls rush into the house, practically bowling me over with big hugs. "Where have you been?" Sophie asks.

"Been busy. That's all. I've missed you."

"Swayze came by to say goodbye. She's moving," Sherri says.

"Where are you moving to?" Chloe asks.

"I don't know. I'm just taking the journey wherever it leads me."

"I'm so jealous." Hayley gives Scott and Sherri this look. They roll their eyes.

"Griffin's coming tomorrow. You're going to miss him."

Everyone frowns at Sophie revealing this to me.

I smile. "It's fine. Tell him hi from me."

A day. I'm missing him by one day. I could stay. But … I'm not going to.

Fate … I have to believe in it for once. I have to believe it's got something really great in store for me.

"We will." Sherri gives me a sad smile.

"Great. So…" I jab my thumb toward the door "…I'd better get on the road."

We share final hugs and lots of goodbyes. I fight every inclination to cry. I want to be strong for them. I want to be strong for me. But more than anything, I want them to be able to tell Griffin that I'm fine.

I am. I am fine.

CHAPTER THIRTY-EIGHT

I T'S BEEN TWO weeks since I set out on this epic journey of self-discovery. I still have no clue who I am, but I've enjoyed traveling without a destination and living without expectations.

I've managed to get a few design jobs done from hotel rooms along the way. Until I find a teaching job, I need to keep some steady income to support my wanderings.

"What brings you to Salt Lake City?" the apartment manager asks me as I walk around the studio apartment with the best view.

"The mountains." I laugh. "I don't know if I'll stay, but since you're offering a six-month lease ... I think it's worth a try."

"You won't leave." She winks. "It's yours if you want it."

I turn away from the window. "I want it."

I SLEEP ON a cot the first night since I put my furniture in storage until I found a permanent dwelling. The next morning, I call my mom to give her an update. She's pretty excited about coming to visit me soon.

After calling the moving company, I head out on this gloriously sunny morning to grab some essentials. I'm just happy to not be hopping from one hotel to the next.

Six months.

Salt Lake City has six months to make me fall in love with it.

"I'm already there," I say to myself, giving the mountain range off in the distance a big smile. Yeah, I love this city. It's new. It's big. It's exciting. And it's mine.

I'm seriously thinking of changing my name to make this new start a truly fresh one.

Abigail, Abby.

Elizabeth, Beth, or Lizzy.

Jennifer, Jenn.

A good three or more syllable name that has an easy nickname. Maybe I'll keep Swayze as a middle name out of respect for my parents.

"Samantha, Sam. Ha! Samantha Swayze Samuels." I snort, as I get out of the car.

I grab a small cart at the entrance. Let's face it, I'm not going to cook at home that much, but a few staples are a must, like coffee, maybe some wine, chocolate … oh, chips too.

I meander down every aisle, finding more than I had on my staple list. Then I head to the checkout with my overflowing small cart. I should have chosen a big one.

"I need to change my tape," the cashier says to me before I start unloading my groceries. "Tanya can help you on aisle three."

I nod, backing my cart out and pushing it two aisles over.

"Shit …" It's a deep, frustrated grumble.

I freeze. That voice. I'm afraid to look up, but I do it anyway.

The gentleman in front of me in Tanya's line, *aisle three*, is giving himself a pat down. "Dammit … I think I left my wallet at home. How the hell did I do that?" With his chin tipped down, he rubs a frustrated hand over his face.

It takes me a few delayed seconds to realize this is not a dream. I fish my credit card out of my wallet and hand it to the cashier. "Here. It's on me."

The gentleman eases his head up like any sudden movement could trigger an explosion.

I know the feeling.

He's handsome. And familiar. The hair is longer but still buzzed short. I notice a new tattoo on his left arm. It looks like a green leaf. Marijuana? No. I actually think it's kale.

I grin, flicking my gaze up to meet his.

"I have over a hundred dollars in groceries," he says, wearing the biggest damn smile I've ever seen.

"I see that." I hold up my bag of potato chips. "Two for five. A lot cheaper than that fresh produce and raw nut crap in your bags."

"How do you know what's in my bags?"

I lift a single shoulder. "Just a hunch."

"I'll need a signature," Tanya says.

I give him a playful nudge so that he moves out of my way. He's blocking the credit card reader. My whole body has a whoa-what-the-hell moment when it feels the two seconds of familiar heat from his arm touching mine.

I don't give him a second glance. He'll see that heat settling in my cheeks, so I slip my card into my pocket and start loading my groceries onto the conveyor belt.

"Thank you," he says.

"Mm-hm." I nod, keeping my back to him.

He leaves the store, and I can breathe again.

"You're blushing," Tanya says. "That's okay." She pats her

face. "I am too. He was hawt! And that was crazy nice of you to buy a stranger's groceries."

"No biggie. He would have done the same."

"You sure about that?"

"Pretty sure." I smile at her.

Tanya shakes her head. "I'm not so sure. Most guys that look like that are too self-absorbed to do something as selfless as pay it forward."

"I don't know." I swipe my card again to pay for my groceries. "Maybe. But I'm going to give him the benefit of the doubt."

When the entrance doors slide open, I spot the recipient of my generosity leaning against the back of my car with his arms crossed over his chest. Yes, looking hawt!

He pushes off the back of it as I get closer with my cart. I press the button and the trunk pops open.

"You have a lot of groceries here for someone just passing through town." He loads my sacks into the trunk for me.

"Ya think?" I grin as he shuts the trunk.

He pulls out his long receipt. "You have a pen?"

I nod.

"Write your name and number on the back of this, so I can repay you."

I trap my bottom lip between my teeth, controlling my grin. He does the same. There's an explosive energy between us that hasn't faded one bit in all these months.

I dig through my purse, internally giggling at fate. After I find a pen, I take the receipt from him and rest it on the car to write my name and number. It's barely legible, my hand is shaking so much.

He reads it when I hand it back to him, a small grin playing with his mouth. "Samantha, huh?"

I nod, biting back my grin.

"You like your name?"

I nod again, several times quickly.

"Huh." He shrugs, folding the receipt and sliding it into his front pocket. "Kind of a boring name for a girl like you. Don't you think?"

"I like boring. Nothing wrong with boring."

He gives me a thoughtful nod and a furrowed eyebrow, but he plays the game. I love him for playing the game.

"Nice to meet you, *Samantha*. I'm Griffin."

I stare at his hand hanging in the space between us. My heart almost stopped when my arm brushed his in the checkout lane. A handshake will do me in for sure.

Wedging my fingers in the front pockets of my denim shorts, I grin. "Nice to meet you too."

"You're not going to shake my hand?"

My head inches side to side, eyes wide.

He chuckles. "Why not?"

"Reasons."

"Reasons ... okay." He withdraws his proffered hand. "I'll call you and get you some money or figure out a way to properly repay you."

"Okay." I clear my throat because I sound like a squeaky mouse. "Okay." That's better.

"Later then." He walks away.

"Oh ... no ..." I whisper to myself.

CHAPTER THIRTY-NINE

THERE IS NO way this is possible.

Fifty states.

Thousands of cities.

Even more grocery stores.

The most heartbreaking part? It's been a week since I saw him. A week since he asked for my number. He knew my number ... it hasn't changed. Why didn't he give me his number? Oh ... that's right, I'm not allowed to call him or know where he lives.

Griffin could be in New Zealand by now. It was an act. Not fate. Not a sign.

Wrong place. Wrong time.

I've been to that same store twice since then. He probably now shops at a different store. There's a Harley dealership here, but I won't go there. I won't call.

This past year didn't rob *all* of my pride.

At least my furniture arrived, giving my apartment more of a homey feel. Too bad my fresh start already feels stale. It's going to be a long six months, constantly thinking I could run into him—hoping for it and fearing it at the same time.

I busy myself with design work, join the fitness center down the street, and contemplate applying for my teaching certification here in Utah. I want to teach, but I have a six-month lease.

Aside from the whole avoiding Griffin thing, I love it here. But hide-and-seek is not my favorite game. Then I think … it's a huge city. He's doing his best to avoid me, if he's even still here. Seriously, he could be in New Zealand.

I go back to fate. If I'm meant to stay here, I'll find a teaching job. It will be a sign.

So that's what I do. I move forward with my new life.

"SWAYZE!" MY MOM squeals when I answer my phone, feet propped up on the balcony railing as I sip my wine.

"Geesh, what is it?"

"I shouldn't tell you this, but I think you need to know. Don't freak out."

I chuckle. "Like you're doing?"

Her long exhale whooshes through the speaker. This must be serious.

"I had lunch with Sherri today. We rarely talk about Griffin … she's very secretive. But I asked how's he's doing. Nothing specific. She said he's good. Then she asked if she could be honest with me, like a friend, not like your mom. I said yes.

"She said it's been rough for him, he likes his job, but he doesn't really have anything outside of his job. But … are you really ready for this?"

I take a big gulp of my wine. "I think so." I'm not sure. I didn't tell her I saw Griffin. Did he tell Sherri we saw each other?

"Last week he went on a date. It's the first date he's gone on since you two split. Sherri said it went well, and she's happy for him. I'm happy for him too. And I want you to be happy as well. He deserves happiness too. I know, deep down, you want that for him."

A week ago. Was that before or after he saw me? That explains why he hasn't called.

Wow. This is a special kind of pain. Deserving? Probably. But it still hurts.

Fate is not awesome today.

"Yeah." It's all I manage to get out of my mouth. Of course I want him to be happy, but for a millisecond, I wondered if I fit in that equation again. False hope.

"There's one more thing ..."

Oh good. There's more.

I tip back the rest of my wine, desperate for every last drop.

"She asked about you. I told her you rented a place in Salt Lake City. She turned ghost white. The next thing I knew, she was making up some excuse for why she had to get home. Swayze?"

"Mmm-hmm?" I keep my lips bit together.

"I think that's where Griffin is at. I think he's in Salt Lake City too."

"Yeah..." I run a hand through my hair "...I actually ran into him last week. I didn't tell you because I didn't want you getting your hopes up."

"Are you serious? When? How ... what was said?"

"Not a lot. In hindsight, it felt like the official goodbye we never had." Half-truth. At the time it felt like the start of something. I misread it. So, yeah, in *hindsight*, it was a goodbye.

"That had to be hard."

Not as hard as this.

"A little. I'm good. I'm hoping to find a teaching job. I really love it here. And it's a big city. I think the chances of running into Griffin again are pretty slim."

"It's amazing how much life changes in a year."

I nod, too emotional to say much.

"I'll let you go. I'm planning on paying you a visit next month."

"That sounds great. Love you."

"Love you too."

I toss my phone onto the chair beside me and pour another glass of wine.

He's twenty-four. Of course he's going to date. I'm a little surprised last week was his first since he left six months ago. But maybe he's been with other women, just not on dates.

He's twenty-four. Young. Sexy.

I'd be an idiot to think he hasn't been with someone else. And while it hurts, I can't be jealous, or mad, or anything. I chose Daisy because at the time it didn't feel like a choice.

But here's the bottom line: Griffin killed Doug Mann to keep me safe. That's an unpaid debt I will carry forever.

So he can date a million women. He can choose to never text or call me again. It's the pass of all passes.

I owe him my life. He owes me nothing.

CHAPTER FORTY

ANOTHER WEEK GOES by. He's not going to call.

Exercise becomes my go-to for my mental health. Whenever I start to feel a pity party coming on, I change my clothes and get my ass to the fitness center down the street. And I don't come home until I'm ready to pass out.

Some days I make the drive into the mountains to climb a long trail. I like the air up there. I like the clarity. I like how small I feel. It's where I always find perspective again.

"After you," a young man holds open the door to my apartment building.

"Thank you."

"You just move in?" he asks.

"Yeah." I retrieve the mail from my box at the bottom of the stairs.

He unlocks a box two columns over from mine. "Well, I've been here for five years. So if you need someone to help you navigate the area, let me know. I'm in 4A. Sam." He holds out his hand.

Sam. I grin. He stole my name. Good thing I didn't make anything legal. Samantha and Sam would never work. I'm not implying I'm looking for anything to work. But since Nate let me go, and Griffin moved on, maybe I should keep my possibilities open for *something*.

I shake his hand. "Swayze."

"Swayze. I like that."

I chuckle. "Don't. Please. If we're going to be neighbors of sorts, I want to like you. But if you like my name, I fear we have nothing more to ever discuss."

Sam laughs. "Fair enough. I hope to see you around soon."

"Me too." I smile.

I climb two flights of stairs behind him, and we share one last smile before he continues to the fourth floor while I make my way down the hallway of the second floor, thumbing through my mail. Mostly junk.

As I fish my key out of my pocket, I look up and stop, a little startled.

"Hey," I say on a breathless exhale.

Griffin pushes off my door, holding up a white envelope. "Grocery money."

"I gave you my phone number, not my address." I take the envelope and slip it into my bag.

"Sorry it took me so long to get you the money." He ignores my address comment.

I slide by him, unlocking my door. He smells of spearmint like he just stuck a new piece of gum in his mouth.

"You didn't have to repay me at all." I open the door and drop my bag on the floor.

"I don't like to be indebted."

I turn. He leans against the doorframe as I hold the door open.

"You could never be indebted to me."

The tiniest amount of tension pulls at his brow. Does he know I know?

A little laugh escapes from my chest, a nervous attempt to break this awkward moment. "You don't have to stand in the hall. You can come inside."

"I need to get going."

How long was he standing by my door? He had to have gotten my address from his mom or mine. He could have mailed me the money.

He owes me nothing. Nate said I wasn't his to kiss. Well, I'm certain no part of Griffin is still mine.

"Okay." I hold the door open with my hip, slipping my hands into the back pockets of my shorts.

Griffin's gaze moves down my body. It's so familiar. He's done it hundreds of times before. I don't let familiarity feed any false hope.

"Why Salt Lake City?"

I shrug. "It felt good. The mountains. The energy. I only signed a six-month lease, just to try it on—the city."

He drops his head into a slow nod, wearing a contemplative look on his face.

These pauses of silence are painful.

"My mom is coming to visit next month. Have your parents and sisters been here to visit you?"

He shakes his head.

Words, Griff. Give me words or leave, but I'm dying here.

"Are you working at the Harley dealership?" I cringe. Why did I ask that? Oh yeah … because he's just standing there saying nothing. I shake my head. "Sorry. You don't have to answer that. I'm just … at a loss for words because you're standing in my doorway, not talking, not leaving, and not coming inside. It's just …"

"Sorry." He takes a step back.

No. I don't want him to leave. But I can't ask him to stay.

This is goodbye. I feel it in my gut. Because if we would

just make the choice, we could have this. But it's too late. I can see it in his eyes, the eyes that shift to my chest. That's when I realize I'm rubbing the heel of my hand over my heart.

Yes. It hurts.

"Take care." He gives me a tight-lipped smile.

Take care. Not, see you later. Not, I'll call you. Nope. Take care is a permanent goodbye.

He pivots on his black boots and makes his way toward the stairs.

"Griffin?"

Boom! Boom! Boom!

My heart crashes into my ribs.

He stops without turning.

"Thank you."

After a few statuesque seconds, his legs shift into motion.

No look.

No nod.

Nothing.

Goodbye, Grocery Store Guy.

CHAPTER FORTY-ONE

"**L**OOKING GOOD."

I jump, shoving my tank top back down over my stomach, all sweaty from my workout.

"Caught ya." Beth winks at me in the mirror as the gym rats file past us.

I bite back my grin, embarrassed, but no one would know since I'm so red from working out. "I have definition in my abs." I giggle. "Don't make fun of me. I've just never had it before. I kinda can't stop staring at those little bumps."

Beth slings her bag over her shoulder. "I think I have twenty more pounds to go before I can properly identify anything bumpy-looking on my stomach as actual muscle."

I giggle some more. It feels good.

She sighs as we walk outside. "Whoa ... hello!"

I follow her gaze down the street. About five parking spots south, there are two motorcycles. A guy and a girl slipping off their helmets.

No. NO. NO!

Before I can duck or make a run for it, Griffin spies me.

"Can you say holy hotness?" Beth fans herself.

"What's the population of Salt Lake City?" I mumble.

"Why do you ask?"

I give Griffin a sheepish smile. He knows I saw him. I can't look away and pretend I didn't, especially with Beth's eyeballs rolling down the sidewalk to rest at his feet. "No reason. It just felt bigger when I got here. But lately it's felt quite small."

"Oh damn … his holy hotness is walking this way."

Yes, he is and so is his female friend. Dang it … why does she remind me of Apple? Only her hair is blond.

Blonder than mine.

Longer than mine.

Thicker than mine.

She's close to my height, but maybe an inch taller.

She's basically me, but *more.*

And she rides a motorcycle.

"I'm out of here. I can't get close to a hot guy when I smell like this. Later."

"Beth—"

She's ten yards in the opposite direction before I can stop her. Great. It's two on one.

"Hi," he says.

Damn, her hair looks like something from a shampoo commercial, even after wearing a helmet.

I know I look just as good as I smell right now—amazingly awful. "Hey. Small world."

Way too small.

"It would seem. Samantha, this is Ginny. Gin, this is Samantha." He winks at me.

I narrow my eyes just for a brief second before shooting his female friend my best smile.

"Hi." She smiles. It's shy and sweet. The opposite of a shampoo commercial woman.

I was shy and sweet like her when I met Griffin.

And she has a great name. It could be longer or short. So many possibilities.

"Nice to meet you," I say without sounding catty. I'm not catty. Okay, I was a little catty with Apple, but she's not Apple.

"What brings you to my neighborhood?" Yes. I've laid claim to this whole neighborhood in just under four weeks.

"Ice cream." Griffin jerks his head toward the ice cream shop right next door to my fitness center.

I nod. When did he start eating ice cream on a whim?

"I see." I smile again at Ginny. It's easier to look at her than it is to look at him.

She points up the street at an angle. "And you live right over in that apartment building." Her finger points right to my place.

"Oh, how did you know I live there?" Does he talk about me with her?

"What?" Her eyes narrow a bit. "No. I mean Griffin's apartment is in that building."

My eyes inch wider. He wets his lips and rubs them together.

No. Fucking. Way.

"She's joking," I murmur.

"Not joking." Her eyes flit between the two of us like he *hasn't* told her about me. "Why is that weird?"

Griffin looks down at her and smiles. "It's not. Let's get some ice cream."

Ginny nods. "Yeah." She gives me that innocent smile again. "Nice to meet you."

I nod slowly. Shock has all of my words held captive.

"See ya." Griffin gives me a quick inspection.

Yes, Griff. Don't give me that look. I know … I know … You've upgraded to Swayze 2.0. Well done.

As I watch him open the door for her, I wonder if she has

little muscle bumps on her abdomen. Maybe I should have told him that I have some now.

Okay. Maybe not.

IT'S A TALL apartment building. People park on all sides of it and down the street in both directions, as well as the parking garage just across the street.

I can't berate myself too much for not seeing his bike or truck. And coming and going from the building is all about timing. I've probably only encountered maybe a dozen other tenants in the four weeks I've been here.

But ... HOLY SHIT! Griffin lives in my apartment building.

And Swayze 2.0 knows where he lives. Has she been to his apartment? Probably. I mean ... we had sex on our third official date. I bet she doesn't vomit at the end of a blowjob. Swayze 2.0 wouldn't do that.

Oh the irony. Griffin didn't want to stay in Madison for so many reasons, but I'm certain the biggest reason was Nate. He didn't want to watch me fall in love with another man.

And here I am, watching him date a better version of me. That's very sweet of you, Fate. It really is.

After a shower, I work on a business flyer for a client, and scroll through a few photos Nate sent me of Morgan. Always just her. He's never in any of them.

There's a knock at my door. The first knock at my door since I moved here. I'm only a little surprised to see Griffin on the other side of the peephole, all freshly showered in a white tee and ripped jeans.

Pressing my head against the door, I take a few breaths to calm myself down.

He knocks three times again. I unlock the door and open it, greeting him with a less-than-chilled smile.

"The day I paid you back, I should have told you I lived in this building. I'm sorry."

Free pass for the rest of his life.

"No apologies. Ever." I manage to get my lips to do something genuine. It feels like the way I used to grin at him.

"Can I come in?"

A shiver of emotions washes along my skin, bringing tears to my eyes that I quickly blink away as I avert my gaze. "Yeah. Of course. Come in."

The apartment is smaller than my last apartment. Everything is in one room except for a tiny closet and the bathroom.

Griffin walks around, stopping at the window. "I'm on the same side of the building. Four floors up."

"I love the view."

He nods, hands in his pockets, back to me. "What are the chances that I see you at the grocery store on the day I forgot my wallet? What are the chances that I see you on the day that I had my first date since you? What. Are. The. Fucking. Chances?"

He faces me, leaning up against the window ledge. I don't react. I'm not sure what the answers are to his questions. My ass stays planted against the front door in case I need to flee for oxygen.

"Don't even get me started on the chances of you renting an apartment in my building."

I am the queen of *what are the chances*. It's amazing that anything surprises me at this point. Pigs could fly and I don't think I'd give them a second glance.

"Ginny moved here two months ago."

Here we go. My hand moves to the doorknob, just in case.

"She's my boss's niece. It's not my style to date anyone related to my boss or even another employee. Things can get messy. I don't like messy."

It's hard to keep this neutral expression. My face wants to contort into shame. I was the definition of messy.

His gaze trails around the room. It's a little messy too. "After meeting her at work, I thought it might not be a terrible idea after all. She's nice. And funny. Easy to talk to."

Stab. Stab. Stab.

It's fine. The man who saved my life is allowed to torture me. I'm completely at his mercy for the rest of my life.

My grip on the doorknob tightens.

"But then you showed up—fucking appeared out of nowhere." His voice permeates a little grit, thickening the air in the room.

The muscles in his jaw pulse several times.

"I'll leave," I say. "I'll go wherever you want me to go. Back to Madison. Seattle. Dallas. New Zealand." I fight the emotion growing in my throat. "I'll go to Hell if you want me to."

Tears fill up my eyes.

He flinches. "Why would you say that?"

I choke out a painful laugh, feeling that old but familiar edge of insanity. "You *killed* a man for me. Every breath of oxygen my lungs draw in has your name on it. I owe you my life. So I'll live that life absolutely anywhere you want me to live it."

His hardened expression fades into pure anguish.

I blink to release the tears blurring my view of him. "The

hypnosis didn't work. I couldn't remember. But I was so scared."

Even now, I still remember how scared, angry, and hopeless I felt banging on Doug's apartment door.

"I went to his apartment with a bottle of sedatives and a knife."

"Jesus ..." he says.

My eyes glaze over, seeing visions of my defeated fist resting on his door when the man told me he was dead.

"I hated you for leaving me without saying goodbye. I hated myself for thinking I would remember what happened to her. And I hated him for killing an innocent child and a young woman. There was this part of me that knew there had to be more. More deaths. More lives lost."

I shrug, shifting my jaw side to side, gaze affixed to the floor between us. "If I didn't kill him, the anger, fear, and guilt were going to kill me."

His black boots come into view. I lift my head, tracking his path to me.

"Do you want to know what he said before he died?"

I wipe my eyes and shake my head.

"No?" He stops just in front of me, so close I can feel the heat of his body.

"No," I whisper, meeting his gaze. Missing the depths of those whisky eyes.

"I think you need to know."

I close my eyes. "No."

Spearmint seeps into my nose. He's close. Incredibly close.

"Ginny is perfect for you." Not a lie.

"I don't want Ginny."

Pain floods my chest, to the pit of my stomach.

"I want you to know what he said before he died."

More tears escape as I squeeze my eyes shut tighter. "Why?" I manage between strangled breaths.

His hand touches my cheek. My body shakes with emotion.

"Because I want *you*. And the only way I can have you is if you know everything." His words carry so much weight, so much anguish.

Opening my eyes, I reach for him. He steps back, dropping his hand from my face and grabbing the doorknob. I step aside, feeling desolate again.

"There's not a middle for us. It has to be all or nothing."

Sucking in a shaky breath while hugging my arms to my body, I nod once.

He starts to shut the door, but stops halfway. "Cash the check." The door clicks shut.

CHAPTER FORTY-TWO

I GET IT.
He killed Doug. I am the indebted one.

But I've come so far. Let so much go. I don't want to relive the past.

Not anymore.

Part of me fears the possibility that a dozen other restless souls live inside of me. I don't want to go backwards. Never again.

It's like the world knows when we need to find each other and when we need space. It's been a week since Griffin came to my apartment, and we haven't bumped into each other since then.

I've thought about going to him, but I don't know his phone number or his apartment number. So either fate puts us in the same place again, or he has to come to me.

Griffin has become Beth's obsession since I told her we used to be engaged. She's twenty-seven with an adoring husband and a three-year-old son—but my story is her happy escape.

"Do you have a tampon?" she whispers a few minutes before our spin class starts.

"Oh … um …" I hop off my bike. She follows me to the cubbies. I dig through my purse and pull out a tampon that looks like it's been buried at the bottom of my purse for a year.

My nose wrinkles. "Sorry. The wrapper is still intact."

"Lifesaver." She snags it from my hand. "Here." She bends down. "This fell out of your purse."

I take the envelope. "Thanks."

She scurries off to the ladies room.

Shit. I was supposed to cash Griffin's check. I slide my finger across the seal of the envelope, opening it.

There's a check and a sticky note with his phone number.

It's been right here in my purse for weeks. I glance at the check. It has his address and apartment number on it.

And because I'm such an idiot who refuses to accept my awesome name, he made the check out to Samantha Samuels.

I grin, shaking my head.

Cash the check.

After class, I shower and run up four flights of stairs because I'm too impatient to wait for the elevator. I knock on his door with one hand while peeling my shirt away from my sweaty skin.

I should have waited for the elevator.

He opens the door. Chatter and laughter spill into the hallway.

"Hi." His eyes widen in surprise.

I crane my neck to see past him. NASCAR is on the TV. Our old TV. And there are a dozen or so people, men and women, mingling in his apartment.

He's having a party and I didn't get an invite. Well, this is wonderfully awkward.

Something tells me he's not wanting to discuss the details of how he killed a man and what that man said before taking his last breath.

"Wow." I hold up my hands and take a step back. "I

should have called. My bad."

"We're just watching the race and hanging out. Come in."

I shake my head. "I don't want to crash your party."

He chuckles. "I didn't say you had to crash it. If you can behave, then you're more than welcome to come in."

Taking a deep breath, I paste on my best smile and step over the threshold to his apartment. He closes the door as I force myself deeper into the small crowd of people, catching a few smiles here and there from a roomful of strangers.

As I worm my way toward the kitchen, praying there's some sort of alcohol, I freeze. There's a blonde with her back to me, just a few feet in front of me.

Swayze 2.0.

I can't believe he invited me into his apartment with her here. Before she turns, I pivot to make a beeline for the door. This was a horrible idea.

Smack.

I run into Griffin's broad chest. Whatever he had in his red cup just slopped down the front of both of us.

I grimace as he holds the dripping cup away from our bodies.

"Shit. I'm sorry."

"What were you doing?" He frowns at his wet shirt.

I lean in and lower my voice. "I was leaving because you invited me to come in and Ginny is here. That's awkward. Why would you do that?"

His brows draw inward. "She's not here."

I jerk my head back, doing a weird eye roll.

Griffin looks over my head and his face relaxes. He leans over and sets his cup on the counter. Grabbing my shoulders, he turns my body so my back is to his chest.

I try to wriggle free before Swayze 2.0 turns around.

"Everybody, meet Samantha. She lives on the second floor. New girl. Be nice. She's easily spooked."

Blonde girl turns, and she's not Ginny.

"Hey, Samantha," everyone replies in choppy unison.

You could fry an egg on my face. I'm so flushed with embarrassment. I don't like being the center of attention, and Griffin just said I spook easily, which is not true. Well, not entirely true. He introduced me as Samantha when I was only trying on that name for a day.

However, the most cringe-worthy part of this situation is he has me positioned so I'm hiding his wet shirt, but my shirt is wet and my nipples are hard because whatever he had in his cup was cold.

Griffin releases me and I curl my shoulders inward to hide my nipple issue. "I gotta go." I start to brush past him.

He grabs my hand and yanks me to the left, straight into his bedroom.

"I need to change my shirt!"

He shuts the door and brings a finger to his lips. I pull the wet material away from my chest.

"You can't leave until you tell me why you came to my apartment." He shrugs off his wet shirt.

I stare. And stare. And … stare.

"You've seen it all before." He yanks a clean tee off a hanger.

I shrug. "Never gets old."

He grins. "Why did you come by? Besides you finally opened the envelope and found my address."

My goofy smile comes out.

"But I still haven't seen the check clear the bank."

"Samantha Samuels. Really?"

"That's what it said on the back of the receipt."

"I can't even cash it."

"Why did you come by?" He steps in front of me and grabs the hem of my shirt.

I squeeze my arms to my body. "Um ... what are you doing?"

"You can slip on a clean shirt of mine."

I stare at him unblinkingly with a death grip on my shirt.

"I've seen it all before. Arms up."

As I relax my grip, he peels the shirt over my head. His gaze goes to my birthmark, something else he's seen a hundred times before. I've never seen him focus on it like this except for the very first time he saw it.

"Why did you come by?" he whispers, keeping a focused eye on my birthmark, like he's mesmerized by it. I've never felt self-conscious about it ... until now.

"I ... uh ... wanted to talk to you." I cross my arms over my stomach to hide the birthmark.

He kneels in front of me. "About?"

What is he doing? His eyes never leave my stomach.

"Doug."

Whisky eyes flick up to meet my gaze for two seconds. He nods and returns his attention to my stomach.

"What are you doing?" I ask as he pulls my arms away.

"Shh ..." He presses his lips to the bottom of my birthmark.

Tears burn my eyes. I don't know why. His touch is so incredibly tender, reverent, and *haunting*. Ever so slowly, he moves his lips up a tiny fraction, like he's trying to ... I don't know.

"He killed Daisy," he whispers over my skin. "But he cut her first ... from here..." he presses his lips to the very bottom again and ghosts them to the top, just on the underside of my breast "...to here."

No ...

"Not now ..." I beg, fighting this miserable reality—this haunting revelation.

"Now," he says.

CHAPTER FORTY-THREE
Griffin

"I SAID I would protect you. I promised to keep you safe. You were my world, even if I wasn't yours."

Her body shakes with emotion as I wrap my arms around her waist, resting my cheek on her birthmark.

"I woke up early that morning before the sun. And I watched you sleep. All I wanted was to scoop you up in my arms and take you with me. I wanted to chase darkness where we could hide beneath the shadows of a million sunsets. If you could transcend time, why couldn't we stop it? Why couldn't our love be immortal?"

"Griff ..." she weeps.

I don't want to hurt her. I want to love her. But I took another life and mine will never be the same. For us to love, for us to live, this has to be *our* burden to bear. I take it to my grave. She takes it to hers. And we both leave it behind in *this* life. We leave no stones unturned between us.

We have to be all or nothing.

"Jett used to be in the Special Forces. He has certain skills and knowledge he shared with me. I didn't have a single weapon. I didn't need one. Nothing to hide. Less accountability. I knocked on Doug's door while blocking the peephole with my other gloved hand. He was fearless, like all idiots are, and he opened the door."

"What the fu—"

I pushed him inside, shutting and locking the door behind me.

"Get the fuck out of here before I call the police."

"Morgan Daisy Gallagher."

He narrowed his eyes, taking backwards steps until his legs hit the sofa.

"Did you kill her?"

"I don't know what you're talking about?"

My lips twisted to the side. "I'm on a tight schedule today. Just indulge me. It will be less painful if you do."

"Think you're going to beat me up again?"

"God no." I shook my head, taking a step closer. "You're going to hang yourself."

He released a nervous laugh. "Fuck you."

"The only question is ... why? Hmm ... do you suppose it's the scar on your face that makes you look creepy as fuck? Is it possible that one day you woke up and couldn't stand to look at yourself in the mirror any longer? Maybe out of sheer anger and self-destructive insanity you cut open that scar. A cleansing of your past, your sins. And then you hung yourself."

I stepped closer.

He fell back into the sofa.

"What do you want? Is this about my accident prone neighbor?"

I shook my head. "I want to know about Morgan Daisy Gallagher. I want to know about that scar on your face."

"It's none of your fucking business."

"Just how much of a sick fuck are you?" I moved toward his kitchen. "Are we talking body parts in your freezer?"

He jumped up from the sofa and came at me. I slammed him into the wall. Not hard enough to leave a mark, just hard enough to restrain him and maneuver him where I wanted him, where my hold on him controlled all oxygen to his brain.

"The scar?" I increased the pressure, using my arms where they wouldn't leave a mark. "One ... two ... three ... "

He flailed. I let up just enough to give him a quick breath.

"The scar? One ... two ... three ... " I let up.

We did this several times until he talked.

"She cut me ... " He coughed. "So I cut her."

"Where?"

He coughed. I applied pressure again. "One ... two ... three ... "

More coughing when I let up. His hand went from clutching my immovable arm to drawing an invisible line on his chest. "I cut her with the same piece of metal she used to cut me—"

"WHERE?" My patience waned.

"H-here." His finger pressed to his ribs and straight up.

The birthmark. He fucking drew the exact path of the birthmark. My jaw clenched. "How many?"

More coughing. More pressure until he clawed at my arm again.

"How many girls? How many? Last chance before I cut. Your. Fucking. Face. Open."

"I-I ... don't know."

I closed my eyes. "I don't know" meant there were many. Too many to count. I didn't open my eyes again. My arms applied more pressure. I counted.

He flailed.

I needed him unconscious, not dead.

When his body relaxed at ten seconds. I let go, eased him to the floor and retrieved the paracord from inside my jacket. I made slip knots at both ends of the cord—one for his head, one for the doorknob—and hoisted him up to hang him. I set a stool nearby. And I left.

No knife.

No gun.

No sign of injuries or a struggle.

Then I drove west. Leaving my whole fucking world in Madison. But ...

I kiss her birthmark again. And again. And again. "You were safe."

"Griff ..." My name rips from her chest.

"I believed you ... ninety-nine percent. But before I took a man's life, I had to know with complete certainty."

I hold her while she grieves. I can't entirely imagine what it must be like to hear details of your own death. So ... I just hold her.

After long minutes, her labored breaths and jerky sobs fade to a silent stillness. She cups my face, forcing me to look up at her red eyes and tear-stained cheeks. "I let her go."

I nod and turn my head to kiss the inside of her wrist.

"I let *him* go."

"I know," I say with my lips relishing the feel of her soft skin.

If she didn't let Daisy and Nate go, she wouldn't be here.

"But my heart ... it never let *you* go."

My gaze finds hers, holding it while I stand. "I know."

She smiles. "All."

I squint.

"You said we're all or nothing."

I grin. "All." Then I grab her a clean shirt and slip it over her head.

"It's a little big." She pinches the front of it and brings it to her nose. "But it smells like Griffin."

I chuckle. "It's a clean shirt."

She shrugs.

I take her hand. "Come on, Samantha. Let's grab some food."

She pulls in the opposite direction. I stop.

Her expression falls serious again. "You took a life."

I took a life.

And while I need her to share some of the burden, I will never tell her that every day for the rest of my life I will think about how it felt to be judge, jury, and executioner. I will never tell her that no matter how much he deserved to die, it's impossible to kill someone without letting go of a piece of your own soul.

"I saved a life. Many lives."

I'll tell myself that every day too. I *have* to think that. I have to *believe* it.

"How many? How many do you think he killed?"

I shrug. "I don't know."

"Why?" she whispers.

I don't answer. I know her question is rhetorical. Sane people can't explain what exactly makes a serial killer.

"He always had these women coming and going from his apartment. I assumed they had to be hookers."

"Could have been. People like him don't kill everyone they associate with. Think of the fucked-up serial killers who have had wives and children."

"So who does he choose? Why Daisy? Why Erica?"

I shake my head. "I really don't know. Your guess is as good as mine. He was clearly upset with Daisy for cutting his face. Did he kidnap her? How long was she missing before they found her body? Did her slashing his face thwart other plans he had for her? He was a sick fuck."

"Other plans?"

"Let's just drop it. It doesn't matter."

She pulls her hand out of mine, hugging herself. "You think he did stuff to her or was planning on it?"

I rub the back of my neck. "It doesn't matter. It doesn't deserve our thoughts."

"How can you say it doesn't matter? How can you believe that I was her, yet say it doesn't matter if that sick bastard did unthinkable things to her—to me."

I hold my tongue for a few seconds. She's here. Alone. She walked away from Nate and that life. She walked away from the past. But she's right. It will always be with her, just beneath the surface.

Just like I will always think of Doug's lifeless body hanging from a noose. And she will always think of dying tragically.

"He's dead. You can't change what happened. So it *doesn't matter*." I grab her face and lean down until my nose brushes hers, until we share the same breath. "We will bear each other's burdens forever. But for us to have everything, the burdens have to live in silence. We can never give them a voice." I close my eyes. "And I want *everything* with you."

She drifts forward to kiss me. I pull back, releasing her.

"Let's live in the now. And right now I want food." I take her hand again and lead her to the door.

"It's Swayze."

I open the door and shoot her a confused look.

"Not Samantha."

I grin. "Are you sure?"

She rolls her eyes. "Yes. And so is my bank. You owe me grocery money."

"I'll work it off later."

CHAPTER FORTY-FOUR
Swayze

AFTER THE RACE ends, I manage to get shoved into the hallway with the rest of the departing crowd. Lifting on to my tiptoes, I try to see Griffin. He's right inside the doorway, chatting it up with some of his friends.

On a defeated sigh, I head to the stairs and back down to my apartment. It's almost ten. I'm emotionally and physically exhausted.

After I get my face washed and teeth brushed, I lift my shirt and stare at my refection in the mirror. He cut me with the jagged piece of metal I used to cut him. I shake my head.

"Unbelievable," I whisper.

Investigators probably dismissed it as a cut from the dock or the boat in my struggle. I don't know. But all this time I've worn my past on my chest.

I crawl into bed. The second I get the light shut off, there's a knock at my door.

"Really?" I throw back the covers and turn on the light.

No surprise, or maybe the best surprise of my life, Griffin's on the opposite side of the peephole. I open the door.

He inspects my nightshirt which happens to be his shirt. "Nice shirt."

"I think so."

He steps toward me. I step back. The door shuts behind

him. He locks it.

I raise a single eyebrow. "Are you staying?"

Griffin exchanged his jeans and boots for exercise shorts and untied running shoes, no socks. "Do you *want* me to stay?" He takes another step toward me.

This time I don't step back. "Wanna crawl under the sheets with me and hide out for the night?" I shrug. "Not because we have to … just because we want to?"

He ditches his shirt. I ditch mine. He slips off his shoes and gazes upon me expectantly. My eyes rove along his chest, jerking to meet his gaze again when he clears his throat.

"Panties. Off."

"You're still wearing two things. I only have one."

"Do I really still have *two* items of clothing on?"

Of course … he's not wearing briefs under those shorts.

I rub my lips together. He still hasn't kissed my lips. It's been seven months. I'm dying. It's a brutal replay of when we first started dating.

"You're toying with me."

Trapping his lower lip between his teeth, he inspects me for a few long seconds. "Am I?"

"The way you toyed with me on our third date."

"Ah … our third date." He smirks. "It was a really good one as I recall."

I nod, hating the rush of insecurities. How many dates did he have with Ginny? Three? More than three?

It's none of my business.

Will he compare me to her now? Was she better in bed?

It's none of my business.

I hate when shit's not my business, but I *need* to know.

"All," he says.

My mind rebounds back to the present.

He steps toward me. I back up. We do this dance until the back of my legs hit the bed.

"I said we have to be all or nothing. There's not a middle for us. To be *all* ..." He curls my hair behind my ear.

I shiver.

"Or everything ... That means I accept your past and you accept mine. And that past includes the months we've been apart."

How does he read my mind?

"I left. You stayed. And life went on for both of us."

I know what he's implying. He thought we were over. So did I. But it still stings.

"I didn't have sex with Nate."

Tension settles along his forehead. "You don't have to tell me that." His fingers ghost up my arm.

"*I* need you to know."

"I already knew."

"You ..." My jaw unhinges and I scoff in disbelief as I sit on the end of the bed, grabbing a blanket to hold over my bared chest. "How could you know? Were you in touch with Nate behind my back? Is this what he meant when he said you told him to keep an eye on me? Is this how he knew you were the one who killed Doug?"

Griffin pushes a heavy breath out of his nose. "Before I left town, I paid him a visit. Yes, I told him to keep an eye on you. I told him to take care of you. And then I told him you were safe."

"You told him you killed Doug. Because he knew. That's how I knew."

Griffin nods.

"What did he say? You told him you *killed* a man. He could have turned you in. You could have been arrested for murder."

Griffin shakes his head. "I knew he wouldn't. We both wanted the same thing—you safe."

"Nothing? He said nothing? Asked no questions?"

"He said 'thank you.' And before I walked out the door, he asked me why I was leaving you."

God, my heart hurts hearing this. "What did you say?" I whisper.

The pads of his fingers brush the angle of my jaw. "I said you weren't mine. And the pain on his face told me you weren't his either."

You're not mine to kiss.

My head bows in shame. Such a painful irony. I've been loved by two men, neither feeling they were the worthy one, when the truth is I'm the one not worthy of this kind of love from them.

In another life, I let Nate go when I should have fought for us. I went to the abandoned property when he told me not to go. Why? I don't know. I may never know why. But for over two decades, he's lived with the guilt.

"I needed to know … everything. How Daisy died. How she felt. Why she went to the property alone. The unknown consumed me like a cancer. Just this …" I grimace. "This unnerving need. A drug. An addiction stronger than anything."

"What changed?"

My gaze inches up to meet his. "You."

His face wrinkles with confusion.

"Doug was the driving force. But when I found out he was dead and I couldn't call you or text you, I felt so fucking empty. *I* felt dead." I shake my head slowly. "I no longer cared. The addiction was gone. The fear was gone. *You* were gone. So I just … stopped.

"I stopped seeing Dr. Albright. The visions in my head were nothing more than whispers, white noise. They no longer fed a need—a curiosity. In some ways they died the day I went to Doug's apartment."

I blink, releasing a lone tear. "I let part of me—her—die with him. And for a while I felt so lonely and filled with anger. Anger toward Daisy for hijacking my life. Anger toward you for leaving. Anger toward Nate for *everything*—sitting in Dr. Greyson's lobby. Putting out an ad for a nanny. Hiring me. Just … everything."

I laugh. "I was so angry. But there was Morgan. She was the innocent one. And my love for her is incredible. So after a while, I thought—okay, life, is this where I'm supposed to be? Here with Nate and Morgan?"

My gaze shifts to the side, trying to figure out how to explain how I got from there to here.

"And what was the answer?"

I grunt. "Nate's answer was I *wasn't his*. In his book, I could never be his when another man killed to save my life. But honestly … I think he knew who I was even when I didn't know."

"And who are you?"

Leaning forward, I press my lips to Griff's abs. My hands surrender the blanket to the floor as I stand slowly. Closing my eyes, I let my lips find the same path up his torso they've taken so many times before, following my favorite lines of muscle and ink. I don't need to see it; I've felt it a million times.

"Ask me again," I murmur over his collarbone before lifting

onto my toes to kiss his neck.

His fingers dive into my hair as he releases a low groan. "Who are you?"

My lips savor the sharp angle of his jaw as my arms wrap around his neck, pressing my bare chest to his.

"Again ..." I grin against his cheek.

He fists my hair with one hand while his other hand slides down my back, grabbing a handful of my ass.

I grunt from the sting of his firm grip.

He grins through gritted teeth. "Answer me."

I bite his lower lip, tugging it hard until he grunts and flinches. "You know the answer."

His eyes narrow. "Samantha?"

I attempt to snag his lower lip again with my teeth.

He pulls back, increasing the pressure of his grip on my ass. "Swayze?"

I shake my head. Our gazes lock and the playfulness dies. I hope he sees that I'm laying myself open for him because of who I am.

Please see me ...

"Who?"

Tears fill my eyes. I *need* him to see it. I need him to say it. I *need* him to believe it. "Griff ..." my lips whisper over his.

His eyes redden a bit when I glance up, keeping my lips hovering over his.

He swallows hard. "Mine ..." That one syllable breaks into two. "You're *mine.*"

"Yours."

He kisses me.

It's closure.

A promise.

An affirmation. In *this* lifetime, my heart—*my soul* belongs to Griffin.

He lowers me to the bed. "I haven't had sex since December. I hope I remember how this works."

His words slay me. Almost as much as that grin. I didn't ask. It wasn't my business. But when a man loves a woman like Griffin loves me, he leaves no room for doubt or insecurity.

He towers over me on his hands and knees. And I feel protected. Safe. And *loved.*

Griffins are mythical creatures—half eagle, half lion. They are believed to be loyal and protective of treasures and priceless possessions.

What were the chances of finding a grocery store guy *and* a Griffin?

Well done, Fate. Well done.

CHAPTER FORTY-FIVE
Griffin

I T'S BEEN A year to the day since I got my second chance. I didn't fuck it up. It was on a trip back home to visit our family in Madison. My parents planned dinner on the deck, yard games, and soaking up the end of summer before Swayze started her first official year as a full-time third grade teacher.

"Don't get sidetracked. Your mom only needs three things, and protein powder is not one of them." Swayze gave me a playful nudge with the basket.

I narrowed my eyes at her, but my grin jumped in and ruined my scowl.

We grabbed strawberries, hamburger buns, and lemonade. I took a fake phone call as we went through checkout lane number three. She loaded the items onto the conveyor belt. I handed her some cash and said a few okays and uh-huhs to absolutely no one. When she took a step forward after the person in front of us finished paying, I winked at the cashier.

The cashier winked at someone over in customer service. While Swayze zoned into her phone, I pulled out a ring—the ring—and got down on one knee.

The person at customer service spoke over the loud speaker, reading off a sheet of paper I gave them the day before. "Attention shoppers, there is a man down on one knee in checkout three."

Swayze's head snapped up at the checkout number on the regis-

ter light, and then her attention landed on me, holding out the ring.

The customer service person continued, "Epic proposal alert. I repeat, epic proposal alert. Griffin Calloway is about to ask Swayze Opal Samuels to marry him."

Swayze turned fire engine red, maybe from the loud speaker, maybe from the fact that I gave away her whole name. Yes, Opal after her grandma—as if Swayze wasn't awesome enough. Her words, not mine. Initials SOS.

"Will she say yes? Let's wait and see ..." The speaker paused.

"Will you marry me, Swayz? I want it all, and I want it with you."

She stood there with one hand over her mouth and the other hand over her chest.

And then the thing I couldn't plan just ... happened. One of the shoppers in line behind us started chanting. "Say yes. Say yes ..." and everyone else joined in.

So. Fucking. Perfect.

I don't think she could have spoken had she wanted to, but she nodded. I slipped the ring on her finger. The crowd cheered.

The customer service person came back on the speaker. "We have a yes! This is the most epic proposal in the history of proposals. Nothing botched up about this, ladies and gentlemen. Congratulations, Griffin and Swayze."

I stood. She threw her arms around me.

"Did I nail it this time? Will this be the proposal you tell our kids and grandkids?" I murmured in her ear.

She still couldn't speak, so she just nodded a half dozen times.

Swayze

"I HAVE SOMETHING for you. It's actually a gift from your groom," Mom says.

I turn, smoothing my hands over the rich silky white fabric of my wedding gown. "Griffin got me a gift?" I deflate a little. I didn't get him anything.

She adjusts my delicate diamond drop necklace. "But your makeup is perfect. We're fifteen minutes away from you walking down the aisle. I need you to hold it together."

"Why would I not hold it together?"

"Just ..." She shoves a wad of tissues in my hand. "Do your best. I'm going to get ready to be seated."

I laugh. "You can't be seated until you walk me down the aisle."

She smiles and opens the door to the room. "Someone else has been requested to give you away."

I lean to the side to see into the hall. In walks a little two-year-old angel in a red dress with tiny white flowers around the neck.

I clench the tissues in my hand. Sorry, Mom, I'm going to need them. It's been over a year since I've seen her except in photos.

"Morgan."

She stops, clearly no longer recognizing me, and turns. Then just to bring out ALL of the tears, Nate walks around the corner. I haven't seen or talked to him since I left the cemetery. He sends photos of Morgan. That's it.

"I heard you needed an arm to hold to get down the aisle. I also heard you didn't have a flower girl. That's not right."

I press my fisted hand to my mouth, tissues ready for me to

blink. The safest bet is to simply not breathe.

Nate's wearing a black suit and a red tie that matches Morgan's dress. Blue eyes make a full inspection of me. And that grin … it's perfect.

"This life looks beautiful on you."

I laugh, but it comes out as a little sob.

Morgan lifts her hands up. Nate picks her up. She gives him that adoring look, the one I always wanted for him.

"Hi." I find one word that I can say without crumbling.

"Hi." He grins.

The familiar no longer haunts me. He will forever live inside my soul, next to Daisy. He will forever know how far Griffin went to give me this life.

Nate and Morgan are my family. They left their fingerprints all over my heart. I feel incredibly honored to have been touched by them.

"Tell me you're even half as happy as you look."

"In this lifetime…" I grin "…I'm certain no man has ever made me as happy as Griffin."

Nate nods. I don't see anything but true love for me—for my life.

"Thank you." I step closer and stretch up to kiss Morgan's cheek and then Nate's cheek.

"For what?" he asks.

"For not letting me be yours."

Nate's lips pull into a tiny grin. "I knew you deserved a real boyfriend."

A real boyfriend.

I can't predict the future. And I don't want to, but I'm certain those three words will tie us together for eternity.

"So we're leaving tomorrow," he says.

"Disney?"

He laughs. "No. The world."

Now I laugh. "That's a bit broad. Is that what your airline tickets say?"

"When Jenna was pregnant with Morgan, we agreed that we would pause our careers and take her around the world. Let her learn from experience. Be a citizen of the world. Cultural immersion."

"Whoa … so you're …"

He nods. "Taking Morgan to experience life."

My smile feels like it could crack my face. "I'm speechless. And really proud of you for doing this without Jenna."

"It feels right." He kisses Morgan's head which prompts her to hug his neck like she's conditioned to give back every bit of love he gives her—times a hundred.

"Ready?" The wedding coordinator peeks in the room, holding a little basket full of red and white petals for Morgan in one hand and my all red flower bouquet in her other hand.

I turn and make one last inspection in the mirror, glancing up to see Nate's reflection and his huge grin. After fixing my eye makeup and lipstick, I turn. He offers his arm.

"Griffin asked you to do this? Really?"

"Yes."

Grocery Store Guy … I love you to the infinite depths of my heart.

The intimate gathering waits in the sanctuary at sunset.

Candles.

A harpist and a flutist.

Griffin's sisters walked down the aisle in their black dresses, holding all white bouquets.

Next is Morgan. She walks surprisingly slow, distracted by

everyone staring at her, but Nate's parents are in the front row, coaxing her to complete her trip.

She does and that brings tears to my eyes.

But I blink them away.

The processional begins and everyone stands—bringing tears to my eyes.

But I blink them away.

There he is. My groom. He looks sinful in that tux, but it's the way he's looking at me that is something beyond beautiful … beyond words.

Nate walks me down the aisle and kisses me on the hand like a true gentleman before giving me away. Tears sting my eyes.

But I blink them away.

I glance at Nate's parents and my mom. More tears threaten my makeup.

I blink them away and hand Hayley my bouquet.

Griffin and I face each other, holding hands. Before the minister starts speaking, Griff leans forward and whispers in my ear, "I can't wait to hear about your day, Swayz."

Tears spill over. He pulls a handkerchief from his jacket and blots my cheeks.

There's an audible "aw" from a few friends and family. I'm sure they're wondering what he whispered in my ear.

I mouth, "I love you, Grocery Store Guy."

There are vows.

Rings exchanged.

More tears.

And the introduction of Mr. and Mrs. Griffin Calloway.

There's a reception filled with good food, even better friends, and the very best family.

The DJ announces it's time for the first dance. Griffin wanted to choose the song, and he wanted it to be a surprise. I just know it's going to be something from *Dirty Dancing*, and we're going to have our first official fight as husband and wife before we leave the reception.

"Don't give me that look, Mrs. Grocery Store Guy Calloway," he says, taking my hand and leading me to the dance floor.

He pulls me into his arms and presses his lips to my ear. "Let's make a lifetime of memories."

And then the music starts: "Boxes" by the Goo Goo Dolls.

Every single word touches me to depths I'm not sure Griffin ever imagined when he picked out this song.

"FINISH ME OFF," Griffins says, shrugging off his jacket and removing his tie, standing before me in the middle of a ridiculously expensive hotel suite.

I give him a curious look.

He grins. "You've already taken my breath away a million times today. Now here I am, just as I said I would be—standing here in awe of the fact that the kindest, most beautiful woman ever said 'yes' to me."

Stepping closer, he kisses me slowly while his hands take their time unbuttoning and unzipping my dress.

"I like this 'unwrapping the best gift I've ever received.'"

He likes delivering all of my words back to me. He did it at the grocery store when he proposed, and he's doing it tonight.

His breath hitches when my dress pools at my feet, leaving me in nothing but a white satin and lace thong, high heels, and my single diamond necklace.

"Dead," he whispers. "You just took my very last breath."

My fingers fumble with the buttons to his shirt. I love that after all this time together, I still can take his breath away, and he can unravel my nerves with anticipation of what's to come.

There's only one thing missing—the one thing to make my day complete.

Say it.

After his shirt is on the floor next to my dress and my hands start to unfasten his pants, he finally says it.

"So tell me about your day, Swayz."

EPILOGUE

A Century Later at a bar in Milwaukee ...

"HERE COMES TROUBLE." My friend Adam nudges my arm.

"I'm pretty sure I'm not looking for trouble." I tip back my beer while eyeing the blonde stomping the snow off her boots by the door.

It's the third night in a row that she's shown up at this bar looking like the forbidden fruit while shooting down every guy in the room who so much as dares to smile at her.

"The usual?" The bartender asks as she sidles up on the stool next to me, her knee brushing mine.

I almost choke on my beer. At the same time, she pauses, sucking in a sharp breath.

"Man, are you okay?" Adam asks, slapping his hand against my back.

I nod, keeping my gaze locked to eyes rich in brown, a few shades darker than my favorite lager.

"Have we met?" she asks, narrowing her eyes a bit.

"Shit. She's speaking to you," Adam attempts to discreetly mumble on the other side of me.

I haven't exactly been a saint during my first two years of college. It's possible I've had sex with more women than my inebriated memory can recall. But I'm kicking myself for not remembering her. The brief nudge of her knee against my leg sent this warm wave of familiarity rushing through my entire body.

It's hard to explain because I've never felt that before.

"You're ..." I try not to mess this up. "Really familiar. But you'll have to excuse me, this is my fourth beer tonight. We're celebrating the end of finals."

Her hand rubs her knee a few times. Yeah, she felt it too, and she won't stop staring at me. Not that I mind.

"Charlotte." She holds out her hand.

"Score!" Adam whispers behind me.

Total dick.

I shake her hand. We both suck in that same breath again, the one that leaves my lungs spasming.

What is going on?

"Mathias," I choke on my own fucking name.

She keeps shaking my hand slowly, her gaze watching our hands in wonder.

Adam continues to nudge my back, making rude comments. His already ugly nose is about to catch my fist.

The bartender sets Charlotte's glass of wine in front of her. She slides her hand out of mine—slowly, until it's just our fingertips touching for a few extra seconds before the connection is broken.

When she turns to take a sip of her wine, I swear she whispers, "Wow."

Wow is right. What the hell was that?

After Adam gets tired of staring at my back, he gives me a quick "later man."

I shift my body, giving my full attention to Charlotte and her messy blond hair and deep lager eyes.

"So tell me about yourself, Charlotte?"

Part of me expects the same fuck off that she's given every guy for the past three nights. Instead, she shifts her body toward mine, scissoring our legs together to make the tight space work.

A million what-in-the-world sparks shoot through my body, and I can see from the excitement on her face that she feels it too. She wants to touch me. It's like we *need* to touch each other.

What the hell?

"I dumped my boyfriend last week. Fourth guy I've dumped in two months. They're always 'too this' or 'not enough that.' You know what I mean?"

"Like the girls that think they're so pretty that they can't stop checking themselves out in every single window or mirror? Or the girls that are so insecure that they won't even look you in the eye. Or my favorite … the ones that have ten layers of makeup on their face and every time they smile, parts of it crack. Too self-absorbed. Too insecure. Too fake."

"Yes!" She lifts her wine glass like she's ready to toast my terribly degrading speech on women. "I pick the guys who are too into their jobs. Too much a mama's boy, not enough brains to talk about anything but the size of their dicks and not enough decency to bring a girl flowers or a sympathy card when her dog dies."

I cringe. "Sorry about your dog."

"Oh…" she waves her hand at me "…my dog didn't die. I just said that to get out of a catastrophic date last week. But *he* didn't know my dog really didn't die. Where were the flowers and sympathy card?"

I laugh. She's definitely trouble.

"Mathias, if my dog died tonight and you knew about it,

you'd send flowers, right?"

Yep. Every single shade of trouble. Why has trouble never looked or *felt* so good?

"Absolutely."

Her lips twist. "You know what I need?"

I grab my beer, tipping back the last two gulps before slamming it onto the bar harder than I intend to do. "I think I do."

And fuck me, déjà vu … I know what she's going to say before she says it, because she's said it before and I've heard it before.

At the same time we say, "A real boyfriend."

"I think a part of you will be mine
to love in every life."

The End

Acknowledgments

Once upon a time I told my mom, Leslie, that I wanted to write a book about reincarnation. This is where my epilogue of gratitude begins.

Mom, your wide-eyed enthusiasm over my idea gave me the courage to follow my creative instinct. You're always there to hold my hand and take this journey with me, researching and sharing information to help make my dreams a reality. You've done this forever.

Tim, Logan, Carter, and Asher—my favorite guys in the world—because you hug me, hold me, love me, and sometimes feed me when inspiration demands all of my attention. Our life is the greatest happily-ever-after.

I'm often asked about where I get ideas for stories. My go-to answer is "everywhere." That's only partly true. While my sister, Kambra, is busy being Super Mom, she texts me story ideas, songs, and where she imagines my work in progress going. She might not get a shower every day, but she does a superb job of feeding my creativity.

Shauna—Queen of Names—stalked me after she read my first two books. I think. She'll probably read this and correct me on that detail. Anyway … what started out as a reader sending occasional messages to an author, has turned into a lifelong friendship which includes a first meeting in Vegas, an epic couples road trip, a car ride through the Midwest with bags of potato chips, and the *most* random daily texts. Nearly every character in this duet was named by Shauna. In real life, Swayze is the name of her favorite waitress and a name that grew on us throughout the book.

Jennifer Beach, aka World's Best Assistant, puts up with me at my worst. She rescues me on a daily basis, holds me together, and solves my problems. And she sends vegan goodies to my house on special occasions.

My newsletter subscribers get a standing ovation from me. Transcend started out as an exclusive newsletter story that I spoon fed to my subscribers, two chapters at a time, for over a year. Not everyone jumped on the slow-burn train, but I owe a huge thank you to those readers that navigated this journey with me. Some of whom had never read any of my other books—a fact that blows my mind! Your feedback helped shape this story. I listened to your wishes, fears, and even your threats. ;-)

So much gratitude goes to my editing team. My beta readers sacrifice their reading enjoyment to catch early errors and find holes and discrepancies in my story. Leslie, Kambra, Shauna, Tim, Sherri, Sian, and Jennifer, you rock! My cantankerous editor, Maxann Dobson with The Polished Pen, has been with me from the beginning. And this could be the end for us if cantankerous doesn't go over well.

Eyes. I like lots of eyes on my manuscript. Thank you to my additional proofreaders, Monique Tarver, Allison Riley, Erika Nielsen, and Bethany Castaneda for raking through my words one last time.

I love these book covers! Thank you, Elias, for having the perfect Nate hair to make the cover of *Transcend* so tastefully sexy. To Wong Sim for capturing the perfect image of Elias.

And a huge thank you to Sarah Hansen with Okay Creations for designing the beautiful covers.

Thank you to Jennifer Watson, Sarah Ferguson, and the rest of the team with Social Butterfly PR for giving my books so much visibility.

Paul Salvette with BB eBooks is a formatting unicorn. I've never seen magic happen so quickly.

And finally to my growing village of friends comprised of readers, authors, and bloggers graciously willing to share my words and support me along my journey, I owe you an infinity of gratitude.

Also by Jewel E. Ann

Jack & Jill Series
End of Day
Middle of Knight
Dawn of Forever

Holding You Series
Holding You
Releasing Me

Standalone Novels
Idle Bloom
Only Trick
Undeniably You
One
Scarlet Stone
When Life Happened
Look the Part
Transcend

jeweleann.com

Receive a FREE book and stay informed of new releases, sales,
and exclusive stories:
Monthly Mailing List
www.jeweleann.com/free-booksubscribe

About the Author

Jewel is a free-spirited romance junkie with a quirky sense of humor.

With 10 years of flossing lectures under her belt, she took early retirement from her dental hygiene career to stay home with her three awesome boys and manage the family business.

After her best friend of nearly 30 years suggested a few books from the Contemporary Romance genre, Jewel was hooked. Devouring two and three books a week but still craving more, she decided to practice sustainable reading, AKA writing.

When she's not donning her cape and saving the planet one tree at a time, she enjoys yoga with friends, good food with family, rock climbing with her kids, watching How I Met Your Mother reruns, and of course...heart-wrenching, tear-jerking, panty-scorching novels.

Printed in Great Britain
by Amazon

30419619R00198